Once Upon an Island Christmas

A Historical Novel of Key West 1859

SUSAN BLACKMON

Dream Publishing

Dream Publishing
Lawrenceville, GA

ISBN-13: 978-1-7358287-1-8

www.susanblackmonauthor.com

Edited by Linda Alston

Proofread by Samantha Mullaney

Printed in the United States of America

Love in Key West series

Salvaged Love

Love in Key West – a novella

Love Again

Enduring Love

Once Upon an Island Christmas – a novella

Divided Love
2021

Chapter 1

Tuesday, November 21st, 1859

Patrick Johnson impatiently watched from the starboard rail as the ship sailed into the busy harbor of Key West. He was anxious to get ashore. More to the point, he was anxious to get off the rocking pile of lumber he had been confined to for more than a week other than a brief stop in Charleston. He may be fine in a rowboat on a quiet mountain lake, but he knew now without a doubt he was not, nor would he ever be, a seaman. He needed firm ground, and they couldn't reach it soon enough.

A curious site came into view as they approached the southern tip of the island. Construction was underway of stout brick walls, their form rising out of the water some thousand yards offshore. Patrick studied the men working on it, noting some of them wore military uniforms. He decided it must be the makings of a fort. He had never known one to be built out in the water.

In the distance behind the fort, a lighthouse rose majestically above the swaying palm trees. Next in view on the coast was a large two story building with a stone foundation. He overheard a nearby passenger say it was the Marine Hospital. It had two docks used for receiving sick seamen. Beyond the hospital, houses, buildings, and warehouses of all sizes became plentiful. The captain expertly maneuvered the ship, bringing it alongside the largest wharf. Patrick was thankful they would directly disembark and not have to go by skiffs to get to shore. Soon he would have his feet on solid ground.

Finally, the lines were cast ashore and tied off. As soon as the gangway was in place, Patrick hurriedly made his way off the ship and down the wooden planks, praying his unsteady, lanky limbs would not fail him now. The last week of sailing from Portsmouth, Virginia to Key West, Florida had been the longest of his life. Despite good weather, his stomach rolled the entire journey. He hoped his apprenticeship with his uncle worked out. He didn't think he could face a return voyage anytime soon.

He stepped off the end of the wooden dock and released a sigh of relief. Odd. He looked down, confirming his feet were indeed truly on the ground. Curiously he still felt the swaying deck under his feet. He frowned. How long was this sensation going to last?

He took a deep breath of balmy salt air to steady his nerves while he took in the large unpainted wooden warehouses before him. At the next dock over, a large amount of barrels and boxes were hauled on carts from the docked ship to the cavernous interior of O'Hara's warehouse. The other passengers from his ship were now passing him by, headed in purposeful directions.

Patrick pulled his uncle's letter from his pocket and read his instructions once again.

> *Make your way from the wharf past the warehouses to Front Street. Turn left and then turn right just past the burned out lots onto Simonton Street. Follow it until you come to the shop on your right.*

Easy enough, he thought. Patrick folded the letter and slid it back into the side pocket of his worn homespun coat. He followed another passenger down an alley between the buildings to a wide, neatly edged, dirt road worn smooth by decades of use. It was a strange whitish-gray. Very different from the brown dirt of his Virginia home.

He stopped to take in his new surroundings. Across from him were the burned lots his uncle mentioned in his letter. Uncle Preston didn't say when the fire happened. It was not recent as the lots were for the most part cleaned up and some rebuilding was under way. Nor could it have been long ago judging by the lack of vegetation and charred bits that remained.

Simonton Street was not far off to his left. He could see it from where he stood. He was instructed to go straight to his uncle's blacksmith shop, but Patrick hesitated. He hardly knew Uncle Preston, but he knew enough about his father's brother to know once he set foot in his forge, he would be put straight to work and have little time to himself. Before him was a new world beckoning to be explored. He wanted a taste of it before he was put to the grindstone, or in his case, the anvil.

To his right, the road followed the coastline and led in the direction of the lighthouse and half-built fort he saw from the ship. His uncle and work could wait a little while. Curiosity irresistibly lured him. Without another thought, he shifted the carpetbag of belongings to his other hand and set off at a jaunty pace. He stepped onto the boardwalk running the length of the next several buildings. Two young ladies approached. Side by side, their hoop skirts were so wide as to take up all the space on the wide boardwalk. Patrick stepped into the street and lifted his cap in greeting. They acknowledged him each with a nod as they passed. He ignored the girlish titter that followed in their wake. They were snuggly wrapped in shawls. It made him smile. He was ready to cast off his coat for it felt quite warm to him. It was the beginning of winter when he left home. There had been a dusting of snow on the ground, bare trees, and a frigid wind whipping across the mountain ridge upon which sat his family home.

This place could not be more different.

So flat! And green. And warm. And crowded.

There were more people on this street than he saw in church on Sundays back home. The closest town of Covington consisted of only a few buildings and businesses. Most of them were thanks to the railroad depot and not the population, which was miniscule. Here there must be a thousand people and they were quite diverse. Already he had heard Spanish, Irish, Scottish, and many other accents he couldn't identify from both the works at the wharves and the men and women passing on the street. The deeper into the city he went, the more he was convinced it was a vibrant cultured city despite the unpainted clapboard buildings.

On his journey to the coast of Virginia, he passed through Richmond and Portsmouth both of which were larger cities than Key West. Much to his disappointment, he didn't get a chance to see either of them other than a few glimpses through the passing train window and from the rail of the ship leaving the harbor. Before going to his uncle's, he was determined to see something more of this town than what he gleaned as the ship sailed into the harbor.

On his left there were a few new buildings and several under construction to replace those burned down. The ring of hammers and the voices of the workers carried far on the breeze. To his right, he passed a grocer, a boarding house, a custom house, ship chandlers, warehouses, and a cigar shop. He deeply inhaled the pungent aroma. It brought comforting reminders of winter evenings spent with his family by the fire while his father smoked his pipe and told stories. It was the first hint of home-sickness he felt, but it was quickly banished as he ogled all the goods for sale through the window of the mercantile. He would have to make a point to return one day to browse inside.

Across the way was the Gem, as denoted by the painted sign above the open door. Raucous laughter spilled from within. Curiosity lured him to the entrance. The rows of glass bottles filled with various shades of clear and amber liquids behind a long bar gave clue to the nature of the establishment. His father would tan his hide to know he was considering entering the premise of a grog shop. The uncouth and rowdy nature of the patrons at such an early hour of the day discouraged him from crossing the threshold.

Patrick forced himself to move on, coming to another cross street. This one was bustling with activity, drawing him to turn left onto Duval Street. He was awed again by what he found. Some of the architecture was simplistic and practical, but many buildings had elaborate artistic trimmings. Each building housed something different; a curio shop, a milliners, a cobbler. He hardly paid attention to where he was walking for reading the signs and peering in the windows. Across the street was a photographers with an advertisement board next to the door displaying various samples of photographs. He was tempted to take a closer look until the rich aroma of roasted beans drew him forward to the coffee shop. He had a few coins left from his journey. Perhaps he could indulge just once and pretend he was a man of leisure like the men across the street lounging in front of the three story Cosmopolitan Hotel. They were well dressed men with fancy top hats and homburgs, neatly trimmed beards and sideburns, nice suits, and elaborate cravats. It made him all too aware of his simple homemade farm clothes and worn out visor cap. He watched the men conversing as he continued walking, wondering how he could change his fate to one day join their ranks.

Oomph!

Patrick's head whipped forward to find he had bumped into a young lady. "Pardon me, miss." He reached out for her arm to steady her, unprepared for the affect just touching her would have upon him. It was as instantaneous as lightening and no less surprising. She lifted her head to reveal the beautiful face that, from his height, was until then hidden beneath the brim of her bonnet.

Her gaze dropped to the hand on her arm. "You can release me now. I am quite recovered."

It was not said unkindly, but Patrick heard the impatience betrayed in her voice. He removed his hand. She moved on past him. He turned to watch her hurried progression down the street while he waited for his heart to resume its normal rhythm. Her skirts swished with the rapidity of her gait. She may not have noticed him, but he certainly noticed her. He couldn't help but notice her. The moment she lifted her creamy complexion to his he was taken with her green-gold eyes and dew kissed lips. He was drawn to her as he was to no other, and it stunned him. Her eyes didn't quite meet his, but if they had, he was sure she would have felt it too.

They were destined for each other.

And he didn't even know her name.

Compelled by need, he followed her. As he tried to close the distance between them, he considered how he, a stranger, could ask for her name. It was against all propriety. His pace faltered. What if she belonged to another? He cast the idea aside, sure he would not feel this way if she was already taken. He caught up with her just as she entered a dressmaker's shop. He couldn't follow her inside. That would be the height of rudeness and she could be in there for hours. He didn't have that kind of time to wait since his uncle was expecting him. There was no choice for it. He would have to wait for another opportunity. Surely their paths would cross again. It was an island, after all, and a small one at that.

She had led him back to Front Street. He considered turning around to continue his exploration, but his enthusiasm to do so was gone. Instead, he turned in the direction from whence he came and soon reached his uncle's shop. The workshop was a lean-to built on the side of a two story building and open on three sides. A brick fireplace took up most of the space on the far side. It was different from one found in a house. There was a lower hearth filled with ashes and above it an open work area where his uncle had a coal fire burning hot beneath a vent to the chimney.

Uncle Preston had his back to the flames, swinging a hammer against heated metal lain across a large anvil strapped to a heavy tree stump. All around the shop were many tools of the trade and the various orders he was working on. His uncle turned back to the fire using tongs to hold the piece of metal in the flames. From behind, he would be hard pressed to tell his uncle from his father, but in the face there were distinct differences in the chin and eyes. Patrick waited to approach until his uncle returned to the anvil and was facing him. He stepped from the bright sunlight to the shade of the roof, but the coolness he expected was not offered, mitigated as it was by the intense fire.

His uncle's hair was a wiry gray, slick with sweat that ran in rivulets down his equally wiry sideburns to the jowl of his chin. The shirt he wore was probably once a bleached white muslin but was now varying shades of gray from age and grime. Likewise, his vest and trousers were also coated in soot and faded with age. It made Patrick feel well-dressed in comparison, although he imagined it wouldn't take more than a week for the forge to take its toll on his clothes as well. He knew his uncle was like his father in that he was brusque, no-nonsense, and a hard worker.

He was fairly certain of what would be expected of him. He only hoped his uncle did not have the same impatient temper as his father.

Uncle Preston gave him an assessing look and said between hammer blows, "Your ship arrived an hour ago."

He didn't say it, but Patrick heard the unspoken question. *Where have you been?* Patrick didn't feel inclined to explain. "Hello Uncle Preston. Pa sends his regards."

The rhythmic pounding of the hammer continued. "Just call me Uncle. Never did much care for my moniker. Always sounded too pretentious to me. Folks around here call me Smithy."

Patrick had no idea what the hunk of metal was supposed to become, but his uncle pounded on it with apparent precision shaping the molten steel as he saw fit. Patrick wiped away the sweat on his brow with his sleeve. It was also beginning to soak the back of his shirt. His uncle turned the piece of metal and hit it some more before returning it to the fire. Patrick watched the process in fascinated admiration. It suddenly settled upon him the enormity of his undertaking. There was more than brute strength needed to shape metal. There was also a well-honed finesse.

He found the whole process utterly unappealing.

Of course, he had some idea of what he was getting himself into by agreeing to the apprenticeship, but the idea of traveling to someplace new and different overrode any concern for the work. Now he was stuck here and he would just have to make the best of it.

Uncle Smithy broke into his reverie, addressing Patrick over his shoulder. "Set your bag down and come give me a hand with the bellows."

He did as he was bid. He set his bag on a bench next to an open door leading into the building. Patrick glanced inside to see stores of all kinds of unshaped wood and metal on one side, and a display of finished pieces on the other. In the corner was a simple desk where his uncle transacted business. He discarded his coat, laying it over the bag, and hurriedly rolled up his sleeves to his elbows as he returned to the fire. He picked up the bellows and gave them a squeeze over the fire, garnering his uncle's immediate, impatient ire. Nope, Uncle Smithy was just like his father. He would have to learn quickly or they were going to have a difficult time getting on together.

"Don't you know nothing? Won't do no good blowin' air that way."

Uncle Preston took the bellows from him and inserted the end into a hole in the bricks that Patrick failed to notice. He gave the bellows a pump and then stepped back for Patrick to take over. The fire flared as he squeezed once, then again.

"That'll do for now but don't go nowhere," said Uncle Preston as he turned the metal to heat it evenly to a glowing red.

Patrick's gaze wandered over the plethora of tools close at hand. There was a waist high wooden rack of varying tongs, another of hammers, and yet another full of tools he had never seen before. A nearby table held what looked like chisels along with more shapes he couldn't identify.

"Hand me the splitter."

When Patrick gave him a blank look, his uncle impatiently pointed to the tool he wanted. He hammered it against the hot metal to make a hole in the piece he was working. He then moved the metal to the brick edge near the fire and turned back to Patrick, taking off his gloves. "You hungry?"

"Yes, sir."

Smithy grabbed the dipper from a bucket of water and drank deeply. He then gave a nod to the stairs behind the lean-to Patrick had yet to notice. Taking up his belongings from the bench, Patrick followed his uncle up the stairs to his living quarters.

Inside, his uncle pointed to the front corner of the room. "You'll sleep on the cot. We eat three meals a day. I expect you to help cook and clean besides learning to forge. I don't allow drink or cards while living under my roof. Got any problems with that?"

"No, sir." Patrick dropped his bag and coat on the cot and then helped his uncle serve the simple meal of salt meat, bread, cheese, and what he learned were sapodillas. He thought it had a slight similarity to a pear he once tried. Spying a whole basket full of them, it was probably a good thing he liked it. While they ate, he dared to speak his mind. "Uncle, I do have a request of my own."

"Do you now? Well, spill it. What's on your mind?"

"I would ask that you show some patience while I learn my way around the shop." He was sure his uncle would take offense to the request. After a tense heartbeat, he raised his eyes to Patrick's and it seemed as if they held a touch of merriment.

"Speaking up for yourself is a good thing and all but don't go overusing it around me."

Patrick didn't know how to respond so he held his peace. After cleaning up their meal, they returned to the forge.

His uncle stopped in the center of the room. "Might as well see what you got for brawn and brains today."

Before Patrick could wonder what he meant, his uncle began rapidly showing and naming all the tools. Patrick tried to remember as many as he could, but he got lost with the hammers beyond which was the ball-peen and the cross-peen. The different pliers were a hopeless jumble of names and shapes as were the drifts, slitters, punches, chisels and more. He thought this apprenticeship would be easy. He was now having misgivings.

Uncle Preston turned to his nephew and took no pity on his confusion. "At the end of each day you are expected to bank the fire, sweep the floor..."

Patrick mumbled under his breath, "You mean the dirt."

"Don't sass me boy."

Patrick cringed. His uncle had keen hearing. "Yes, sir."

"You will empty the ash from the hearth into the bin by the door and leave it outside for Sandy Cornish. He comes by at odd times to pick it up for his crops in exchange for fruit. You are also to make sure all the tools are put away. We work six days a week. Sunday's we go to St. Paul's Episcopal Church. You have free time after dark and after church. We'll discuss wages at week's end." He turned to face Patrick. "Understood?"

"Yes, sir."

"Now let's test your brawn, shall we?" He thought he heard his uncle chuckle to himself as he turned away. Smithy stoked the coal fire. He handed Patrick the tongs with a billet of steel and proceeded to direct him in heating it to the proper color before taking it to the anvil to wield the hammer in shaping it. Patrick soon learned the advantage of the open structure. It allowed the breeze to offer some cooling relief to the hot and strenuous work.

And so the rest of the week continued just as Patrick expected. He was put straight to work upon arrival with no time for exploring. His uncle was a hard taskmaster but fair. He was gruff, not given to any soft emotion or sentimentality, but he was also hard-working and honest. Patrick easily gave him his respect, if not his affection. Each day his uncle gave him more of the heavy hammering to do while he did the lighter more detailed work. Each night Patrick fell into an exhausted sleep.

Every moment in between, he thought of *her*, his destiny with no name. How was he ever going to find her again?

* * *

November 27th, 1859 First Sunday of Advent

Patrick dressed with care for church services in the hopes of seeing *her*. He was thankful his uncle allowed them to close shop a little early yesterday so they had time before dark to bathe in the sea. It was a novel experience for Patrick. Although the water was chilly, it was worth the discomfort to be rid of nearly a week's worth of sweat and grime. He was contemplating making it a nightly ritual even if he had to do so after dark.

As he donned the homemade unbleached linen shirt, he was thankful that his mother insisted he have new Sunday clothes. As he buttoned the cuffs, he noticed the sleeves were tighter around his biceps. The charcoal gray trousers fit him well. He wished he had a new hat and shoes as well. He decided to forego the stained brown cap, but made do with dusting off his work shoes. Recalling the dandified gentlemen in front of the hotel, he vowed to buy a new hat as soon as he had the funds. For now, he combed his hair until it lay smooth.

He was ready to leave when Uncle Preston stepped out of his bedroom door looking right smart in a blue ticked shirt, navy vest, and polished shoes. He plopped his 'going out' bowler on his balding head and left the apartment, expecting Patrick to follow. Patrick's eyebrows rose at his lack of a coat but he said nothing. His upbringing would not allow him to forego his coat no matter how much he would like to be rid of the excessive warmth the extra layer provided.

They only had to walk a few blocks further inland to reach the church on Eaton Street. It was a finely built wood frame structure on a stone foundation with batten siding. All the windows and the double front door where arched. A decorative belfry rose above with a simple wooden cross atop. The chimed bells sounded upon their approach. Patrick followed his uncle through the gated white picket fence, passing the parishioners visiting in the yard with a silent nod to those who greeted him, and entered into the church. He scanned all those milling about on their way in but didn't see *her*. From the walk he took last night he knew there was at least one other church and there could even be others. He had to accept it was likely she wouldn't be here. Still, he sat slightly turned to surreptitiously watch the door until his uncle gave him a scathing look, forcing him to face forward. They were in the second pew, which meant if she did arrive, he wouldn't be able to see her without turning.

And he didn't turn once during the service. His uncle took to nudging him every time his gaze strayed from the pulpit or the bible in his hand. Once the service began, his uncle sat like a statue, giving the reverend his undivided attention except when he cut his eyes at Patrick's every movement. At the service's end, his uncle didn't immediately leave the pew either. He lingered in devout prayer until most of the others had left the church. Patrick was seething with frustrated impatience. It seemed his uncle was determined to be first in and last out. By the time they reached the door, more than half the parishioners had already left the church yard. Despairing of hope, he scanned those who were left. His shoulders dropped. He didn't see her. His gaze swept back across the yard. A movement arrested him. A man in the street was talking to a couple and stepped back, revealing a lady by his side. She turned her head giving Patrick a glimpse of her face.

It was *her*!

His uncle was still speaking to Reverend Herrick. The lady and man were walking away. He had missed his chance at an introduction to her. Although it would be rude not to speak to the reverend, it would be sheer torture to wait another week to learn her name. There was another option, but he had to hurry. He couldn't wait. Respect be darned, he wasn't going to lose this chance. "Excuse me, Uncle, Reverend." He gave a nod and ran, leaving the two men flabbergasted. He would apologize later. *Now* was vital. He couldn't chase down the lady; to do so would ruin any chance of an introduction. Instead, he cut diagonally across the yard to intercept the couple with whom she, and he assumed it was her father – he hoped it was her father and not a husband – were speaking with. The young man had visited the forge this week to order sponge hooks. Patrick was trying to remember his name as he hurdled the picket fence. Something with a 'W'. He ran in front of them and skidded to a halt.

"Oh my!" The lady's hand flew to her chest as she and the children by her side came to a halt.

The man shifted the child he carried to his other shoulder. "What is the meaning of this, sir? Surely you do not mean to accost us?"

Patrick stammered between breaths. "No, sir. Sorry, sir. I have a question."

"Do I know you?"

"Patrick Johnson. I'm the nephew of Pres... Smithy. We met the other day at the forge. You are Mr. Whitmore."

"Ah yes. I remember. Did your uncle send you?"

"No, sir. My question is for me."

"And what question of yours could I possibly have the answer for?"

Patrick glanced at the openly inquisitive Mrs. Whitmore and ducked his head to hide his embarrassment. He took a breath, steeled his resolve, and raised his gaze to Mr. Whitmore. "I was hoping you would tell me the name of the lady you were just speaking with." He gave a nod to the lady disappearing around the corner behind the Whitmore's.

Emily Whitmore raised her fan to hide her smile.

Henry Whitmore gave Patrick a stern look. "What interest do you have in my sister?"

His sister! Patrick's shock made it hard to answer. "Uh... hmm...well, sir... I think she's beautiful." He cringed at blurting out the truth, having lost all ability to prevaricate.

A giggle escaped Emily but a harsh glance from her husband made her suppress her mirth. The man was clearly taken with Emmaline. How delightful! She waited with curiosity to see how her husband would answer.

Henry turned back to the young man in front of him. He was clearly discomfited but also determined to get his answer. The impression Henry got at the forge was that his uncle, while not outspokenly proud of his nephew, was not disappointed in him either. That spoke volumes for his character, for Smithy was not known for his tolerance. Another point in the lad's favor was that he attended church. Although, Henry could well imagine, Smithy would not give him a choice in the matter. "You see her in the church yard, determine she is beautiful, and now demand an introduction?"

"No, sir. I saw her earlier in the week. We passed on the street. I have had to wait until now to learn anything of her. And no, sir, not demand, respectfully request an introduction."

"I'll think about it. Good day, sir." Henry stepped around the man, expecting his family to follow.

Patrick's jaw dropped. Disappointment swamped him. He spun around to plead, "Could I at least know her name?"

Henry refused to answer. He would know more of this man before he did anything to encourage a liaison with his baby sister. She didn't need the added heartache of a fickle affection or worse, a scoundrel.

Emily had seen the crestfallen look upon Mr. Johnson's face. Her instinct led her to believe his feelings were true. She turned to say over her shoulder, "Emmaline." His face lit up with joy. Catching her husband's shocked look, she patted his arm. "I have a good feeling about him."

Henry knew better than to argue with her. At least not in the middle of the street.

Patrick whispered the name to the wind brushing across his shoulders. "Emmaline." He inwardly smiled, happy for now to have a name to go with the sweet vision haunting his dreams. It would suffice today. Somehow, someway, he would make sure he was properly introduced to her next Sunday.

Chapter 2

Thursday, December 1st

Morning sunshine streamed across the floor hewn from Dade County pine as Emmaline Whitmore adjusted the hoop skirt beneath her favorite purple and aquamarine plaid silk taffeta plaid day dress to sit down at her mother's writing desk. She moved aside the stack of household receipts to open the ledger. Usually, she found this chore calming and methodical. Today as she dipped the quill in ink 69prepared to write the date, she hesitated. It was the first of December. She had been both dreading and looking forward to the holiday season. The past two years they had been a house in mourning, and still were in essence. She was determined to bring back the joyful spirit of Christmas this year. She just wasn't sure it was going to make a difference with her father.

Putting aside the troubling thoughts, she set the pen to paper and neatly wrote the date. She picked up the first bill from the stack and entered the amount the cook paid to the butcher last week, then her father's tailor bill, and another for Mr. Wall's tobacco shop, Mr. Tift's dry goods, plus the week's wages for the housekeeper, cook, and her maid. With each entry she adjusted the account balance and when done she would check it against the actual amount left in the money box in the desk drawer.

"Miss Whitmore?"

Emmaline looked up from her task to look inquiringly at the housekeeper. "Yes, Mrs. Paden?"

"Did you want to approve the week's menus?"

Emmaline turned her graceful palm up to receive Mrs. Paden's neatly printed list. She skimmed it and looked up. "It is fine, though I would suggest a different cake. Spice cake is likely to upset my father."

"My apologies, miss. I forgot about the cinnamon. Will pound cake do?"

Emmaline nodded. "Rather nicely, I think. Thank you." As she watched the housekeeper leave, she was assailed with memories of her mother pulling fresh baked cinnamon bread out of the oven. She could almost smell the sweet spice filling up the air and see her father's wolfish grin as he threateningly teased to keep it all to himself. The memory was bittersweet.

She adored the father of her childhood. He was kind, jovial and loving. Now, he was bitter and often angry. She did everything she could not to upset him. She was the last child living at home and had assumed the duties of mistress of the house. She might as well have occupied the large house all by herself for as much company as her father provided. She pushed the thought aside and forced the remembered aroma of cinnamon to dissipate. It wouldn't do to dwell on the past.

She picked up the next receipt which happened to be for her dressmaker. The sudden reminder of her forgotten fitting appointment made her look to the wall clock. Quarter 'til nine o'clock. "Oh my!" She had better be on her way if she wasn't going to be late. She capped the ink and rose from the desk chair, crossing the room in a fast walk to reach the foyer. She donned her gloves as no proper lady would leave the house without them. She lifted the finely woven, wool shawl from the wall peg and wrapped it around her to ward off the chill of the winter breeze. Lastly, she tied a bonnet over her smoothly twisted, strawberry braids. A glance in the mirror made her reach up to pinch some color into her pale cheeks and bite her lips. If only there was a way to hide the light smattering of freckles across her nose. She wished her skin was as pure as Brianna's, but at least her freckles were not as dark as Agatha's. Turning from the looking glass, she was thankful her maid appeared at the top of the stairs, saving her from leaving without notice.

"Jane, if anyone asks, I have gone to the dressmaker."

"Yes, miss."

Emmaline glanced at the grandfather clock in the hall. She had only ten minutes to walk across town or she would be late. She was never late. It went against her pride. She could only hope no one would stop her to converse. Even worse than being late, she abhorred being rude.

* * *

Emmaline turned again in front of the oversized mirror in Mrs. Keats's dress shop, admiring the drape of deep royal blue silk from her narrow waist over the expanse of hoop skirt and petticoat to brush the floor. The skirt was two-tiered, which was all the adornment Emmaline would tolerate. She preferred a simple style rather than all the elaborate trimmings currently in fashion. The bodice was low, dipping down from the roundness of her shoulders. The sleeves were short and similarly unadorned. The gown was for the Eatonton's Christmas ball and was a splurge expense. Her dark green velvet gown could be worn again, but she wanted something lighter in weight and different in color, having worn green at Christmas for as long as she could remember. It was one of the ways she was trying to brighten her spirits this holiday.

Esperanza Keats said, "Are you happy with the length?"

Emmaline had known the petite Cuban seamstress all her life. She was one of her mother's dear friends. Emmaline met her gaze in the mirror and noticed for the first time the streaks of gray in Mrs. Keats's hair. She lightly smiled at the seamstress' reflection. "It is perfect."

"Good. Then it should only take another week to finish hemming it."

The tolling of a bell from the wharf drew both ladies' attention and brought delighted smiles.

Excitement fluttered in Emmaline's chest. "The *Isabel* is early today."

"Here, let me help you get out of this. I know you must be anxious to hear from your sisters."

"I am for more reason than you know."

"Why is that?"

"I am expecting confirmation my siblings will come home for Christmas."

Esperanza nodded in approval. "Their visit would be good for your father, especially James."

"I am hoping he can take holiday leave from West Point. There seemed to be some question of it in his last letter."

Esperanza lifted the ball gown from Emmaline with help from her assistant. "Surely they don't hold schooling through Christmas."

"No, they do get a break. It was whether or not he would have time enough to travel here and back." Emmaline stepped out of the ridiculously large hoops and waited for it to be exchanged for her everyday hoops. She was thankful to have them as the metal wires held together with ribbons of fabric tape were cooler and lighter than the layers of starched petticoats and crinolines she used to wear. Once the hoop skirt was in place, she donned her day dress over her chemisette. The style was falling out of fashion, but Emmaline refused to be a slave to fashion except on the most formal of occasions.

At last fully dressed, she bid farewell to Mrs. Keats and her assistant and made her way to the wharf to wait with friends and neighbors for the arrival of the post. The arrival of the bi-monthly mail brought most to gather in anxious anticipation of receiving letters and periodicals, allowing the tiny community to once again feel connected to the outside world.

* * *

Patrick looked to his uncle for explanation of the unexpected bells.

"That would be the *Isabel* arriving from Charleston with the mail. I suppose you would like to go get ours."

"Yes, sir. I would."

"Off with you then but don't dawdle. We have orders to finish this afternoon."

"Where is the post office?"

"Go towards the wharf. You'll find it easy enough. It's where everyone else will be gathered."

Patrick lifted his hat from a peg on the post holding the shed roof and took off towards the docks. A tremor of excitement filled him in the hopes he might see Emmaline among those gathered.

Townsfolk were streaming from all directions to meet the steamer coming into port. There weren't many people when Patrick arrived, but the numbers rapidly swelled in size as he stood on the fringe of the gathering to have a better view. His heart leapt when he saw her walking alone. She drew him to her like a beacon. He simply couldn't look away. He was almost unaware of his movement towards her. It wasn't necessarily his intention to intercept her, knowing he needed an introduction first, he merely desired to get closer.

Emmaline could not help but notice the young man walking towards her, mainly because he was the only one walking against the flow of people anxious to receive their mail. The arrival of the *Isabel* twice a month was always met with great anticipation. His lean length also made him stand out. He was bearded, hair in need of a comb, and wearing the worn clothing of a tradesman. She was sure she had never seen him before, for despite his less than polished appearance, he was an attractive man.

The closer he came, the more she became certain his gaze was focused upon her. She glanced behind her to see if he could be looking at someone else, but there was no one directly behind her. She turned back to find his gaze hadn't wavered. Why her? It was as if he knew her, but she had never met him. She moved a little closer to the side of the street opposite him and tried to pretend indifference while keeping her eye on him. His gaze followed her. The intensity of it disturbed her. She had full intentions of ignoring him, sure that in this crowd she was safe from any unwanted advances. But then a rare burst of anger overtook her. The man was simply too rude to be born, and she intended to tell him as much.

Patrick's heart began to gallop at Emmaline's determined approach. She firmly held his gaze as she walked towards him. He stopped and waited, anxious and not a little afraid of what she might say. He was aware his actions deserved rebuke. Had he ruined his chances with her before he had any right to claim her attention?

Emmaline came to a stop in front of him and angrily held his frank gaze for a moment before speaking. He was tall. Taller than she first surmised. She had to tilt her head to keep eye contact. She stopped a yard from him, instinctively knowing any closer would be too disturbing.

She attempted a frosty tone, but she was not able to carry it off as well as her sister, Agatha, who could issue a scathing put down with an icy effect. "What is the meaning of your rudeness, sir? Surely, you must know it is impolite to stare, especially at a lady you don't know."

Patrick ducked his head. "My apologies, Miss Whitmore."

She was taken aback to hear her name. "You seem to have me at a disadvantage, sir. Have we met before? I can't seem to recall."

"No, we haven't, much to my disappointment. My name is Patrick Johnson."

"You presume I wish an introduction." In truth, she was intrigued by him despite her better judgement.

"Pardon me. I apologize for my assumption."

"Well, Mr. Johnson, as long as you insist on going about this in a most unorthodox manner, at least tell me something of yourself to instill my trust and to even the table, so to speak, since you seem to know more of me than I of you."

"I only know you are the most beautiful creature I have ever met, you are Henry Whitmore's sister, and your given name is Emmaline."

"How do you know my brother?"

"He brought work into the forge."

"And he told you my name?" She seemed to recall the blacksmith's last name was Johnson though everyone called him Smithy. Perhaps this man was a relation.

"No. Your sister-in-law did when he refused."

"Henry refused you an introduction?"

"Not exactly. He said he would think about an introduction. He refused to give me your name when I asked."

"And Emily did?" *Why would she give a stranger my Christian name?*

"If that is his wife, then yes, and I am ever grateful."

Emmaline giggled, captivated by his honesty. "Grateful, just to know my name?"

Patrick grinned bashfully. "You could never know how much you have tortured me since the day of my arrival."

Her eyebrows rose. "Since your arrival? And when, pray tell, was that?"

"Nine days ago."

"You confuse me, sir. How could I possibly torture you when we have never met?"

"We bumped into each other on Duval Street."

It took only a second for Emmaline to recall the incident. She had looked down to check the time on her watch fob when she bumped into a gentleman. She looked at him, but hadn't really seen him, noting only his height and dark hair. "That was you?"

Patrick grinned. "It was, and you have intrigued me ever since."

Vanity made her want to ask how she intrigued him, but she held the question, deciding it best not to wander into such intimate conversation. "You haven't told me anything about yourself."

"What would you like to know?"

"Where are you from?"

"The Algonquian mountains of Virginia."

She had no idea where that was in relation to the state, but she had a more important question to ask, "Why are you here?"

"To apprentice with my uncle."

"Smithy is your uncle?"

"He is. Uh, Miss Whitmore, your brother is headed this way."

Oh, no! Henry could be overly protective of her and this meeting would not sit well with him. "Then quick, you best escort me closer to the wharf. He won't make a scene in the midst of the crowd."

Patrick was more than willing to comply with her request. He held his arm out to her and smiled as she placed her gloved hand upon his shirt sleeve. He was thankful he had the presence of mind to unroll the sleeves and button the cuffs as he walked into town, for even her gloved hand on his bare arm would be considered scandalous. As it was, without a jacket, it was uncouth enough to worry about creating gossip. He turned them to the docks and didn't stop until they were in the midst of the clustered group.

Henry soon joined them. "Emmaline, I see you have met Mr. Johnson."

"I have. He just told me he is from the mountains of Virginia."

Henry turned his attention to the interloper. "I suppose your home is quite a contrast to our island."

Patrick nodded, more than thankful her brother seemed to easily accept his sister's acquaintance with him. "A pleasant one, I assure you. I don't mind missing a Virginia winter."

"How did you two meet?"

Patrick swallowed hard. He should have known he would not pass her brother's protection so easily.

Emmaline took Henry's arm. "Oh look. The letters are ready. Will you escort me to the window, please? Good day, Mr. Johnson."

Patrick knew it was best not to follow and give Mr. Whitmore a chance to continue his questioning. So, as much as he didn't want to, he would wait off to the side until they left to retrieve his uncle's mail. As he recalled their conversation, it occurred to him that she had yet to smile. Her look and tone were light but any merriment, and even happiness, was missing. He longed to help her find it again.

Henry looked down at Emmaline as they waited their turn. "You imp. You are not fooling me. You were not properly introduced, were you? What did he do, walk up to you on the street?"

Something in his deriding tone provoked her to renounce his assumption. "I approached him."

Henry sputtered in shock. He had never known Emmaline to do anything untoward. Before he could find a response, it was their turn at the postmaster's window. They were each handed a stack of mail. They moved from the window to both quickly review the handwriting of each address. Emmaline was pleased to find a letter from each of her siblings addressed to her and one from Brianna addressed to her father.

Henry said, "I have one from Brianna."

"We do too."

"Is she coming for Christmas?"

Emmaline looked at him in surprise. "How did you know I invited her?"

"I didn't. Why would you need to invite her to come home?"

"I more or less wrote to implore all three of them to come home this Christmas in the hopes it will please Poppa and improve his spirits."

"And are they?"

She held up her letters. "I am hoping these replies are favorable."

"Well open them."

"Very well. Will you hold these?"

Henry took the other letters from her so she could open Brianna's first. She scanned the first lines and looked up with a closed smile. "Brianna and Garrett are coming." She traded the letter for James'. She sadly shook her head. "He still feels there is not enough time to make the trip." She exchanged the letter for Agatha's. Her smile grew. "She is coming, and she promises one way or another to bring James with her."

"Well then, we shall have a grand family Christmas."

Emmaline grinned but then she sobered. "Do you think it will work?" At her brother's blank look, she added, "Do you think it will help Poppa?"

Henry brushed his knuckles down Emmaline's cheek wishing he could ease her concerns. "I don't know dearest, but it certainly won't hurt."

Henry walked Emmaline home and left soon after speaking to their father. Emmaline approached the study after he left. She peered inside the door. "Poppa?"

Theodore put down his paper. "Come in."

"I have a letter for you from Brianna." She handed it to him along with the rest of the mail.

He placed Brianna's letter on the desk. "We'll read it at supper." He sorted the rest of the mail. "What are we having tonight?"

"Turtle soup and poached fish."

He said nothing. He didn't really even acknowledge that she spoke. He opened the New York paper he received and began reading, effectively dismissing her. Used to, if not resigned to, his diffident distraction, Emmaline turned and left the room. She took her letters to the morning room to read in solace. It was a place in the house that reminded her most of her mother, perhaps, because it was her mother's favorite room. She sat down in one of the Queen Anne chairs facing the front window to read her letters in full.

Brianna's letter was long, as usual. Her eldest sister lived in Pennsylvania with her husband Garrett. She and Garrett had a whirlwind romance the summer before her mother's passing. Emmaline barely got used to the idea her sister was in love before she was married and gone. She dearly missed her. The best part of her letter was the news she was departing a week after writing it, meaning her sister would likely arrive next week. Emmaline looked forward to seeing her again and to meeting her newest nephew.

Agatha's letter was short, as usual, which always struck Emmaline as odd considering she was employed as a writer for a New York paper. She read the letter in full while with Henry but did so again now, taking comfort in her assurances she could bring James with her by paying extra to travel by steam ship.

James' letter, while not as long as Brianna's, was more than Agatha's. He told of life as a freshman at West Point and gave a grand description of the Hudson River flowing next to the campus. After explaining why he couldn't come home, he lamented that he would miss celebrating the holiday with his family. He closed with concerns for Poppa.

Emmaline set the letters aside.

Step one of her plan was complete.

She was glad they were all coming home, or hopefully all would be home. Christmas hadn't been the same since her mother passed away two years ago. The rawness of grief made it difficult to celebrate the joyous season just months after her death. Last year wasn't any better. Agatha was too busy to come home, and Brianna was in the family way and couldn't travel. Emmaline was determined this year would be different. And the first step was to bring the family together.

She was the youngest of her father's daughters and the last child left at home. Her younger brother, James, the baby of the family, left a few months ago, having been accepted to West Point as soon as he turned seventeen. Her two elder sisters had left the island; Agatha to seek adventure in New York and Brianna followed her husband to his family farm. Her step-brother, Henry, the eldest of her father's children, was settled on the island and doing quite well with his sponge fishing enterprise. He was now a father of six, ranging in age from three to twelve.

It was just Emmaline and their father now occupying the grand Victorian on Elizabeth Street that was once filled with laughter. Meals were often taken in silence. Her mother told stories of how her great Aunt Agatha used to demand silence while eating. It sounded awful to Emmaline as a child. The reality proved even worse to endure. Her father was never gregarious, but until her mother's passing, he had a generous spirit, especially for his children. Since her death, he had withdrawn from the world.

She was counting on the Christmas season to bring about a change of spirit for herself and especially for her father. Now that the family was coming, she needed to turn her attention to decorations and menu planning. She would need to get started now to secure the ingredients needed to make her father's favorite dishes. Turkey and sweet potatoes were some of the many things that had to be imported to the island, meaning she couldn't wait much longer and still hope to find some available. She had to make sure they would be on hand.

* * *

December 4th, second Sunday of Advent

The need to see Emmaline was a physical ache for Patrick. It had been three days since they met at the wharf. Three days of torture waiting for his next chance to see her. He was determined his uncle would not prevent it this Sunday. He had a plan and for it to work, he had to leave now, before his uncle was ready.

He shrugged into his coat and picked up his cap so there would be no delay in stepping out of the door. He approached his uncle's bedroom, took a deep breath, and spoke the rehearsed line to the closed wooden door. "Uncle, I am leaving early to run an errand. I will meet you at church."

Smithy opened his bedroom door still buttoning his shirt. "What errand could you possibly have on a Sunday morning?" He was startled to find he was speaking to an empty room.

It was a blustery morning, threatening of rain. Patrick hoped it would not thwart his encounter with Emmaline. As he walked down Simonton and turned on Eaton he was debating if he should linger in the street or wait in the church yard. He supposed the yard would seem more appropriate. It appeared he was first to arrive. He entered the gate in the white picket fence and was greeted by Reverend Herrick.

"Good morning, young Mr. Johnson. How are you?"

"Good morning, Reverend. I am well. And yourself?"

"Good. Good. I see you have come ahead of your uncle. Are you so anxious for the Word of God?"

"No, sir." Patrick realized the truth would not serve him well with the pastor. "Uh, I mean, yes, sir."

The reverend eyed him speculatively. "The way you took off last Sunday, I rather imagine your early arrival has more to do with a young lady than with your spiritual needs."

Patrick blanched. Embarrassed by his transparency, he couldn't think of a reply.

Reverend Herrick patted his shoulder. He nodded in the direction from whence Patrick had come. "You will find the view best from over there. Keep an eye on the road opposite from your walk."

Astounded, Patrick watched the Reverend enter the church chuckling to himself. Had he just received the minister's blessing to pursue Emmaline? If not his blessing, at least his aid. He walked to the indicated corner of the churchyard to lounge against a shade tree giving him an unobstructed view of Simonton Street. It wasn't long before parishioners began arriving, but as the minutes ticked by, growing ever closer to the hour, he began to despair. He could not walk into the church late. His uncle would give him a tongue thrashing such as he had never heard.

And then he saw her.

She was a vision in a straw bonnet the color of wheat just before harvest and a light sky-blue dress with a cream woolen shawl. He studied her as she approached and walked past him on the arm of her father. As he turned to follow them around the corner, trepidation seized him. He had been so focused on seeing her, he wasn't prepared for meeting her father. The sternness of his eyes and jaw did not help Patrick's confidence.

He timed his approach to meet them on the walkway to the church. As he hoped, Emmaline spoke first.

"Hello, Mr. Johnson. Good to see you again."

Patrick removed his hat and bowed his head. "Likewise, Miss Whitmore."

Emmaline said in an overly cheerful voice, "Father, this is Mr. Patrick Johnson. He is Smithy Johnson's nephew here from Virginia to apprentice with his uncle. Mr. Johnson may I present my father, Mr. Theodore Whitmore."

Patrick held out his hand. "Pleased to meet you, sir."

Theodore grudgingly shook his hand. "Hmm."

Emmaline grimaced. Her father was rarely social, but she thought he would at least be cordial. She was forced to move with him as he turned and resumed walking.

Disappointed, Patrick trailed behind them. Their family pew was five rows back on the left. Patrick slipped into the second pew on the right next to his uncle who had arrived while he waited by the tree. He tried to focus on the service, especially the Gospel reading of John the Baptist, but his mind kept reliving her father's curt greeting. What was the meaning of it? Did he disapprove of him? If so, why? He could hardly know him. Perhaps it was his forwardness in approaching them. His mind spun with any number of reasons for his dislike or distrust. Between her father and brother, it was going to be darn difficult to get to know her.

His uncle nudged his arm because he was not reciting the Lord's Prayer. Patrick made a more concerted effort to pay attention to the service. As soon as it was over, he left the pew, unwilling to wait for his uncle. His height allowed him to see Emmaline and her father. More than a dozen parishioners were between them, including Henry Whitmore and his family. Reverend Herrick winked at him as they shook hands to convey his understanding of Patrick's impatience to follow Emmaline. In the yard, people gathered in clusters to visit. A group of ladies joined Emmaline. Nearby, her father and brother talked. It did not give him an opening to speak with her. He did take heart in the glance she cast his way as if she too lamented the lost opportunity.

Two men near his age approached him, one openly friendly, the other stern in demeanor wearing a soldier's uniform. The friendly one spoke first.

"Heard you was Smithy's nephew."

"That's right."

"Name's Nate Eatonton. This is my brother Thorn."

"Patrick Johnson. Nice to meet you." They shook hands.

"I see the ladies have caught your eye. We've a few eligible belles around town. Some easier to catch than others."

Patrick frowned. "What do you mean, catch?"

"Well, some are looking for husbands and are easy to talk to, others are more cautious."

"What do you know of Miss Whitmore?"

Nate chuckled. "You do like a challenge. She rarely speaks to men."

"Why is that?"

"It's not that she dislikes them, she's just never taken an interest in them."

Thorn said, "Your intentions better be true if you plan to court her. Hurt her and you'll have more than her father to deal with."

Patrick gravely looked from one brother to the other.

Nate smiled, "She is like family to us."

Patrick thought it best to change the subject. "Obviously your brother is a soldier, what do you do Mr. Eatonton?"

"Call me Nate. I think we're going to be pals. I sponge fish for my brother-in-law, Henry."

"Ah, yes. Henry Whitmore. I've met him."

While they talked, Patrick wondered just how difficult it was going to be to get to know Emmaline, but at least he had made a friend today.

While the other ladies were discussing the latest dress design from France, Emily whispered to Emmaline, "It seems Mr. Johnson has set his cap for you."

Emmaline blushed. She whispered in reply, "Whatever has given you that idea?"

"Last week's demand to know your name, and this week his eyes have hardly stray from you. Henry told me of you speaking to him in town. It seems he is not the only one smitten."

Smitten? Was she? She certainly thought he was handsome, but she hoped she wasn't making a fool of herself over him. She abhorred girls who did so, especially when the gentlemen in question seemed to have little regard for the lady. No. She liked him as an acquaintance, but he certainly was not husband material, at least not for her. "I am hardly smitten with him. A few moments of polite conversation doesn't mean anything. Besides, he is too bold for my liking."

"Or maybe it is his boldness that has captured your attention. He is the first man I have seen you taken any notice of, polite or otherwise."

"I am sure you are mistaken."

"What have you learned of him?"

Emily's question pulled Kate Geiger's attention from her conversation with the other two ladies. "Learned of who? Do you mean the new blacksmith apprentice? He's a fine-looking man."

Emmaline pasted a friendly smile over the glare she wanted to cast at her sister-in-law. The last thing she wished to do was openly discuss Patrick Johnson.

Urania Geiger said, "He's nice I suppose."

Rebecca, a lawyer's daughter, turned up her nose. "If you like a man who does menial labor."

Mariah Watlington said, "Are you to tell me you are offended by his muscles?"

Emmaline's eyes widened at Mariah's shockingly bold reference of Patrick's body. She saw Emily cut her eyes at Mariah in disapproval.

Rebecca said, "I assure you I wouldn't notice his physique. It is his dirty hands that I abhor."

Emmaline surreptitiously looked Patrick over. It was not easy to see in his jacket, but she had felt the strength in his forearm when he escorted her to the wharf. She hadn't given any thought to a man's muscular attributes before. Mariah's forthright comment awakened her awareness and her curiosity.

It was too bad the windy gusts made the day unpleasant, shortening conversations. Theodore and Henry came to escort Emmaline and Emily home, leaving no opportunity for Emmaline and Patrick to speak.

Patrick sadly trudged beside his uncle back to the shop to face another week of hard labor before he could see Emmaline again. He had managed to overcome the obstacle his uncle presented, but now her father stood in the way. He was an obstacle Patrick wasn't sure he could overcome. He had heard rumors of other suitors who tried and failed. He wouldn't give up, he just needed to figure out how to earn her father's approval.

"Uncle, what do you know of the elder Mr. Whitmore?"

"Not much. Different social standing. He used to have a print shop. Produced a good newspaper until the fire burned it down. He was in a bad way before the fire, grieving for his wife, but it seemed like after he lost his business too, he gave up on life."

"When did his wife pass?"

"Guess it's been two years now."

"And the fire?"

"That was earlier this year, in May."

They walked the rest of the way in silence. Patrick had a lot to ponder and what his uncle told him revealed a lot of what made Mr. Whitmore so bitter. He wondered if he could find a way for the knowledge to help in his pursuit of Emmaline.

Chapter 3

Wednesday, December 7th

Having eaten their midday meal, Emmaline retreated to the morning room while her father returned to whatever he was doing in his study. She lingered by the front window, anxiously waiting for her sister's arrival. She refused to consider the steamer might be delayed. Her excitement and anxiety over her father's reaction made it difficult to focus on the novel in her hands. She was glad Brianna wrote him of her pending arrival as she wasn't sure she could find the words, but her father had not found pleasure in the news, at least not that he displayed. She wasn't near as concerned for Agatha's arrival or even if James couldn't come. It was Brianna that so favored their mother in looks and manner that Emmaline feared her presence would increase rather than diminish their father's melancholy.

It was nearly time for tea when Emmaline saw their approach. She hurried to the study unable to control her own excitement. "Father, they're here." He looked up and gave her a nod. She had a sense of his tightly held emotions behind his somber mask. She retreated to the front door, praying this reunion went smoothly.

Emmaline opened the carved paneled wood door wide as Brianna and Garrett, who carried baby Elijah, stepped onto the veranda. The joyfully reunited sisters rushed into each other's arms with tears and laughter. When they parted, they entwined arms to enter the house. Their father was waiting in the hall watching the reunion with hooded eyes. Brianna broke away to greet him with a hug. Emmaline saw the emotional pain cross his face as he embraced her.

As Brianna and her father parted, Garrett stepped forward to shake his hand. "Sir, good to see you. May I present your grandson, Elijah?"

Brianna smiled proudly at her prodigy.

Theodore reached out to touch the ten-month-old, but Elijah shyly turned away to hide his face in his father's shoulder.

Brianna stepped forward. "I'm sure Eli will warm up to you by

27

supper time. For now, he would do well with a nap."

Emmaline led her sister and nephew upstairs to Brianna's old room while Garrett and Theodore went into his study for a cigar, drink, and to discuss politics, which these days was all about slavery, state's rights, and possible succession. Brianna changed Eli's diaper and then settled on the edge of the bed and undid her top layers to nurse him.

Emmaline took a seat on the bed next to her and smiled at her sister. "Motherhood suits you."

Brianna looked up from her son with a radiant smile. "I love being a mother even more than I love being Garrett's wife. I feel very blessed." She gave her sister a searching look. "Is there not anyone who has caught your eye?"

Patrick's face immediately came to mind, but Emmaline shook her head. "Not really."

"You say no, but your eyes give you away. Who is he?"

"I don't know him well enough to know if I fancy him."

"Fancy has nothing to do with how well you know him. Fancy is usually about attraction first and the rest after. What is his name?"

"Patrick Johnson."

"What is your impression of him?"

Emmaline cast about for how best to describe Patrick. "He seems modestly educated, a bit forward, but polite."

"And his looks?"

She calmly answered her sister, but she felt her heart speed up as she focused on his image in her mind. "He's handsome. Dark hair and eyes, and tall." Needing her sister's advice, she made a confession. "For some reason, he makes me irrational."

Brianna's eyes widened in surprise. "What do you mean?"

"Well... for instance, before we were introduced, he was rudely staring at me on the street. His audacity made me angry, so I walked right up to him and demanded to know why."

Brianna's jaw dropped. Her sister was as cautious and proper as they come and normally a bit shy. Such temerity was not in her character. "What was his excuse?"

Emmaline frowned. "He never gave one. He caught me off guard by knowing my name."

"Well that certainly speaks to interest on his part."

"I suppose so."

"Do you have any reservations in his character to cause concern?"

Emmaline carefully considered the question. "Other than being forward, not really."

"And how do you feel about him?"

"I don't have feelings for him."

Brianna was determined to get her to admit the truth. "Are you trying to tell me if he was in front of you now, you would have no interest in him?"

Emmaline opened her mouth to say no but she couldn't speak a lie. "Curiosity is not the same as feelings."

"Sometimes it is, or at the least one will lead to the other. How many times have you been in each other's company?"

"Only once, or I suppose you could say three times."

"Why is that?"

"First, we bumped into each other on the street the day of his arrival. I didn't notice him, but he did me, which led to him asking Henry and Emily for an introduction, and failing that, asking for my name."

"Did they give it to him?"

"Henry refused but Emily did. Next was the meeting in the street I told you about, and then he approached father and I before church this Sunday, but father gave him little regard."

"And afterward church?"

"Others kept us apart."

"What does he do?"

"He's a blacksmith apprentice to his uncle."

Brianna grew silent considering how to arrange another meeting between the two.

Emmaline sighed as she watched her nephew suckle. Daydreams of having a baby of her own filled her mind for a moment. With a wistful smile she brought her attention back to the present. "I wanted to talk to you about our Christmas plans."

"Ah, yes. The Christmas plans. When do Agatha and James arrive?"

"Agatha will be here a few days before Christmas. James says he can't leave, and Agatha promises to bring him anyway, so I guess we will see what happens."

Brianna smiled. "My bet is on Agatha. When she sets her mind to something..."

Emmaline grinned. "She is a force to be reckoned with."

"So, in the meantime, we have some decorating to do and food to consider."

"I wanted all of our traditional dishes, so I have already made up the menu and ordered what was needed. I only hope father doesn't get upset over the extra expense."

Brianna heard it in her tone. "You've had a difficult time dealing with our bereaved and taciturn sire."

Tears welled in Emmaline's eyes as she nodded.

Brianna shifted Eli's weight to pat her hand in comfort. "You poor dear."

Emmaline confessed her fear. "Brianna, I don't know what to do if we can't pull him out of his grief. Every day is a little worse. He's a little more quiet, a little more bitter, a little more withdrawn. Some days I feel as if I live in this house alone."

Brianna leaned over to hug her sister's shoulder, dislodging Eli who promptly let the ladies know of his dissatisfaction. Brianna pulled away and laughed. "Just like a man. Now, where were we? Decorations I suppose. Have you been up to the attic?"

"Not yet. I wasn't sure if we should decorate as mother used to or keep it simple."

"Oh, we should definitely put up all the decorations. This house has been in mourning for too long. It is time to live and celebrate again."

"And what if it upsets Poppa?"

"Upsetting him is the point. Allowing him to wallow in self-pity is not doing him any good. And that reminds me of his gift. What is the latest?"

"Henry expects it to arrive next week. Are you sure about this? What if Poppa wants nothing to do with it?"

"That is a chance we'll have to take, in which case we'll sell it, but at least we will have tried." Brianna cocked her head and grinned. "Now, do you know what I need?"

Emmaline shook her. "No. What do you need?"

"Momma's cinnamon bread."

Emmaline blanched.

Brianna frowned. "What is it?"

"Poppa has forbidden it."

"Forbidden it?"

"Yes."

"He's worse than I understood him to be. When was the last time you tried making it?"

"Last Christmas."

"Well this Christmas is different. Momma always made it for guests and Garrett is a guest. He tells me I haven't the knack for it, so he is counting on you."

"Alright, I'll make it, but not tonight. Your arrival is upsetting enough."

Brianna sobered. "I know. I felt his reserve in our greeting. Very well. We'll save the bread for another day." She checked her drowsy son. "Let me put this boy down for his nap, and we can continue our visit."

"I had the cradle brought down from the attic." Emmaline looked from Eli to the cradle. "But I suppose he's too big for it."

"It was a thoughtful gesture. We'll find something else for him later. For now, would you like to hold him?"

Emmaline smiled a very full and genuine smile. It felt like the first in years. "I would."

Brianna gratefully transferred her chubby son to her sister's arms, having supported his weight during the feeding.

Emmaline studied the soft features of the sweetly sleeping babe and inhaled the unique scent of babyhood that clung to little Eli. She kissed his forehead. She had at various times helped to care for all six of Henry's children but for some reason Brianna's son was extra special. She could only suppose it was because of the close bond of sisterhood. Henry and Emily were so much older than her. The family dynamics between them were different, and so her relationship with their offspring, while close, was also different.

Brianna's heart was full at the sight of her youngest sister holding her son. "Will you be his godmother?"

Emmaline's hazel eyes rose to meet Brianna's bright blue ones. "I would be honored."

"I was hoping we could baptize him Sunday."

"And his godfather?"

"Garrett's elder brother."

"Won't that create a conflict if the worst were to happen?"

"Whichever of you is married then will take custody."

"And what if neither of us are or both of us?"

"If neither, Eli will stay with Garrett's family. If both of you, then he will come to you."

"I see."

"It's not ideal, I know, but I wanted Eli to have a strong connection with my family. Having you as his godmother secures that." Brianna rose and looked about the room. "You haven't changed it much." Emmaline looked up to see to what she was referring. Brianna said, "The room."

"I have touched nothing except to dust and to have the bed linens cleaned. There hasn't been any reason to change things."

Brianna brought her gaze to Emmaline's face. "Has it been so bad being here alone with Poppa?"

The sympathy in her voice nearly released a flood of tears. Emmaline had to work hard to contain her emotion. Eli squirmed in her tightened hold. She closed her eyes and breathed deeply, forcing her arms to relax and the tears at bay. "It has not been bad."

"Your eyes betray you."

Emmaline grimaced. "It has been lonely and sad to live in this house. Poppa gets upset at any added reminders of Momma and clings tightly to others, like her portraits."

"What makes you think having Christmas will help?"

"I don't know that it will. It was all I could think of to try and pull him from his grief."

Brianna sat down and placed her arm around her sister's shoulder. They leaned their heads together. "Then we will do all we can to make this work. And at least for the next few weeks, you are not alone."

Emmaline closed her eyes and sighed. Brianna's assurance, gentle spirit, and comforting presence brought peace to Emmaline for the first time since her mother's passing. Even if it didn't help her father, at least her Christmas plan was helping her.

* * *

Supper was lively for a change. Not only was there Garrett and Brianna to talk to and the antics of introducing Eli to new tropical foods, but Henry's family also joined them. Emmaline had planned for the large gathering with their cook, Mrs. Faraday, preparing a feast for their evening meal to be served at the table beneath the old mahogany tree and a sunset sky. She was glad the weather was cooperating.

Henry and Emily's children were anxious to meet Eli, especially their eldest, twelve-year-old Ella Rose. They gathered around the youngest family member almost from the moment they entered the door. Eli did well being surrounded by strangers and allowing Ella's attentions. With five younger siblings, she was quite adept at tending the baby. The ten-year-old twins, Alexander and Benjamin, soon lost interest and went outside to play until supper. Six-year-old Margaret tagged along after her eldest brothers. Four-year-old Henrietta, on the other hand, preferred her Aunt Emmie's attention while three-year-old Lawrence refused to be parted from his mother. It took until the family was nearly ready to leave before Laurie warmed up to his Aunt Brianna and Uncle Garrett.

The family had an enjoyable evening visiting with each other and sharing a good meal. Emmaline even caught a hint of a smile creep into their poppa's face. Afterwards, they adjourned to the parlor. Emmaline listened as Brianna and Emily shared their stories of the joys and woes of motherhood. Across the room, the men spoke of politics, the topics varying little these days. Between them were the children, with Ella watching over the youngest.

Brianna said, "Emily, would you mind watching over Eli tomorrow morning? I have an errand to run, and I would really like to have Emmaline join me."

Emily smiled. "It would be a joy to get to know my nephew better. Why don't you make a day of it? You two probably have lots of sisterly bonding to do and holiday plans to attend to."

"That would be lovely. Are you sure it's not too much of an imposition? You already have your hands full."

"Not at all. Ella Rose is a God's send when it comes to taking care of the younger ones, and we would love nothing more than a chance to spoil Eli."

"Well then, I will certainly take your offer. I haven't had a day to myself since he was born."

"Why that's a shame! My mother gives me a day to myself at least once a month. It helps restore my good humor as nothing else can and makes me a better mother for it."

"I can well imagine."

"Tomorrow you shall know for yourself."

* * *

Emmaline closed the door behind her on Emily's boisterous household to join Brianna, who seemed almost giddy with excitement to have a day to herself. "Now, will you tell me what this mysterious errand is all about in which you insisted I must look my best?"

Brianna linked her arm around Emmaline's printed cotton sleeve. "Not yet, sister dear." She led her further into town to Front Street as they chatted about the weather and the latest news of Key West friends. As they reached Front Street, Brianna paused, seeing for the first time the now empty lot where their father's print shop and newspaper office once stood. The ground had been cleared of debris, with little evidence remaining of the lost livelihood or of the tragedy that destroyed it. She whispered, "At least Poppa wasn't lost in the fire."

Emmaline said, "I know. If it had happened during the day, I'm sure he would have tried to save it or done more to stop the fire, harming himself more than he did. At least all he suffered was singed hair and smoke inhalation."

"He has not mentioned rebuilding?"

"Not once."

Brianna's brow wrinkled with concern. "I pray you are right that it is because without a press he doesn't see the point."

"He won't spend the money for a new press and the building."

"Hence the reason we are giving him one. It is an expensive gift if that is not the real reason."

"Henry agrees with me. Poppa needs purpose again."

"That I agree with. I am only saying, he may not appreciate the gift, nor the interference."

"I too worry about that, but I don't know of anything else to motivate him."

Brianna turned them away. "Only time will tell. Now tell me, is the blacksmith's shop in the same place?"

Emmaline was stunned by the question. "The blacksmith? Why ever are we going there?"

"To order a Christmas gift for my husband and to see about getting you one, a husband that is."

Emmaline stopped walking and turned to stare at her sister. "Brianna Kate, I will not parade myself in front of a man."

Brianna softly smiled. "You are not parading. You are accompanying me on an errand. If it gives you a chance to get better acquainted with a certain young man, so be it."

"I couldn't."

Brianna pulled Emmaline to continue walking. "You can and you will. I insist. Poppa is not the only one wallowing in grief. It is time you were settled."

"I'm not against being settled, but this is not the way."

"It is for you. Waiting for chance encounters on Sundays is going to take entirely too long. This gives you at least two more chances to meet, and if I have my say, it will be three."

Emmaline's voice was filled with concern. "What are you scheming?"

"You will see him today when we place the order, again when we come to pick it up, as I will distract the uncle so you two may visit, and a third when he and his uncle come to dinner."

"Come to dinner?"

"Yes. I plan to invite them to dinner."

Emmaline was overwhelmed. She would have never thought her

sweet sister to be so cunning. That was Agatha's territory. They turned on Simonton Street.

"Ah, I see it is still in the same place. And is that Patrick shoveling coal?"

"It is."

"He's nice looking."

Emmaline didn't comment but knew her blush told her sister more than enough.

Brianna approached the forge with seeming nonchalance. She paused just outside the shed covering to speak to Patrick. Emmaline trailed behind, garnering Patrick's attention. He set the shovel against the coal bin, dusted his hands against his pants, and approached them. He doffed his visor cap. "Good morning, ladies."

Brianna nudged Emmaline to speak.

"Good morning, Mr. Johnson. This is my sister, lately arrived from Pennsylvania, Mrs. Cade."

"Pleased to meet you, ma'am."

Brianna turned her gaze on her sister. "Nonsense, Emmie. When have we ever adhered to such formality with family friends?" She turned her blue gaze to the strapping young lad. "You may call me Brianna."

Just then Smithy approached.

"Good morning, Miss Emmaline, Miss Brianna. Oh, pardon me, ma'am, it's Mrs. Cade now, if I recall correctly."

"Yes, that's right. Good morning to you, Smithy."

"What can I do for you?"

Brianna took his arm and turned him into the shop giving Emmaline a private wink as she did so. "I am here to see if you can make a special sign. It is to be a Christmas gift for my husband."

"How large of a sign?"

As Brianna and Smithy moved deeper into the forge area to discuss details, Emmaline and Patrick were left alone. They both looked at each other and their eyes darted away to the surrounding area, the murmur of voices from within the forge, and back to each other in the search of something to say.

Patrick was thrilled with the unexpected weekday encounter with Emmaline.

Left alone, they both were suddenly unsure of what to say. They glanced at each other and looked away and then back again.

Patrick finally said, "Your sister is forward." Realizing his word choice might offend, he quickly added, "I mean in a good way."

Emmaline gave a puzzled look towards Brianna. "It is not in her nature to be so. Agatha is the forward one of us three." She redolently smiled. "And quite happy to be so, I might add. I think she enjoys shocking people, though she means no harm."

"It sounds as though you admire her a little."

Emmaline's gaze swung to his as she pondered his statement. "I suppose you're right. Being reticent myself, I do admire her for boldly seeking what she wants of life rather than conforming to society's dictates."

"And what is it she does?"

"She's a writer for the New York Weekly."

"So, it runs in the family. I heard your father used to produce a paper here."

"He did. He also was a partner with the founder of the paper Agatha writes for. I suppose that made it a little easier for her to get started."

"It still took a whole lot of gumption."

Emmaline nodded. "I daresay you're right." Her gaze was drawn to the brawn of his exposed forearms. She could see the muscles she had felt beneath her hand on their walk to the wharf. She raised her eyes to his. "How is your apprenticeship progressing? Do you find you enjoy the work?"

"I like it better than farming. Whether or not it is my life's calling, I've not enough experience yet to know. Uncle lets me wield the hammer for the brunt of the work, but he has not let me try my hand at some of the creative details. If I have a talent for that then I may stick to the work. It 'tis important work, especially to the ships needing replacement parts."

"You could ask permission to make an anchor. Those don't have to be perfect to function and they are in high enough demand around here that some won't care what it looks like."

Patrick smiled. "I like your thinking."

Brianna emerged in the sunlight still speaking to Smithy. "When do you think it will be ready?"

"Next Friday should be time enough."

Patrick inwardly sighed. His moment with Emmaline was at an end. Desperate to keep his tie to her he said, "Could I walk you home from church on Sunday?"

Emmaline tried to hold back her excitement. "Yes, you may."

Brianna gave Smithy a nod. "That will do. Thank you, sir."

Smithy gave her a lopsided grin. "Thank you, ma'am." He turned his gaze on his nephew. "Patrick, hurry up with that coal. We've got work to do. Good day, ladies." He hurried off to stoke his fire.

Patrick tipped his hat with a smile. "Good day, Emmaline. Brianna." He waved to Emmaline as he turned away.

Brianna gave him a nod. "Good day, Patrick."

Emmaline smiled shyly as she returned his wave. She reluctantly turned away to walk with Brianna.

"So?"

Emmaline gave her a questioning look.

Brianna huffed. "What did you two speak of?"

"Oh. Mostly of Agatha."

"Agatha? Whatever for?"

"Well it started out with you and drifted to her. But it doesn't matter. He asked to walk me home from church."

"Good boy. I knew I liked him." Brianna turned a concerned gaze to her sister. "You did accept and not give him the idea he must ask Poppa first."

Emmaline threw her a saucy look. "I am not that meek and subservient. Of course, I said yes. Besides, I know from last Sunday Poppa is likely to turn him down if asked."

Brianna already heard of last Sunday's meeting. "I'm sure you're right." She inhaled the salty air. "I miss that."

"What?"

"The ocean breeze. Pennsylvania's pretty country, but I miss this island." She took another deep breath as they followed Simonton Street southeast towards home.

Emmaline said, "Shall we venture into the attic for the decorations when we get home? Unless you need to stop and nurse Eli first."

"Heavens, no. Thankfully, he is past the stage of constant feedings. He will be fine until supper. Starting on the decorations will be fun, and I can't think of a better time than now, while Eli is being cared for."

A short while later, the girls climbed the second story staircase to the attic door. The narrow steps were a tight fit for their wide hoops. Emmaline was feeling the strain of pulling the squeezed cage by the time she reached the top. She opened the door inward and felt a rush of warm air pass over her. Even in December, the sunbaked roof heated the space beneath. At least it was not as terrible as summer. Her hem left markings in the dust coating the plank floor as she moved into the arched space beneath the rafters. Dust motes danced in the filtered sunlight of the gable vents. Her gaze swept over the mélange of items cast aside over the years. Empty trunks were stacked closest to the door, vainly awaiting their next adventure. Further in was a mixture of old furniture, crates of miscellaneous items, and trunks full of old quilts and blankets. One thing they would not find up here was old clothes. Her mother did not believe in saving them as fashions changed, and there were always those in need.

Brianna turned to Emmaline. "I expected to see some of mother's things in here."

"Poppa has not allowed any of her things to be moved. Especially from their room."

"Another way in which he isn't healing."

Her sister's tone pricked Emmaline with guilt, but really, there was nothing she could have done different. Her father refused to allow her mother's things to be removed, and Emmaline wasn't willing to face his wrath by doing so without his consent.

Brianna happened to catch the distress on her sister's face. "Oh dearest, I'm sorry. I didn't mean to imply you were at fault. It is father's failure, not yours. Somehow, we have to make him face his sorrow. Now enough of this maudlin thinking. Where is the Christmas box?"

"I'm not sure." They made their way to the steep ladder-like stairs in the center of the room. Brianna wistfully looked up the narrow steps leading to the hatch in the roof. "I swear I'm going to leave off my hoop skirt one day so I can visit the cupola."

Emmaline's face brightened as she looked at Brianna as if she had come up with a brilliant idea. "Why not today, Bri? There's no one else in the house but the servants, and it would certainly make searching in this attic easier. These skirts are dreadfully inconvenient at times." She brushed at the dust marring her skirt. "I don't know why it didn't occur to me sooner to change into some of my old clothes for this."

Brianna smiled. "I like your thinking."

The girls eagerly made their way to Emmaline's room to help each other undress. They donned old blouses and cotton skirts sans the petticoats and hoops. As they left the room, Emmaline turned to whisper, "I feel indecent." She ran her hands down the sides of her straight skirt. "We're only a corset and chemise away from nightclothes in midday. It's shameful."

Brianna smiled. "Only if we're caught."

They hurried back to the attic stairs, anxious not to be spotted by any of the servants.

Once inside the dim shadows of the attic, Emmaline once again turned to Brianna. "To the cupola first or save it for last?"

Brianna smiled broadly. "First."

Emmaline looked down again at the skirt clinging to her legs. "Perhaps we best not go up at all."

"Nonsense. The railing will hide us from view. No one will be the wiser."

Emmaline smiled at Brianna's girlish giggle as they raced to the steps in their lightened clothing. Brianna reached it first, eagerly leading the way up the stairs to unlatch the hatch, and out into the bright sunlight of late morning. She turned to help her sister up. They walked the perimeter of the railed platform perched on the roof's peak. The cupola was uncovered, as her mother requested, so she could gaze at the stars to her heart's content. Their cupola was not as grand as the Eatonton's Captain's Walk but it was still a special place to visit.

From their vantage point they could see to the cleared ground of the new cemetery not far beyond the house, the roofs of the barracks on the northern beach, the church spires in the direction of town, Mr. Tift's lookout tower on the bight, and the lighthouse off to the south. The canopy of trees, mostly palm, obscured the rest of town from view. Only the roofs of the taller houses and businesses could be seen. They were too far inland to get much of the coastal breeze, but it was still enough to play with the tendrils of their hair.

Brianna smiled. "I love it up here."

Emmaline turned to gaze upon her sister's profile. "I've missed you."

Brianna heard the wistful tone. She turned her head to her sister with affectionate, tender feelings brimming in her chest. "I have missed you too."

Emmaline impatiently wiped a leaking tear away. "Not as much. You have your husband and son."

"True, but they cannot replace a dear sister." They linked arms and stared out to the distant blue horizon smattered with puffy cotton clouds.

After a moment's peaceful quiet, Emmaline said, "We should have thought of bonnets. I can feel the freckles popping out on my nose."

Brianna laughed. "You always were sensitive about them. Shall we get to our task, then?"

It didn't take long to find the Christmas box near the stack of empty trunks. It wasn't very large, containing mostly red velvet ribbon and a few keepsakes.

Brianna gave a lingering look of longing at the closed hatch before shutting the attic door behind her. Maybe she and Garrett could sneak up here tonight for some star gazing of their own. She secretly smiled at the idea.

Emmaline carried the box down to her room where they first redressed in their normal clothes. It was fun for a bit to shed the heavy garments, but it felt right to once again be properly dressed. They took the box down to the dining room to spread out the bows and unroll the ribbon used for garland. They used a damp rag to dust them and fiddled with plumping up the sad looking bows.

Emmaline gave Brianna a concerned look. "Do you think we should buy new ribbon?"

Brianna turned the bow in her hand and shook her head. "By the time we add these to the greenery, no one will notice. They will do fine."

Under the ribbon was a small wooden box. Emmaline ran her hand over the cover before undoing the catch, prolonging the moment and letting the memories wash over her. She gently lifted the globe from the velvet lining.

It was just an ornament. A hallow ball blown from ruby red mercury glass with an embossed copper cap suspended from a red silk ribbon. It was called a Kugel. To anyone else it was just a pretty decoration, but to her it was exquisitely special. It embodied every beautiful memory from a long-ago Christmas spent in Austria with her father's parents. It represented soaring spires and domed roofs set against majestic snow-covered mountains, her first encounter with Christmas trees, and the breathtaking beauty of all that was for sale in the Christkindlmarkt. The ornament was a gift from her Grandmama. It was the one and only time she and her siblings met their paternal grandparents. She may have perpetually shivered in the cold climate, but it didn't matter. Innsbruck, Austria was becharming to her young eyes. Now over a decade later, the ornament still brought to mind the magical place where she learned about sleigh rides, muffs and woolen undergarment, ice skating, the beauty of newly fallen snow, and the love of her grandparents.

Brianna appeared at her shoulder. "That was a wonderful Christmas. You were smart to forego the sweets and ask for the ornament."

"It wasn't intentional. I just wanted the ornament more than I wanted the treats. I can't believe Grandmama would purchase something so expensive for me and not for each of you." Emmaline careful laid the ornament back in its velvet nest.

"I think she was a very smart woman who gave us each our heart's desire that day, no matter the cost."

Emmaline nodded in agreement. "It was really sweet of her. How was your gingerbread heart?"

"Tasty."

"And then James generously shared his bag of peppermint sticks and comfits."

"Yes he did. What did Agatha ask for?"

"I don't recall."

Brianna reached into the box. She held up a mold made of pear wood to study the carving of a courting knight and lady. "Do you remember the springerle biscuits?"

"I do. We enjoyed them so much Momma bought the mold."

"And do you remember trying to make them here?" They both smiled.

Emmaline shook her head. "Too much heat and humidity. What a mess we had trying to get the dough out of the mold, and it would never sufficiently dry to get a good impression. They baked out into a flat biscuit. Agatha declared them to be nothing special and refused to touch them."

Brianna shook her head. "That was just an excuse. She doesn't care for anise."

"I didn't know that. They were still good to eat."

"Yes, they were. As I recall, Poppa had more than his fair share. All this talk of sweets has made me hungry. I hope it's time for lunch?"

Emmaline consulted her watch fob. "It is. We should move these ribbons and bows to the morning room to keep until it's time to put up the greenery."

Brianna picked up the Kugel and handed it to Emmaline. "You should hang this in the window first."

Emmaline took the ribbon from her and walked to the parlor window with Brianna trailing behind. She reached up beneath the curtain with her free hand to find the nail still in the window frame. Carefully she hung the ornament. Both girls watched the sunlight play upon the crimson glass before turning their attention back to the ribbon.

* * *

They retrieved Elijah after lunch, to the relief of mother, son, and Aunt Emily. It was now after teatime. Brianna and Emmaline were playing on the parlor floor with a happy baby just awake from his afternoon nap.

Brianna grew concerned when Emmaline retreated into silence for a spell. "Is something bothering you, Emmie?"

Emmaline looked to her sister's concerned gaze. "Maybe I shouldn't have said yes to Patrick."

"It's just a walk home from church."

"Shouldn't he have asked Poppa first?"

"Of for heaven's sakes. We are allowed to say if we want to walk with a gentleman or not. It's not as if he was proposing marriage, though I bet he will one day."

Emmaline's jaw dropped. "Marriage? No. He is just being nice. He probably hasn't had a chance to meet any of the other girls. When he does, I'm sure he will pick one of them. That is, if he doesn't have a girl in Virginia."

Brianna smiled. "He wouldn't look at you the way he does if he didn't hold you above all others."

"What if I'm not ready for courtship?"

"You are only worrying because it's something new. You're nineteen. More than old enough for courting."

"Maybe old enough, but it doesn't mean I want to be courted."

"Why ever not? Courting is the fun part. Marriage is the work."

Emmaline tried a different argument. "I should tell him I've changed my mind. I couldn't possible leave Poppa."

"Who said anything about you leaving Poppa? Your husband could live here."

"What if he doesn't want to? He may want to return to Virginia. I don't want to leave Key West."

"My, aren't we putting the cart before the horse. It's just a walk Em. You can worry about the rest when it comes to pass."

"And what of Poppa? He's very likely to say something horrible when Patrick comes to me on Sunday. He was very cold to him last week."

"You leave Poppa to me."

"Very well." Emmaline frowned. "What if we have nothing to talk about?"

Brianna sighed with exasperation. "Then talk about the weather. Ask about his family. Ask his favorite color. You can find something to talk about Emmaline."

Her sister's continued silence made Brianna turn her head askance. "Is something else bothering you?"

Emmaline bit her lip as she worked up the nerve to ask her question. "How will I know if he likes me?"

"By how he treats you. He will make you feel special and do anything to please you. That is important. If he's not willing to please you now before you're married, he won't even try afterwards. You can't change a man Emmaline."

"How will I know if he's the one?"

Brianna smiled with a faraway look. "You'll just know. You will want to be with him all the time. You'll miss him when you're apart. Your insides get all jumpy when you see him. You would do anything to make him happy. When you're in love, his world becomes your world."

Emmaline couldn't imagine what that must feel like. She wasn't a selfish person, but she couldn't imagine being that giving to another person. Brianna interrupted her thoughts.

"Do you want Patrick to walk you home?"

Emmaline thought of the excitement she felt when he asked and the way she answered without hesitation. In the moment, she wanted nothing more than to continue their liaison. Her lip quirked as she accepted the truth of her feelings. "Yes."

Chapter 4

At his uncle's impatient call, Patrick put away the trimming scissors. His mustache was as neat as it was going to be. He had to shave his beard a few days ago, having singed it being careless with a stick of heated iron. He was fortunate he hadn't burned his face too. As the days were passing, he found less and less to like about forging. He couldn't quit unless he came up with another means of earning a livelihood.

He donned his necktie and checked his image. It was as good as he could make it. He shrugged into his Sunday coat at the door, smoothing it down in a nervous gesture. He was even more anxious to see Emmaline this Sunday than last. Knowing he would have more time with her increased his excitement.

Stepping outside the door, the ominous clouds dampened his spirits. Please don't rain.

* * *

Sunday was upon her before she knew it. Emmaline dressed with extra care for church, more than aware of the butterfly fluttering of her stomach. She had never before experienced such nervousness. She chose a winter pink shirtwaist that flattered her complexion and paired it with a navy skirt and black velvet sash. She glanced out the window to check the weather. The sky was gloomy and threatening this morning. She hoped it would clear away or their walk would be postponed. It could even prevent them from speaking to each other altogether. As she dressed, she kept glancing out her window in the hopes of seeing signs of the clouds breaking.

Poppa's call from downstairs had her rushing for the door where he waited to hand her into the carriage to join Brianna, Garrett and Eli. That her father had called for the transport to travel the equivalent of three blocks was not a good sign.

* * *

Emmaline felt guilty for praying more for the weather to clear than for the sanctity of her soul or the needs of others. It was especially shameful being the third Sunday of Advent. Still, she asked it of Him.

She could see Patrick's bowed head several pews ahead of her. He was seated before her family's arrival, so she had only caught a glimpse of him, and much to her surprise his beard was gone. The strong line of his chin in profile was surprisingly provocative. She had a hard time keeping her gaze from continually straying to him. It was a great relief when the final hymn began, bringing an end to the wait.

They exited the church to find the sky was still overcast, but the clouds were light. She stopped midway down the walk in expectation of speaking with friends. Her father continued to the street, but Brianna and Garrett paused with her. They were soon joined by Patrick with his uncle trailing behind. Garrett and Smithy were introduced to each other.

After a few moments of mundane conversation Patrick said to his uncle, "You can go on without me. I'm going to see Miss Whitmore home." His uncle gave him an assessing look making Patrick nervously shuffle his stance. He breathed easier when Uncle Smithy gave a slight nod, bid the others good day, and parted company. Patrick turned to Emmaline with an eager smile.

Emmaline shyly met his gaze. Something about his clean-shaven chin made him seem more... virile, she supposed. It definitely upset her equilibrium. The beard had somehow made him seem more approachable and harmless by softening the planes of his face. Now he had the hard edge of a young, strapping man. A man who watched her with a disturbing intensity unlike any man before him. She wasn't sure she liked it, but she didn't dislike it either.

Brianna turned to her husband. "Garrett, be a dear and take Eli to Poppa. Tell him the three of us will walk home."

Garrett said, "You want me to leave Eli with your father?"

"Yes, I do. It will be good for both of them."

"What if he starts crying or your father refuses?"

"Hand over Eli, tell Poppa we're walking, shut the door, tell the driver to go, and walk away fast without giving either one of them a chance to gainsay you. Poppa has plenty of experience to take care of Eli long enough to return to the house. Mrs. Paden will be more than happy to take over from there."

Garrett shook his head as he turned away. "Yes, dear."

Brianna winked at Emmaline secretly reminding her, *a man in love will do anything to please you.*

Garrett returned as the carriage pulled away. They looked to him expectantly and he answered, "He wasn't happy about it."

Brianna smiled demurely. "Which one?"

"Neither to be truthful. Eli looked at me as if I had betrayed him, and I think your father would have yelled at me if not for Eli."

"It will be fine. They need time to bond."

"And you think this is the way to do it?"

"It was a good way to force them into it."

Brianna took Garrett's arm and together they turned towards the gate and walked out to the street. Patrick offered Emmaline his arm and they followed behind.

* * *

Theodore held fast to the child on his lap, knowing how quickly they could move. He watched as Eli's expression wavered between curiosity and distress. He felt the same. The rhythmic clop of the horse's hooves eased them both.

He couldn't believe Brianna would place her baby in his care. It wasn't that it had been so long since he had held a baby, Henry's youngest was three, but it had been a long time since one was left solely in his care. The two of them studied each other in the shadowed confines of the rocking carriage. He didn't know what Eli saw in him, but in his grandson he saw many similarities to his youngest son, James.

The first year of James' life was some of the best memories he had of being a father. Unlike with his other children, he was there for every first moment. His first smile, his first steps, his first foods, even his first breath. Witnessing the miracle of James' new life helped put into perspective the trials of Theodore's own life. He wondered now if Brianna was trying to do the same by forcing him to tend to Elijah.

He knew he had shut the world out since Betsy's passing. Her sudden death from heart failure had left a hollow emptiness inside him. The ache of it made him withdraw from everyone. Watching life go on as if it hadn't happened was too cruel for him to face, but it didn't stop it from continuing. This grandson was proof of that. Somehow, he had to find a way to rejoin the land of the living, no matter how much it hurt.

* * *

Emmaline was unsure how to behave on this planned outing. She had seen other girls act coy and flirtatious, but she didn't know how to begin in such a manor. It was not in her nature. She glanced at his profile and her gaze caught again on the angles of his jaw. This close she could see the faint skin irritations from the straight edge. She wanted to ask why he shaved his beard, but it was too personal a question. Unfortunately, her curiosity about his grooming kept her from thinking of anything else clever to say so she commented on the weather. "It seems as if the storm has passed us by."

"So it has. Is it wrong that I prayed that it would?"

Emmaline smirked. "If so, we are both guilty."

"Really? I would not have thought it of you."

"You think me so pious? Though I do try, I assure you I have my selfish failings."

"I doubt they are many."

Emmaline gave him a self-deprecating shake of her head. The look he cast her made her pulse skitter. The intensity of his gaze was like no other. She blinked and still his gaze did not falter. It wasn't threatening, but still, it made her nervous and self-conscience. It was as if he were absorbing every detail of her face and every nuance of her expression. The intense scrutiny made her uncomfortable, but she couldn't seem to pull her gaze from his either.

"You are the most beautiful creature I have ever seen." When her eyes widened and her cheeks took on a rosy hue, Patrick realized he had spoken the thought aloud.

Now that the spell was broken, Emmaline lifted her hand from his arm in a pretense of checking her bonnet ties. She put a little space between them.

Patrick grimaced. "Forgive me, Emmaline, for being so forward. I'm afraid I didn't realize I had spoken aloud. You make me forget myself."

"Speak no more of it, I beg of you." She took several breaths to calm her racing pulse.

"As you wish. I will say no more of your beauty. What of your kind heart? May I speak of that?"

Emmaline glanced at his face to see it matched the hint of humor she detected in his tone. "You would still tease me?"

"I assure you, I don't mean to tease. I do find you beguiling, enchanting, tempting, enticing..."

Emmaline could bear no more. "Enough of your sweet talk. If that is all you have to say you may go home now and leave me in peace."

"Has no one ever complimented you before?"

"I have received compliments aplenty. Just not from the likes of you."

"And what am I?" He was anxious to know what she thought of

him.

"A... Um... Well..." She grew as frustrated with herself as with him. "You're a silver tongued devil is what you are."

"No, not a devil, I assure you. I mean you no harm."

She gave him a measuring look. If he didn't mean her harm than just what was he meaning? She turned her gaze forward and bit her lip. She was so unsure of what to say or how to act. Was he flirting with her or stalking her like prey? If this was courting, she didn't like it. She didn't like this unsettled feeling at all.

Patrick's intrigue grew as he watched her nervously worrying her lower lip. He affected her. He was upsetting her equilibrium. It assured him his were not the only feelings disturbed between them.

Emmaline became aware of their surroundings and was surprised to find they were only halfway home. She had to turn this conversation to safer ground or she would walk into the house with a face that was beet red. "How many brothers and sisters did you say you have?"

Patrick's grin went lopsided. He would let her pull away. For now. "Eight. One older and one younger brother and five sisters, all younger."

"So you are the second oldest and the second son."

"I am."

"You mentioned farming before. I take it that's what your family does?"

"Yes."

"What crops do you grow?"

"Mostly hemp which is sold to a company that makes rope. It grows well in our mountains."

"I see."

"Have you ever left this island?"

The doubt in his voice made her answer defensively. "Of course I have." Derisively she turned the question on him. "Have you ever left your mountain before?"

"No. This would be the first."

Instantly, she felt contrite for her tone. "Oh. What do you think of our island?"

"It's beautiful." He would have added that she was more so but didn't want to upset her again.

"Even so. I'm sure you must be homesick."

"I have had moments, especially missing my family. Uncle Smithy is not a very garrulous fellow except when giving orders and my family is anything but quiet. I also miss the peaceful beauty of a dewy mountain morning or sitting on my favorite rock below the tumbling water of Falling Spring."

"Is that a waterfall?"

"It is. A rather pretty one spilling over a sharp, tree lined ridge to fall upon a pile of moss-covered boulders."

Her voice grew wistful as she looked off into the distance. "I would love to see a waterfall. Henry took Emily to Niagara Falls on their honeymoon."

Patrick laughed. "Mine is nothing so grand as that one, or so I've heard. I've not seen it myself. Something else I've not seen is a waterspout."

Emmaline's gaze returned to his. "Where did you hear of waterspouts?"

"One of the sailors visiting the forge told a tale of water spinning in the air. He was probably pulling my leg."

Emmaline shook her head. "No. He was telling the truth, likely embellished a bit, but nevertheless the truth." Unaware of the coy smile she cast his way, she added, "I have seen one."

If Patrick hadn't been enamored before, he surely was now. Her half smile captured his heart. It was a good thing they had reached her house. Another five minutes and he might have declared himself to be in love with her.

They entered the house to discover her older brother, Henry, and his family were there too. Patrick later learned they alternated Sunday dinners between his family and Emily's and on holidays both families joined together. Patrick cordially greeted Emmaline's father who returned his handshake with a speculative look and only slightly more warmth than their first meeting. He said little afterwards to Patrick or to anyone else in the family. The patriarch mostly sat brooding either in a wing-backed chair by the window in the parlor or at the head of the table during the meal. The rest of the family acted as if it was his typical behavior. Patrick wondered if it had always been so, but discarded the idea, for there was an underlying tension in the room belying their outward appearance.

From the moment of their arrival Emmaline was carefully keeping busy. He suspected she was doing so to avoid him. He would be discouraged by it except that every once in a while her gaze would stray in his direction and she would blush adorably when he caught her eye. The third time, he winked.

Emmaline was feeling sympathetic for the mouse that was chased by the cat only to be toyed with before being eaten. It was the way she was feeling about Patrick today. He was toying with her, and she was trying not to get caught, but dinner was looming, and she knew Brianna would make sure Patrick was seated next to her. She thought of herself as steadfast and grounded, but his open flirtation made her feel fidgety and unsettled. She wanted to avoid him, but he seemed to be everywhere she looked.

And then he winked at her.

The first time took her by surprise and took her breath away. She felt the burn in her cheeks and turned away from the room to hide her blush. A deep breath soon restored her composure. She cast a wary glance in his direction expecting to see a smile or smirk for having affected her so. Instead, she encountered his sober and intensely interested gaze. She quickly looked away.

Discomfited. That was how he made her feel, and she didn't like it. Didn't like it one wit. But she had to endure it for she couldn't throw him out before the meal, though she longed to do so, at least that's what she told herself. What she wasn't willing to acknowledge, at least not yet, was that one part of her secretly liked his attention, was even flattered by it. It was different than the other men who had tried to court her. They appreciated her looks, but they never really saw her. Not like Patrick did. His gaze made her soul feel bare to him. Perhaps that was why she wanted to flee from the room. It was the instinct to protect herself.

Emmaline barely tasted her meal. She was too aware of Patrick sitting next to her. He didn't touch her, not even when he held her chair for her to be seated. But her pulse raced as if his hand was constantly brushing hers. They conversed mostly with her siblings other than when she asked if his uncle let him do any more forging. He turned pensive in his reply even though he confirmed he was learning to do more skillful work.

When the last dish was consumed, they adjourned to the parlor once more. The men soon left the room to have brandy and cigars in her father's study. Nervously, Emmaline watched them leave the room, surprised that Patrick chose to join them rather than go home. Her father certainly hadn't given him any reason to stay. He had been less than cordial since Patrick's arrival.

Brianna and Emily joined her on the sofa, one on either side of her. She should have pleaded a headache and fled to her room.

Emily said, "I like your Patrick very much."

"He's not *my* Patrick."

Brianna smiled. "Mark my words. He will be soon enough." She leaned forward to say to Emily, "Did you see him wink at her?"

"I did." Emily frowned at Emmaline. "Why aren't you encouraging him?"

"He doesn't need any encouragement."

"You wouldn't want to lose him to another girl. You must let him know you're interested."

"But that's just it, I'm not interested."

Emily scoffed. "Fiddlesticks."

Brianna shook her head. "You can pretend indifference all you want, but it's as plain as the nose on your face, you are anything but disinterested."

Emily looked at her with concern. "Why are you holding back?"

Emmaline was confused. "Are you telling me to be forward? We are taught from the cradle to hold ourselves aloof to avoid folly."

Brianna picked up her hand and held it in both of hers. "With him, yes, but not with yourself."

Emily asked, "What are you afraid of?"

Emmaline blanched. It was true. She was afraid. But what exactly was she afraid of? "Change, I suppose."

* * *

Patrick wondered what he was doing walking into the proverbial lion's den. He hadn't been directly invited to join the men. He breathed a sigh of relief not to be rebuked as he walked into the room. His eyes roved over the masculine room. The left wall was lined with bookshelves filled to capacity. A heavy oak desk was centered in front of a large front window and faced the door. Behind it was a heavy leather chair. A small leather sofa was on the left side of the door and two chairs and a small table occupied the other side. The right wall had a sideboard with a selection of decanters and cut-glass tumblers. Above it was a painting of an Indian in ceremonial clothing with ostrich plums adorning his head covering.

Henry handed his father and Garrett each a glass of brandy. He turned to Patrick. "What would you like? I'm having whiskey."

"That will be fine." It wasn't his first taste of alcohol, but near enough. His family kept one jug of mountain whiskey on hand for medicinal purposes. He snuck a sip a few years back when curiosity got the better of him. He sputtered as the liquid burned like fire down the back of his throat and then ran when he heard his mother coming. Now he accepted the glass with trepidation.

Henry raised his glass in a silent salute which the others returned before taking a swallow.

Patrick took a cautious sip, prepared this time for the burn. It wasn't as harsh as he remembered. Still, he had to swallow hard to keep from sputtering and embarrassing himself. He hated showing weakness, uncertainty, or ineptitude. He would not cough and reveal his inexperience.

Garrett asked, "You hail from Virginia?"

Patrick cleared his throat. "Yes, sir."

"Where do they stand on secession?"

Patrick was thankful he had participated in the discussions his father had with his neighbors. It made him feel capable of answering the inquiry. "Divided, sir. The eastern half of the state is of course in support of slavery and states' rights to keep slavery for the plantations while the western half is siding with abolitionists."

"And your family? Where do they stand?" The question came from the stalwart man seated behind the desk smoking a cigar.

Patrick glanced from Mr. Whitmore to Henry and Garrett standing on either side of the room and back, trying to gauge their feelings on the subject. "Well, sir. We reside in the middle of the state and have neighbors hardly speaking to each other over the matter. My father would prefer to remain neutral. Publicly, he tries not to take either side. Privately, he disagrees with slavery but is bitter about the government's threatened involvement in what is believed to be the state's decision."

"And you?"

Mr. Whitmore was the first to ever ask him directly how he felt. He hoped his feelings would not offend his host. He was aware some of the islanders owned slaves. He had seen them working on the fort and in attendance to their owners. He had yet to see any in the Whitmore household but that did not necessarily mean he didn't own any. "To be honest sir. I don't like slavery. I would like to see it end."

Henry clapped him on the back. "As would we all in this room."

Patrick breathed a little easier.

Theodore rose from his chair, turned to the window, and clasped his hands behind his back. "That's not to say we would not support secession. State's rights are not something to be thrown over or cast aside by the President or Congress. It goes against the principles of the founding fathers."

Garrett said, "Secession must be a last resort. It will lead to war."

"I agree." Theodore sighed. "With the election coming up next year, the slavery issue is likely to get more heated. It will take a strong man to keep this country from tearing itself apart, and so far, our Democrat candidates are not proving worthy."

"With your view on slavery sir, I would have thought you to be leaning towards the new Republican party." Patrick gulped. He had spoken before he considered how the question would be taken.

Theodore swung around to face the young man who threatened to disrupt his household. He saw the concern on his face and for a brief moment held sympathy for the man who dared to hold his own in essentially a room of strangers. "I have considered it, yes. Are you a Republican?"

"I haven't rightly given it sufficient consideration as next year will be the first election I can vote in, having just turned twenty-one."

Garrett said, "Doesn't Virginia require a man to hold property to vote?"

"The law was changed in '51, removing the requirement." Patrick looked to Mr. Whitmore with a nod to the portrait. "May I ask about the painting, sir?" Patrick watched in fascination as the man's demeanor softened for the first time in their acquaintance. "That is a painting by George Catlin of Chief Osceola. It was done shortly before his death." His gaze grew distant. "You wouldn't know it to look at this, but he was in a great deal of pain and weak at the time. Too weak to stand for long periods and yet he did to have the portrait made."

Patrick heard the deep respect laden in his voice. "You greatly admired him."

"Yes. Do you know of him?"

"Only what my father read to me from the papers."

Henry nodded. "He likely was reading from the articles my father wrote."

Patrick's eyes widened. Emmaline had said he was a journalist and produced a paper, but he never imagined he was a famous journalist. "If so, you made him seem larger than life, a true hero to his people."

Theodore stared at the portrait, remembering the man he called a friend. "He was."

Henry approached the desk. "Poppa, where is the last article you wrote?"

Theodore reached into his desk and pulled out a yellowed newspaper page to hand to his son. Henry passed it to Patrick who sat down on the sofa to read it while the others in the room spoke of local politics.

* * *

53

Brianna patted Emmaline's hand. "Everything changes sooner or later and marriage is a wonderful change, especially if you marry for love. Surely you don't aspire to become a spinster?"

"Of course not. I simply hadn't aspired to be a wife just yet, either."

Emily chuckled. "Well you better start aspiring because if he isn't asking to court you today, mark my words, he will be soon enough."

Emmaline cut her eyes at her. "Brianna thinks so too." She bit her lip in consternation. What would she do if Patrick did have more than a passing fancy for her?

An argument amongst the boys pulled Emily away from them. Ella came to sit beside Emmaline holding Eli. "Are you courting Mr. Johnson?"

Emmaline could have groaned. Even this child was attuned to her affairs. "No, I am not."

Brianna smiled. "Not yet anyways."

Ella looked off dreamily. "I can't wait till I'm old enough to be courted."

Emily returned to them in time to hear her daughter's pronouncement. The look of horror that crossed her face made Emmaline and Brianna turn to each other to hide their mirth.

* * *

Patrick left the Whitmore house with a lively step. He felt as though he had made headway in winning Mr. Whitmore's approval, and he had thoroughly enjoyed his time with Emmaline. He only wished he had been able to visit with her more after leaving the study, but Henry ushered him to the door after a brief moment to bid her farewell.

Chapter 5

Emmaline was startled awake from a dream of Patrick as he leaned in to kiss her. It had seemed so real she was almost surprised not to find him in her bedroom.

A knock on the door preceded Mrs. Paden's voice. "Emmaline, are you awake child?"

She realized it must have been Mrs. Paden's knocking that pulled her from her dream. She wasn't sure if that was good timing or bad. Did she want Patrick to kiss her? It was a disturbing thought.

"I'm awake," she called out to the door. She must have overslept this morning. It wasn't surprising as it took her thoughts a long time to settle down before slumber overtook her, and of course those too were of Patrick. The man had managed to thoroughly upset her peaceful existence.

She opened the door to find a disgruntled housekeeper standing before her. Mrs. Paden opened her mouth to speak only to be interrupted by Brianna's sudden appearance.

"Oh good. You're up. I can't seem to find Momma's recipe for cinnamon bread. It's not with the others."

"Give me a moment to dress and I'll be right down."

Brianna left them as quickly as she arrived, not running, but not walking either.

Mrs. Paden said, "That's what Mrs. Faraday asked me to come tell you. Your sister is intent on making the bread and nothing will sway her otherwise."

"It's alright Mrs. Paden. She thinks we need to stop protecting Poppa."

"And you agree with her?"

"I don't know if this is the way, but something needs to pull him from his despondency."

Emmaline arrived in the outdoor kitchen to find Brianna and Mrs. Faraday arguing. Her sister was accusing the cook of hiding the recipe. Emmaline reached into her pocket and pulled the stiff paper card with her grandmother's flowing script from her pocket. "Brianna, I have it here."

Brianna looked properly contrite and eloquently apologized to

Mrs. Faraday.

Several hours later, Emmaline inhaled deeply as she pulled the two loaves of bread from the brick oven. It had been too long since the aromatic spice filled the kitchen. She closed her eyes for a moment and in her mind pictured her mother standing there, turning the bread out to cool on a wire rack and smacking her father's hand as he tried to snitch a bite.

"That smells heavenly."

Emmaline opened her eyes to find Emily standing before her.

"The aroma drifted down to my house. As soon as I could get away, I had to come see if I was dreaming."

Brianna appeared in the doorway behind her. The cook had gone home for a few hours before returning to prepare supper, so they had the kitchen to themselves.

Brianna perched on the stool and picked up a nearby knife. "I can't wait for it to cool."

Emily smiled broadly. "Neither can I."

Emmaline shook her head. "We made this for Poppa, and he's not home."

Brianna shook her head. "Poppa was an excuse. I helped make this for me, and I'm not ashamed to admit it. We can serve the second loaf after supper unless you think it would be better for breakfast." She made an attempt to cut the loaf, but it was still too hot to hold on to, so Emmaline handed her a towel. Brianna transferred the loaf to a cutting board and cut off three thin slices. "Wouldn't want to spoil our dinner."

All three ladies smiled at the oft heard admonishment which Emily now used with her children.

Emmaline tore a corner from her slice and popped it in her mouth. Her taste buds sang with the burst of sourdough, cinnamon, and sugar. She closed her eyes again and let the memories of her mother flow; of helping her in the kitchen, creating and sewing new dress patterns, and tending the garden. She fondly recalled her mother's smile, and of her twirling and laughing as she danced with her father at Brianna's wedding. Emmaline opened her tear-filled eyes to find the other two ladies in a similar state.

Brianna whispered, "I miss her so."

Emily said, "I do too. Your mother was a very special lady. I'm so sorry you lost her."

Brianna was quick to say, "We lost her."

Silence ensued as coffee was poured and they moved to the

wrought iron table and chairs set under the shade of a mahogany tree. Soon they were sharing their favorite memories of their mother and mother-in-law amidst smiles and tears, sorrow and laughter, to the accompaniment of coffee and cinnamon bread, in the lush garden Betsy so lovingly tended.

Emily said, "Did your mother ever tell you about helping my mother escape a pirate?"

Brianna frowned. "A pirate? No."

Emmaline said, "Don't you mean an evil wrecker? I believe his name was Talmage."

Emily grinned. "Yes, you're right, he was a pirate of a wrecker."

Brianna shook her head. "Why did you change it?"

"Embellishment, I suppose. A wrecker wasn't exciting enough for my boys when their father, grandfather, and uncles all at one time or another have been wreckers." Emily held her last bite of bread to her mouth, hating that it was the last, when inspiration struck. Her hand lowered and her bright gaze swung to Emmaline. "You should take some bread to Patrick and his uncle."

Emmaline frowned. "It won't keep until Friday."

Emily said, "Why Friday?"

"That is when Brianna and I go to pick up her Christmas gift for Garrett." Emmaline grew worried as Emily's smile turned mischievous.

"Oh, I was thinking of something much sooner, like today."

Emmaline gulped. "Today? But we have no reason to go there today."

Brianna joined in the conspiracy. "I'm sure we could come up with something."

Though Emily and Brianna tried, suggesting many reasons why she could visit the forge, Emmaline remained steadfast in her refusal. She was not going to encourage Patrick's attentions, and she especially was not going to give cause for anyone to call her forward, or worse, desperate.

The ladies had just finished cleaning up the kitchen when Mrs. Faraday arrived to begin making supper. Emmaline handed Emily the second loaf of bread wrapped in cloth to take home.

Emily said, "I can't take the whole loaf. Let me have the cut one."

Emmaline shook her head. "You have more mouths to feed. We'll serve this one already sliced, and no one will be the wiser."

The ladies walked to the front yard where they bid good day to Emily. Brianna and Emmaline settled into the wicker chairs on the front porch. Garrett brought Eli to Brianna, having just woken up from his afternoon nap. He then returned inside the house to finish reading the paper.

Brianna let Eli play with her fingers while she rested her head against the back of the chair. "I forgot how nice it was to leave the cooking to someone else. I shall have to encourage Garrett to let us visit more often."

"We would like that." Emmaline nervously turned to Brianna. "How do you think Poppa will react?"

Brianna turned her head, still resting against the chair. "To the cinnamon bread? I'm not sure. How did he react before?"

"It wasn't cinnamon bread. Our previous cook served sweet potatoes with butter and cinnamon. As soon as he smelled the spice, he grew angry. I have never seen his jaw so tense. His hands fisted upon the table on either side of his plate. Then he stood up and left the room, leaving his food untouched. Later, I overheard him tell Mrs. Paden to be sure he was never served anything with cinnamon, or she would be fired. It upset the cook so much, she quit the next day."

Brianna cringed. "Oh, my. No wonder the cinnamon jar was covered in dust, and no wonder Mrs. Paden was so upset with me this morning. We'll have to make it clear to Poppa that this was my doing, not hers."

Emmaline nodded. Her anxiety grew as the sun descended. Her father had gone to visit with the city leaders today. He would be home soon. "Maybe we should wait 'til after dinner, when we are gathered in the parlor, to serve the bread."

Brianna's looked askance. "Perhaps after he's had his brandy."

Emmaline was a fluttering bundle of nervous anxiety by the time Brianna gave her a conspiratorial nod, rose from the settee, and left the room to retrieve the plate of sliced bread. She worried her bottom lip as she waited for her return.

Brianna stepped into the room balancing the cloth covered plate on one hand, held high before her. "I made us a special treat for tonight." She approached her father with trepidation. She knew he already struggled to relate to her because every time he looked at her, he saw her mother. Now she was about to present him not only a living, breathing visual representation of his lost love, but an olfactory one as well. It wasn't going to be easy for him, but she refused to help him hide from his feelings any longer.

Theodore was rooted to his chair trying to take normal breaths while his heart constricted against the pain of memories and loss. His daughter approached giving him no means of retreat. Her steady gaze held his as she uncovered the plate and presented it to him. The cinnamon wafted his way and he couldn't help inhaling deeply. He swallowed hard. His eyes blurred and through them he saw not Brianna, but Betsy. He allowed himself to pretend, just for this one moment. He smiled as he had all the times before when his love presented him with his favorite treat. He took the offered napkin and chose a slice of bread. The wavering image of Betsy turned away from him. He knew it was Brianna who next offered the plate to her husband, Garrett, but for another moment he lingered in the pretense that it was his beloved. He took a bite of the bread, savoring the taste and the memories that came with it.

As Brianna approached the settee to offer Emmaline her piece, she risked a glance at her father. Her gaze swept to Emmaline's to share her relief. So far, he was taking it well.

Emmaline reached for the offered slice of bread. She breathed a sigh of relief, thankful her father was not angry with them. He seemed to be handling the situation well.

No sooner had the thought crossed her mind, she saw him place the bread and napkin on the end table, toss back the rest of his drink, and rise from his chair. He was behind Brianna before Emmaline's alarm registered with her sister.

Theodore placed his hands on Brianna's shoulders, preventing her from turning. His emotions were too raw to face her directly. He placed a kiss on her head and managed to say gruffly, "Good night, girls." He strode from the room, desperately seeking the sanctuary of his study. The second bite of bread had turned to dust in his mouth as the bitter and distressful memory of Betsy, prone upon her bed in a faded dressing gown with sallow skin, taking her last breath, banished the sweet memories of her.

Emmaline and Brianna looked to each other, both unsure whether or not they had succeeded or failed in their campaign.

Garrett approached to caress Brianna's shoulders. "I caught a glimpse of a smile before the darkness returned if that gives you any comfort, dearest."

Brianna reached up to touch the hand resting on her left shoulder as she leaned back into her husband's chest, seeking his comfort. "It does, I suppose."

Chapter 6

It was Thursday and the family was gathered in the parlor having drinks after supper. Emmaline guardedly watched her father from across the room. It had been four days since the cinnamon bread, and her father hadn't said a word about it to her or Brianna, nor to Mrs. Paden. Brianna talked of making it again for Christmas, but Emmaline had misgivings. He may not have lashed out as before, but it still upset him. With all the other things that were going to be difficult for them during the Christmas celebrations, Emmaline felt baking more bread was an act of cruelty. Brianna said it was just such thinking that had kept them living in limbo for too long already.

Brianna spoke to the room in general. "Shall we go down to the wharf and join the fun?"

Today was the fifteenth and the steamship *Isabel* was late with the bimonthly mail. She usually arrived before midday but here it was evening and still there had been no bell to announce her arrival. It happened occasionally. She ran late for one reason or another and by sunset the townsfolk began gathering at the wharf. The longer the delay, the merrier the gathering became as everyone waited for news from the outside world.

Garrett said, "What of Eli?"

Brianna shrugged. "We'll take him with, of course."

Theodore stood. "There's no need to disturb the baby. I'll stay behind to listen for him. You three should go and enjoy yourselves."

Brianna rose and crossed the room to kiss his cheek. "Thank you, Poppa. He shouldn't be any trouble. I don't expect him to wake until morning." She turned to Garrett. "What do you say? Shall we go?"

Garrett drained the rest of his drink and set the glass down. He rose from his seat as he said, "My dear, your wish is my command."

Emmaline smiled and rose from her seat to follow the couple from the room. She paused before her father's chair. "You're sure you don't want to come too?"

"I'd rather stay here in the comfort of my chair. I'll hear all the news tomorrow at the custom house."

Emmaline stepped as close as she could to his knee forcing the hoops under her skirt to press against her legs and tip to the back of her.

She leaned forward to kiss his cheek. "There was a time nothing would keep you from the news."

His eyes took on a faraway look. "Everything changes in life, especially one's priorities."

"I supposed it does." Her emerald skirt brushed his leg as she turned to leave, reluctantly leaving him behind to brood.

The three of them approached the bight, eager to join the others gathered under the glow of gas lanterns to talk and laugh as they waited for the arrival of the mail steamer.

Garrett said, "Would you ladies like some ice cream? It appears they are selling it just over there."

Emmaline pulled her shawl a little tighter against the chill of the night air. "Thank you, Garrett, but I think not."

Brianna gave him a nod. "Yes, please. I'll take some. My blood is not as thin as it once was. Tonight feels quite pleasant to me. But would you mind if we shared one?"

Garrett came back with a small dish of frozen vanilla cream and two spoons. It wasn't long before some of Brianna's old friends joined them. Emmaline wandered away in search of her friends as the conversation turned to married life and parenthood.

She wove her way around the different small groups of friends and neighbors, young and old, enjoying the carefree moment to visit with each other. Some greeted her as she passed but most paid her no mind as she was one of many milling about the crowd. She was rarely out after supper. The cloak of darkness just beyond the lantern's glow gave her a thrilling feeling of doing something naughty, even though she wasn't. She discovered a few of her intimates clustered together and headed in their direction, looking forward to sharing female gossip of her age set. Focused on her destination, she was startled by the sudden appearance of Patrick in her path.

"Hello, Miss Whitmore. How are you this evening?"

She did her best to appear calm despite her raging pulse, which she hated to admit had as much to do with his good looks as it did with his unexpected proximity. "Good evening, Mr. Johnson. I am well. And yourself?"

"Better now that I'm in your presence."

The corner of her mouth quirked. He was flirting with her. To recognize it as such was novel for her. Privately, she decided she liked it, but she knew nothing about him. Was he sincere or toying with her? "Do you flatter all the pretty ladies so?"

A flash of hurt crossed his face before he hid it behind a smile.

"Only you."

She felt contrite for her poor words and woefully inexperienced to mend the slight given. Pure honesty was the only way she knew to proceed. "Why me?" Part of his face was hidden in the darkness. She studied the side that faced the feeble light of the lanterns for traces of his true feelings.

"You're different than any other." He placed his open palm against his chest. "I feel it here. No one else makes me feel as you do, as though I am man enough to conquer anything and yet woefully inadequate to speak to you."

Horror gripped her. "I apologize if I have made you to feel that way. I certainly never meant to imply you were beneath me."

Patrick reached for her hand as he took a step closer. "That's just it. You don't make me feel inferior despite my lowly status as apprentice and new to this island. You treat me as an equal. It is your inherent goodness that makes me feel unworthy of you."

"Do you not believe yourself to be of good character?"

"Well, when you put it like that, of course, I would say I am of good character."

"Then you must believe my character to be more than it is. I assure you, I have faults, the same as any other."

Patrick smiled warmly. "Not in my eyes."

The warmth of his gaze reached deep in her soul. It pulled her to him. Her heart beat a rapid staccato. Not a word was uttered between them while his brown eyes held her hazel ones and within their depths she discovered desire – his and hers. Her breath grew shallow as one part of her longed to step forward and experience more and the other demanded she turn and run. Her instincts screamed at her to flee from him least she be changed forever.

The bell rang announcing the Isabel's arrival in the harbor and broke the spell. They both looked to the ship's silhouette moving in the darkness.

Emmaline was left shaken by the emotionally charged moment they just shared. Never had someone else claimed such a hold on her emotions. It was as frightening as it was...thrilling, she supposed, to have someone want her in that way.

She cautiously brought her gaze back to his and was relieved to find his open and friendly once again. She smiled in response and hoped he didn't notice the slight tremor in her bottom lip. "I should find my family."

Her smile, the first full smile she bestowed for him, made him feel like the luckiest man in the world. "May I escort you?"

She licked her bottom lip and felt the cool breeze dry it. His eyes were drawn to the action bringing color to stain her cheeks. She hurried forward to hide it from him.

* * *

Emmaline entered her bedchamber lost in thoughts she held in check until she was finally alone. The downstairs clock struck midnight as she slipped into her white cotton nightdress. She sat down at her dressing table to run the brush through her hair before braiding it for slumber.

Tonight had been a revelation and an awakening.

Once she and Patrick joined Brianna and Garrett, she tried to act as though nothing had happened; as though she had not had a life changing experience; as though she hadn't momentarily glimpsed beyond girlish notions of love to the hidden depths of feelings that can exist between a man and a woman.

The brush stilled. Absently she set it down. What was she to do? What did she want to do? She would see him again tomorrow. How should she act when she couldn't decide if she wanted to encourage or discourage his favor? She wasn't ready to handle the feelings he invoked in her. Tonight made it clear this was an attraction well beyond mere flirtation. What she wasn't sure of, and indeed the question to be answered, was what were his intentions? It wasn't that she was worried he would take undue advantage of her, but she didn't have the impression he was ready to settle down. For that matter, she wasn't sure he intended to stay long in Key West. He had intimated he was not happy with his apprenticeship. Didn't that mean he might leave at any time?

One thing she was certain of, she did not want to leave her island home.

Avoidance.

She must avoid any more private interactions with him.

Having made a firm decision, she slid under the covers and fell easily to sleep.

* * *

Sleep did not come easily to Patrick. Tonight's encounter with Emmaline replayed over and over in his mind and in between was nervous anticipation for tomorrow's meeting when she and her sister came to pick up the Christmas gift. At least, he fervently hoped Emmaline would accompany Brianna tomorrow.

Tonight was a revelation for him. He thought her more than a pretty face from the moment he met her, but tonight, he felt something he had never experienced before. His feelings for her ran deep. The mail bell was timely. He wasn't sure he would have acted honorably had the moment lasted longer than it did. The urge to pull her to him and kiss her had grown too strong to deny. Especially when she moistened her lip. He nearly groaned with the pain of his longing for her.

He knew he wouldn't be able to act on any of his feelings tomorrow. But even so, the need to see her was undeniable. The hours between now and then stretched interminably before him.

* * *

Emmaline seated herself at the table to await breakfast. Her father was already there, drinking coffee and reading his mail. She had read her letter from Agatha last night confirming her travel details. She expected to arrive on Monday. When she wrote the letter, she still couldn't confirm if James would be joining her or not. Emmaline cast a prayer heavenward that Agatha could manage it, for no one could cheer her father like James could. He would make their Christmas complete and without him there would be an emptiness to the celebration.

Garrett and Brianna, carrying Eli, entered the room the same time as Mrs. Faraday appeared with a heavy tray laden with breakfast food. Garrett gallantly took it from her and received a scowl in return. Emmaline thought she mumbled something about not being a feeble old woman just yet as she left the room. Garrett gave them a sheepish shrug as his gaffe registered. He set the tray in the middle of the table. Emmaline served the food as she normally did in the mornings.

The arrival of mail brought news of the outside world and one particular event was the primary topic of conversation all around the island. They heard of it last night and Garrett was quick to share it with her father this morning. "Sir, did you hear yet of the John Brown hanging in Virginia?"

Theodore dropped his paper to address Garrett. "I was just reading about it."

The two men would have soon been deep in debate over the validity of the charges and the resulting execution if Brianna hadn't intervened. "Please, there will be enough talk later on. Let us not speak of murder and mayhem at the breakfast table. I would have one meal not spoiled with politics."

Theodore gave Brianna a look of acceptance and snapped his paper straight to continue reading.

Garrett leaned towards his wife to whisper, "Without politics, I have nothing to speak of with your father."

"Then you'll be thankful to save the discussion for later."

He contritely began his meal.

Emmaline watched her sister manage feeding Eli soft bites of food in between feeding herself and trying to keep his hands from reaching for her plate. It was amusing to watch, but as soon as she finished her meal, she offered to take the little boy so her sister could finish eating.

"Thank you, Emmaline." Brianna finished her meal and as she sipped the rest of her coffee she said to Emmaline, "Shall we run our errand first thing this morning or wait till later?"

Emmaline looked up from playing patty cake with her nephew. It was on the tip of her tongue to tell her sister she would be staying home, but Brianna saw it in her eyes and with a look conveyed her devote intention to be accompanied. Emmaline knew well her sister would prevail, so she gave in gracefully. "I suppose sooner rather than later may be best. Unless you would prefer to wait until Elijah takes his nap?"

"Emily offered me the use of her pram, so I don't see why we shouldn't take him with us. Let us leave as soon as we are done with breakfast."

Emmaline's stomach did a nervous flip-flop knowing she would see Patrick again within the hour. With last night's resolve to avoid him now thwarted, excitement and trepidation warred within her.

* * *

Brianna held a nearly one-sided conversation as they walked to the forge. Emmaline merely responded enough to keep her going. She didn't breathe easy until they reached Smithy's yard and discovered Patrick was nowhere to be seen.

Brianna sighed. "Well that is unfortunate."

Emmaline uncomfortably wavered between relief and disappointment. Her head felt one, and her heart the other. She took charge of the pram and Eli while Brianna concluded her business with Smithy. The suffocating heat from the fire led her to push the baby buggy into the shade of a palm tree to the side of the forging shed. Eli had fallen asleep soon after they started walking. Emmaline watched his cherub face in slumber and smiled ruefully to note he was sucking his thumb. Brianna was going to have a time of it breaking that habit. He was really too big to ride in the pram comfortably. There was not enough room for him to stretch out. The poor dear had to curl up.

"Hello there."

Startled, Emmaline gasped as she turned towards the familiar voice behind her.

"I'm sorry. I didn't mean to frighten you."

Emmaline sucked in a breath to steady her racing pulse. "You didn't." It was clearly a lie, but she said it anyway. He couldn't know how much he affected her, although her impertinent question likely gave it away. "Where did you come from?"

Patrick gave a nod to the stairs leading up to the residence. Her eyes followed his gesture. He stepped closer to her. "I was hoping to see you today."

"Were you?" Her gaze darted back to him, uncomfortably aware of his nearness.

"Of course."

Her eyes lifted to his and tangled in his gaze. The intensity was there again. She felt as if she was suffocating and looked away to break his hold on her. She took a deep breath to clear her head.

Patrick felt her withdrawal and keenly watched her. A frown marred his features as the thought occurred to him that she may not care for him as much as he did for her. He had the impression she wished to flee from him. "Emmaline?"

She heard the questioning note in his voice. It drew her gaze back to his. She was relieved not to find the smoldering heat in his gaze. His questioning vulnerability drew her to him like a moth to a flame. "Yes, Patrick?"

The concern in her eyes was unexpected and robbed him of thought. He couldn't remember what he was going to say nor think of anything to say now.

Brianna emerged from the shadowed interior to find the pair staring at each other with a loss for words. Smithy trailed behind her carrying the wrapped sign she had purchased. To give the young couple more time she gave Patrick a conspiratorial wink and quickly pretended interest in an iron gate leaning against a post on the opposite side of the building to pull his uncle away. "Did you make this too Smithy? I would love to have something like this for my garden gate. A little more ornate perhaps."

Emmaline inwardly groaned at her sister's machinations.

Patrick leaned forward a little to murmur in a joshing manner, "I seem to have your sister's approval."

Emmaline's lip quirked despite herself. "You do, but I'm afraid she is taken."

Patrick blinked at her unexpected comment. He wasn't sure how to respond until he saw the twinkle in her eye. "Well that is too bad. I suppose I will have to make do with another. Do you have any suggestions? I know so few of the ladies."

She expected him to make some reply referring to her. That he didn't took her aback. He was teasing. She knew he was and yet the thought of him paying attention to any other, even in jest, gave her a sharp pang of jealousy. Could she have mistaken what she read in his gaze yesterday and just now? She didn't think so but then again... She raised her eyes to his to search their depths for the truth.

Patrick saw the flash of hurt at his careless words. He had to reassure her before she retreated even further from him. "The trouble is, the only person who will do for me..." His voice dropped as raw emotion filled him. "....Is you."

Emmaline stared at him, dumbfounded. In just a few moments, everything had changed. The imagined threat of loss had dramatically shifted her feelings from wanting to run to wanting to embrace his feelings and hers. She felt faint with the realization of it. She placed a hand against her abdomen, wishing her corset were not so tight. She needed a deep breath to steady her. Now she finally understood why an otherwise sound woman could faint. She was in danger of it now. She turned her gaze to Eli and forced herself to calmly breath.

Patrick took another step closer and reached out to grasp Emmaline's upper arm. She looked as if she would keel over at any moment. He felt a spasm at his touch, but she didn't pull away. His heart beat out the rapid seconds as he waited for her to say something. He dropped his hand from her arm at Brianna's return.

"Emmaline, are you well?"

Emmaline turned to her sister with a falsely bright smile. "I am fine. Are you ready to return home?"

"I am." Brianna turned to Smithy who held out her cumbersome parcel. The sign was nearly four feet in length. It gave her an idea. "Smithy, would you mind sparing your apprentice long enough to carry that home for me?"

"Not at all. I'm sorry you had to ask. I should have suggested it." He handed the wrapped and tied sign over to Patrick.

Brianna turned as if to leave and then turned back to the gray-haired blacksmith. "Would you and your nephew care to join us for dinner tomorrow? Consider it a token of appreciation for the timely execution of your good work."

"Your payment is enough. A meal is not necessary, Mrs. Cade."

"Oh, but I insist Smithy. If you're not comfortable with an evening meal, then we shall make it midday. Will noon be good for you?"

Smithy noted the determined set of her chin and gave in gracefully. "Yes ma'am. Thank you."

"We will see you then."

Emmaline steered the pram towards the street but was soon nudged aside by her sister and encouraged to fall in step with Patrick. They clung to the meager shade of the left side of the street as they made the return journey.

Brianna said, "I'm glad your uncle accepted lunch instead."

Patrick gave her a speculative look. "Why is that?"

"It will free you to spend the afternoon however you please."

Her tone gave no hint of an ulterior motive, but Patrick clearly perceived the implied implication. She was suggesting Patrick spend tomorrow afternoon wooing Emmaline. He smiled. He had no objection to her plan.

Brianna quickened her pace to get ahead of them and moved sideways to put herself clearly in front of them. A horse and open buggy passed them by, and the ladies returned Mr. Patterson's greeting.

Patrick said, "I suppose we have that in common. I know everyone from my hometown as you know everyone here."

Emmaline shook her head. "Not quite the same. While it is true I am acquainted with just about everyone who lives here, we have many strangers about on any given day due to the port. Some stay a few days but most travel on before I may even be aware they were here."

"I forgot about the ship passengers, as you have recognized everyone around you since we met."

"Just coincidence, I suppose."

She gave him a beguiling smile that made his breath hitch. Something had changed between them. She was openly engaging with him. He wasn't going to question it, but he would take advantage of it. "Will you take a walk with me after luncheon tomorrow? I've heard of a plantation where you can buy fruit."

"Uncle Sandy's place. I would love to go there."

"What about a chaperone?"

The reminder sharpened her thoughts from the ease of friendship to the uncharted waters of romance. It no longer frightened her as it did yesterday, but it did bring a return of nervous tension. She swallowed against it. "I'll think of someone."

"I wouldn't mind if it is Brianna and Garrett. I like them."

Emmaline glanced towards her sister and was surprised to find her several paces ahead of them. Too far to ask her now.

Patrick said, "How far is it to Uncle Sandy's?"

"About the same again as from the forge to my house, further inland."

"Have you been there before?"

She laughed. "Many times."

Patrick's gut tightened. He loved her laugh and dearly wanted to hear it again.

Emmaline added, "Actually, it will be fortuitous to visit tomorrow as I have an order of sweet potatoes to pick up from him for Christmas dinner."

"For sweet potato pie? It's one of my favorite dishes."

"Ours is more of a pudding than a pie. Momma called it a soufflé and it is a family favorite."

"Can you believe Christmas is just over a week away?"

"It will be a busy week of preparations." She looked at him with concern. "Will this be your first Christmas away from your family?"

"Yes. Though I suppose that is not entirely correct as I will celebrate with Uncle Preston, I mean Smithy."

"I never knew your uncle's name was Preston."

"That is likely because he hates his name. He told me to call him Smithy, but it is hard for me to do so since I have always heard my father call him Preston."

"Would you like to join us for Christmas? We always have more than enough food." She surprised herself in issuing the invitation without qualms. It felt right to include him. "You and your uncle, of course."

"I would be honored to, but I suppose it will depend on my uncle's acceptance."

"Of course."

Reaching the house, Brianna directed Patrick to hide the sign in the outdoor kitchen. The one place she felt sure her husband wouldn't enter. She offered him a tip for his trouble which he adamantly refused to take. He doffed his hat to both of them. "I bid you good-day ladies. Until tomorrow."

Patrick gave Emmaline that intense look again before he turned to leave, but this time it thrilled her rather than frightened her. He made her feel special. No man had ever done that before.

Brianna admired the soft smile wreathing Emmaline's face as she watched Patrick walk away and congratulated herself. Emmaline was as good as married, of that she had no doubt.

Chapter 7

Patrick was impatient for noon to arrive. He was pining to see Emmaline again and it showed in his work. His uncle was growing frustrated with his inattention. The morning hours moved frustratingly slow for him but as the sun rose high in the sky, so too did his excitement. And now that it was almost time to leave, his uncle was taking a rather complicated order from a regular customer. Patrick inwardly groaned when the man changed his mind, forcing he and his uncle to start the process all over again. They were in danger of being late for lunch. Patrick gave a deep frustrated sigh when he saw one of his uncle's friends approaching. The order was stalled as the three elder men eagerly began conversing.

Patrick took his vexation out on the piece of metal he was hammering hoping the noise would be loud enough to bring an end to the conversation. He was only half listening while they speculated about the coming repercussions of the John Brown hanging that occurred on December 2nd in Charles Town, Virginia. He had read the newspaper article that came in with the mail of John Brown's sentence to hanging for leading the raid on Harper's Ferry. Even though Harper's Ferry was two hundred miles north of his home in Virginia, the October raid brought fear and unrest to his community. He could well imagine they were facing it again with the hanging. The overwhelming consensus here in Key West, as he was sure it was there too in Virginia, was John Brown's death would not be the end of it. Many feared it was a significant step towards more violent acts that eventually may lead the country to war.

Patrick paused mid-strike as he realized the visitors' words had become heated. It was clear they were at odds in their views. The two men let passion get the better of them, shouting at each other with clenched fists. His uncle bravely stepped between them, asking the one to come visit another day as he and Patrick had an appointment. Searing looks passed between the adversaries before the one man turned to leave. The other finished his business and left too. He supposed it shouldn't, but it surprised Patrick that tempers were as heated on this faraway island as they were back home.

His uncle stood at the edge of his domain, shaking his head, as he watched his customer leave. He turned to Patrick. "I don't know what this world is coming to. Those two were once close chums and now they can't speak a civil word to each other." He pulled out his pocket watch. "Bank that fire. We'd best hurry and clean up or we'll be late."

* * *

Emmaline hurried to answer the knock at the door. She laid a hand over her heart in a futile effort to calm her racing pulse. This morning's buoyancy in her step was all to do with seeing Patrick again. Yesterday's encounter had been an awakening. Never before had she taken more than a passing interest in boys, much less men. In her school days, she had been polite but not particularly chummy with the boys. When she came of age, she was more interested in books than courtship, and then her mother died and for a time she lost interest in everything. She wasn't sure how it came to pass, but Patrick had lifted her spirits. Yesterday, she was still in denial of the growing attraction between them. Today, she was eager to see where it would lead her.

She opened the door and her smile naturally bloomed for Patrick, standing on her porch, hat in hand, wearing a smile just for her that made her feel special in a way she never had before. His hair was slicked back as if he had just washed it, and his face was cleanly shaven. She curled her hand to keep from reaching out to trace her fingers along his jaw. Behind him stood his uncle, also hat in hand.

She stepped back with the door wide open. "Please, do come in." Her breath hitched when Patrick winked at her as he passed.

Brianna and Garrett came forward to greet their guests. Patrick fell behind to walk with Emmaline as Brianna and Garrett led the way to the parlor, followed by Smithy. Patrick reached for her hand, but she pulled away, giving him a look of reproach for his impropriety.

They went directly to the dining room since the meal was ready to be served. Brianna directed Smithy to the chair next to her father. Patrick gladly assumed the seat next to Emmaline that he had occupied the last time he dined with the family.

The afternoon meal went smoothly thanks to Brianna. With Garrett's help, she kept the conversation from lagging between Smithy and their father. It wasn't long before the men diverted to politics and the John Brown incident. Brianna grimaced but didn't gainsay them.

Emmaline lifted her concerned gaze to Patrick's. "All this talk of Charles Town has made me wonder, is that near where you live?"

"Compared to here, yes, but not really. It's about two hundred miles north of us. It's actually close to Baltimore."

Brianna said, "If I remember my geography, does that mean your home is closer to North Carolina?"

"We are more towards the center of the state, about two hundred miles west of Richmond."

Garrett said, "I believe you mentioned your family are farmers. Is it a large farm?"

"I would say it is a modest one."

"And do you..." Emmaline thought better of asking her question.

Patrick was curious of what she hesitated to ask. "Go on."

Emmaline shook her head. "Never mind."

"No. Please ask whatever it is you want to know."

Emmaline saw the determination in his gaze. "I was going to ask if you have slaves."

Her hesitancy was understandable. Slavery was a very volatile subject these days. "My father has two to help work the fields. He talked of purchasing a third because of my leaving but didn't think he could afford it."

Garrett said, "I'm surprised he would let you leave if your help was so important."

"Me too. I tried to talk him out of sending me away."

Brianna said, "Then coming here was not your idea?"

He shook his head woefully. "No." When he saw Emmaline's consternation, he quickly added, "But I'm not sorry I came. Far from it."

Their eyes met and held, saying far more than words could convey, especially since the words could not be said in the dining room.

Theodore's gaze caught on his youngest daughter's upturned face. Emmaline wore an expression of adoration not unlike the one her mother used to bestow upon him. He swallowed hard, not just to suppress the unbidden memory but also the sudden fear his youngest would soon leave him too. "Mr. Johnson, how goes your training as a blacksmith?"

Patrick abruptly turned from Emmaline to her father sitting at the head of the table. "You might best ask my uncle that question."

"But I am asking you."

Patrick nervously cleared his throat. "I believe I am meeting his standards." He glanced to his uncle and received a confirming nod.

Theodore scrutinized the young man. "And do you like forging?"

Patrick swallowed hard. He couldn't lie to Mr. Whitmore, but he wasn't ready for his uncle to know the truth. "I don't believe I know enough of the trade to make such a determination."

"Meaning, so far, you've only done the grunt work."

Patrick released his held breath. "Just so."

"Or have you other ambitions?"

Patrick sharply sucked in another breath. Mr. Whitmore was not a man easily fooled. "No, sir."

"I see."

And Patrick was afraid he did see, entirely too much. No wonder he was a good journalist. "Might I ask sir, if you still write for a paper?" He sensed Emmaline's unease next to him.

Theodore's jaw tensed. "Nothing recent."

"Why not?" Patrick had the distinct impression he was poking an angry bear and wasn't sure why he felt the need to do so.

Emmaline harshly whispered, "Patrick!"

Theodore gave him a pointed look. "I've not been so inclined."

Patrick held Theodore's gaze with sincerity. "That is a shame, for your readers, I mean, as your writing is quite good. Perhaps you will again one day."

"Hmm."

Patrick took his response for the close of discussion it was meant to be. He wondered that he dared as much as he did in asking, but he saw in Mr. Whitmore a soul that had lost its way. Emmaline tread lightly with her father's feelings, but Patrick sensed he was a man in need of a cause or at least motivation to get past his grieving, and somehow his lack of writing was part of it.

Emmaline brightly asked, "Have you read his articles?"

"On my last visit, I read his editorial on Osceola. It was a fine piece." He turned again to Mr. Whitmore. "I admire your way with words. I wish I could write like that."

Emmaline smiled. "Most consider that piece to be his best work. It was reprinted in almost all the papers of the day. My sister is the journalist these days. She writes for the *New York Weekly*."

"Another sister?"

"Yes, Agatha. She's coming home Monday."

"I look forward to meeting her."

When they had finished their midday meal, Theodore invited Smithy to his study and Brianna suggested the four young adults take a walk. As they were preparing to leave, the maid rushed down to say Brianna was needed to tend to Elijah. It was then arranged for the maid to accompany Patrick and Emmaline as chaperone. They weren't far from the house when the maid began trailing further and further behind. Emmaline looked to Patrick with a half-smile. "This is Brianna's doing. She planned for us to be alone."

"Are you suggesting she contrived to keep her and Garrett home?" He glanced back at the maid. "And instructed your maid to give us space?"

"That is exactly what I am suggesting."

He gave her a wicked smile. "I knew I liked your sister."

Emmaline's nerves tingled as she felt the predatory warning his smile engendered. "As long as we're on our own, come this way. There's something I want to show you."

"I thought we were going to Uncle Sandy's. Isn't it in the other direction?"

"It is. We'll go there after." She led them past the church and into town by way of Duval Street. Fluffy white clouds frolicked against the azure sky and the sun's warmth made it a pleasant day for a stroll.

They turned right on Front Street and came to a halt a block later facing a plot of land in the burnt district. Patrick patiently waited for her to tell him why they had come here. She lifted sad eyes to his. "This was my father's newspaper office. After my mother died, he buried himself in his work. He was rarely even home for supper except for the night of the fire. I threw a fit that morning. Said something about hurting too and needing him. I guilted him into coming home that night. I choose to believe I may have saved his life in doing so, but I fear he blames me for the loss of the paper as much as he does the fire."

"Surely not."

"Oh, he hasn't said it, but things have not been the same between us since then. He's not been the same since that night. First my mother and then his business..." She turned her troubled gaze to Patrick's. "I wanted you to understand why my father is the way he is. He was never an openly social man, but he used to be friendly and... well, not so sullen all the time."

"He must have loved your mother greatly."

"He did."

Patrick frowned. "I think I understand him a little better now. He's lost his sense of purpose and his sense of self, maybe even his self-worth."

Emmaline turned her soulful eyes on him. "You think so?"

"I sensed it before but after telling me this, yes, I do believe so. When did this happen?"

"My mother died almost two years ago. The fire was this past

May."

"How did it start?"

"At Mr. Shaefer's warehouse. It stood on the corner we just passed. There is speculation that it was purposely set but there have not been any charges brought. As you can see, all but two houses were destroyed. It burned for twelve hours. Everyone pitched in with buckets and blankets as best we could."

"A town this size doesn't have a fire pump?"

"It was employed but wasn't sufficient enough to stop the fire with so many large warehouses and stores to feed it. We had all but given up hope of saving anything. It became too monstrous to fight anymore. The wind was pushing it onwards towards more housing. If not for Mr. Henry Mulrennon, the town might have been lost or at least a larger majority would have been homeless."

"What did he do?"

She turned to Patrick with a smile. "He blew up his house."

"He what?"

She nodded and then led him onward down Front Street and turned down an alley that cut back to Green Street as she retold the events of that fateful night. "The fire was about to overtake his house anyway. He somehow procured a keg of gunpowder from the fort. By the time he returned to his house, it was aflame. I watched him disappear inside. He returned a few minutes later leading a train of fuse. He lit it without any hesitation, and then we were all scrambling to get away. I remember rushing to the waterfront with everyone else, someone was pulling me along, but I don't remember who it was now." She huffed. "I kept thinking, how in the world could an explosion stop a fire?" She shook her head. "I still can't believe it worked. We had no sooner reached the water's edge when the keg exploded. The flash of the explosion was louder and brighter than the roar of the fire. For a moment, it eerily lit up the cloud of smoke hovering over the city. Afterwards, we cheered when the fire wasn't able to cross the road. A few complained of broken windows from the blast, but most were thankful for Mr. Mulrennon's actions."

Patrick whistled. "That is quite a story."

"It's a day I won't ever forget."

"No. I suppose you wouldn't."

She paused at the corner of Green Street to turn around. "The only day more horrific was the great hurricane. Would you believe all of this area we just passed from here to your uncle's shop used to be a tidal pond? Our house was just over there, at the edge of the pond until the awful hurricane of 1846. Hardly a building was untouched by it and many, like our house, were blown down. The lighthouse and Mr. Curry's house were washed out to sea. The pond was filled in. That storm changed a lot about this island."

He heard the emotional pain that still lingered behind her words and in response reached for her hand. "Have you ever thought of leaving the island?"

She turned to him, surprised he asked the question. She frowned as she shook her head. "No, I've never thought of living somewhere else. I don't think I would want to. This island is my home." Patrick's frown disconcerted her. What if he withdrew his interest because she wouldn't leave the island? Would she leave it for him? She couldn't say but she didn't want to risk disaffecting him over the idea. "That is to say, I've never had a reason to want to leave." She breathed a sigh of relief when his frown vanished with a twitch of his lips, not a smile but certainly a lightening of his demeanor.

Emmaline pointed further ahead. "Mr. Mulrennon's house was there on the corner of Fitzpatrick."

Patrick nodded. They were now retracing their steps heading to Sandy's farm at a leisurely pace. "What was your mother like?"

Emmaline's smile grew wistful. "Momma was kind and gentle and beautiful. Brianna's nearly her mirror image, but they all say I take after her in spirit. She loved to work in her garden or to sew. She was a seamstress before she and Poppa married."

He heard the strain of sadness in her voice and was sorry he had asked the question. To lighten her mood, he nodded towards the gentlemen standing in front of the hotel they were passing. He smiled to realize this was where they first bumped into each other. "Do you think I would look good in a top hat?"

Emmaline looked from the gentlemen to Patrick giving his profile careful consideration. His face was long with a high forehead and cheekbones. His eyes were of a nice size with pleasing eyebrows and a straight nose. "I think you could carry it off quite nicely."

"Good. I mean to have one someday."

"When you do, I think you should let your beard grow out to balance it."

He rubbed his hand on his smooth chin. "I do miss it but after nearly singeing it, I've been reluctant to grow it back."

"How did that happen?"

"Carelessness. Not to be repeated, I assure you."

Another couple strolling down Duval in the opposite direction caught her eye. It was Kate Geiger and her beau. Emmaline returned her friend's wave and ducked her head to hide her blush. She supposed it was the novelty of being with a man that embarrassed her. It certainly wasn't the man himself. Several of her friends had commented on Patrick's handsomeness and charm.

Patrick noticed her shyness but didn't comment on it. "You told me the other day you have traveled. Where did you go?"

"I've been to Pennsylvania several times to visit my mother's family and to Alabama once when I was a child to visit the plantation of Emily's great uncle."

"You've been to a real plantation?"

She nodded. "And there was one wonderful Christmas we spent in Austria with my paternal grandparents." Her tone always grew wistful when she thought of that trip. It was as if it happened in a storybook and couldn't be real.

"When was that?"

"Oh my, many years ago. I was just a child. It was soon after the new house was built following the hurricane, so it must have been 1847. I would have been seven years old."

"So I am two years older than you."

She looked at him in surprise. "I suppose I did just give away my age."

Patrick laid his hand over his heart. "I promise to hold your confidence."

She smiled in response to his teasingly serious oath.

With her smile as encouragement, he asked, "What was Austria like?"

Emmaline's eyes took on a faraway look as the memories flooded her mind. "Beautiful."

He prompted her when she didn't elaborate. "How so?"

"My grandparents lived in Seefeld. It's a quaint little town nestled in a valley surrounded by soaring mountain peaks, all of it covered in a deep blanket of snow. I'd never seen snow before. I was mesmerized by it from the moment we got off the ship until we left. There is nothing prettier than falling snow. The softness of it falling in the dark of night or the glittering brilliance of it as the ice crystals capture the sunlight. After sunset one evening we went sleighing across the frozen lake. It was as if we were flying over the snow beneath the moonlight. It was breathtaking." She was so caught up in her memories, she was almost surprised by the heat and humidity when her mind returned to the present. Her glistening eyes turned to his. "I suppose you can't imagine it."

"Actually, I can imagine it. My home usually gets a few inches of snow in winter. It is beautiful when it covers everything in white. I've heard the water freezes over when it's as cold as you say in Seefeld. Did you go ice skating?"

She grinned to recall the exhilarating joy of moving so fast once she got the knack of it. "Oh, yes. A few times on a lake by an odd church with a domed roof. St. Oswald's, I believe it was. Even seeing the frozen lake, it was hard to conceive that water was beneath it or that in summer it was freely moving water. Another day my grandparents took us to a Christkindlmarkt."

"What is that?"

"It was like an open market and a fair at the same time. There were many vendors selling food items and various Christmas decorations unlike anything I have ever seen, not even in catalogs. So many beautiful things. My grandmother bought each of us one thing we dearly had to have."

Softly he asked, "And what did you find dear to your heart?"

Her eyes shone brightly as she recalled the reflective brilliance of the display. "A glass tree ornament called a Kugel. They were made in so many colors I had a hard time picking one."

"You chose red."

She looked at him in surprise.

He answered her unasked question. "I saw it hanging in the window."

She smiled and nodded. "Yes, a red one, but it was the deepest red of all of them."

"It is beautiful."

She smiled to herself. "That was my favorite Christmas." She turned to him. "Do you have a favorite Christmas?"

Patrick returned her charming smile with a teasing grin. "All of them." He turned his gaze ahead to answer her more seriously. "I have never gone anywhere for Christmas. In fact, this will be the first one I've spent away from my family." He frowned as the significance of it registered for the first time.

"Then you must spend Christmas with our family. You and your uncle, of course."

"I'm not sure how my uncle usually celebrates Christmas, but I will extend your invitation to him, and thank you for your consideration."

Emmaline asked, "How does your family celebrate Christmas?"

"Well, about a week before Christmas the whole family goes out into the woods to find the perfect Christmas tree. My siblings and I usually get into a fight over who has found the best tree. Mother usually decides. Sometimes there's snow but more often it is a bleak winter landscape of browns and grays relieved only by the evergreen trees. Anyway, once she picks the tree, we chop it down and all of us together carry it home. We decorate it on Christmas Eve with popcorn, candles, and gingerbread cookies and then, when the candles are lit, we sing Christmas carols until bedtime. Christmas morning we go to church services and afterwards we have a light lunch, share presents, and in the evening we have a big celebration dinner that my mother has spent all day making."

"What do you have for dinner?"

"Roasted turkey, mashed potatoes and gravy, green beans, winter greens, beans and ham, and an iced Christmas cake."

"That sounds perfectly wonderful."

"It is."

"You'll miss them, won't you?"

He could only nod in answer suddenly choked with homesickness.

Emmaline saw the great emotion he was struggling to hide and gave him a moment to recover. They passed the church rectory and were now crossing Fleming Street. The homes grew sparse and the vegetation dense as they continued their south-easterly walk. Curiosity made her risk further upsetting him to ask, "Would you tell me what your home is like?"

Patrick was surprised by her question. "Oh, it's nothing like yours."

She softly said, "I didn't expect it would be."

"Meaning?" The disparity in their family's income made him feel defensive.

"Just that your home is in the mountains and mine is by the sea. Yours, I imagine is isolated and mine is at the edge of a populous town."

"Oh." He felt ashamed for having attributed anything other than genuine interest to her curiosity. "It is a simple two-story log cabin my father built when I was still in leading strings, but it sits atop a mountain ridge with a grand view of the facing mountain."

"Is it part of the Blue Ridge mountains?"

He smiled. "It is."

"Why are they called that?"

'Because in summer or winter, where the distant mountains touch the sky they appear bluish in color."

At a rough crossroad, Emmaline paused to gesture towards the right. "The lighthouse is just beyond those trees if you would like to see it."

"Yes, I would. I haven't been able to explore this far before. And I've only seen this lighthouse and the one in Portsmouth from a far distance."

Emmaline led the way as they followed the shady path between Duval and Whitehead Street. As they came closer to the corner, they could see the clearing enclosed by the picket fence and the faded gray keeper's cottage, but it wasn't until they reached the crossroads that the lighthouse became visible due to the dense canopy of trees. Patrick's excitement grew as they approached the cylindrical tower. His stride lengthened, taking him a few steps ahead of her but then he turned back with a grin and called out to her, "Do you think we could go to the top?"

Emmaline raised a finger to her lips. "Shh." Patrick's instantly contrite look was endearing. He waited for her to come closer. "Mrs. Mabrity and her grandson will be sleeping this time of day." Emmaline looked back to the cottage but saw no one about. "I don't see why we couldn't. The lighthouse belongs to the city. It isn't as if we are trespassing."

She swished through the gate Patrick held open for her and together they walked to the wooden door of the freshly whitewashed brick tower. As Patrick held the door open for her, she lifted the front of her skirt and stepped over the threshold into the cool interior. She eyed the narrow spiral stairs with trepidation. It was not going to be easy to climb with her hoops. Patrick followed behind and waited for her to proceed him up the steps. Emmaline grasped a handful of skirts and hoop with her right hand and used her left to hold on to the railing. The first few steps weren't so bad, but then she had to force the full width of her bottom hoop to compress between the central pole and the wall, making the climb more difficult. Worse, she worried that her hoop was being pushed too far backward and exposing her ankles – or more – to Patrick. She glanced over her shoulder. He was right behind her so perhaps he couldn't see much after all. Emmaline breathed a sigh of relief to reach the top of the tower but found the way no less easy to navigate. The walkway was only half as wide as her skirt. She was deeply regretting taking Brianna's advice to wear the dratted hoops. Her crinoline would not have done her dress justice but at least it would have fit in the space. She moved forward giving Patrick space to join her. The view drew her gaze. It never failed to thrill her to get this bird's eye view from above the trees. Today, being alone with Patrick made it even more exciting.

Patrick reached the landing and had to wait for Emmaline to circle halfway around before he could enter the lantern room. He had hoped for a more intimate moment, but her skirt forced a yard of space between them. It was more effective than a chaperone, of which theirs had long since disappeared. It was likely a good thing. He had a strong desire to do more than touch her hand, and he had a feeling one kiss would never be enough.

Emmaline turned to say something to Patrick, but the words were lost as she encountered his heated gaze. Somehow, it gave her the feeling of being caught like prey. Flustered, she gave him an uncertain smile and was relieved when he returned it and the look in his eye softened.

Patrick felt guilty when he realized he had made Emmaline uncomfortable. He pushed the lustful thoughts from his mind to give her a reassuring smile. When the worry left her face, he pulled his gaze from her to the island view before him and frowned. "I thought lighthouses were always built on the coast?"

Emmaline was relieved to speak of something common place. The tension of a moment ago was not something she knew how to handle. What was the proper reaction? Should she be flattered, mortified, scared, thrilled, curious? She felt all of those at once. And how should one react? With outrage or encouragement? She should ask Brianna for advice, but she knew she would be too embarrassed to even broach the subject with her. She put the moment and the worry from her mind.

What was his question? Oh yes, the lighthouse. "The first one was on the coast." She scanned the horizon to the right, taking note of the fort's location, and then turned her head back to the left. With a lift of her chin she indicated to the southern coast. "It was right over there, but the great hurricane washed it out to sea."

"I remember you mentioned it earlier."

"It was decided to keep that from happening again to build it here."

"Why here?"

"Higher ground. The flood waters didn't reach here. It is the same reason my father chose to rebuild our house outside of town. The highest part of the island spans from here to the cemetery. Poppa bought the closest lot available to it." The intensity of Patrick's warm brown eyes heated again. She looked away, but it did not ease her discomfort, for she could still feel the weight of his gaze. "Do you see the fort?" He shifted beside her. She moved further to the right so he would have a better view.

"I do. How long have they been working on it?"

"Fourteen years now. They started in 1845 but the hurricane wiped out all they had done, and so they had to begin again. The footings are ten feet below water. My brother, Henry, worked on the fort before and after the hurricane until his sponge business grew too large to do both."

"He does well at sponging, it seems."

"Yes, he does."

She moved a few steps further along so they could look out over the roofs of town nestled between the trees. Church steeples and the lookout tower at Tift's warehouse rose above the rest. The burnt district was distinct by its lack of buildings and trees. From this distance, sailing ships appeared to glide smoothly in the harbor. "Before the hurricane you could hardly see the roofs for the trees. The tallest of the trees are the ones that survived the storm. The rest were planted afterwards."

Silence ensued as they took it all in. After a few minutes, Emmaline moved further along the circle. She pointed to a roof not far in the distance. "That is Sandy's place and if you look out to the edge of the island you can see the six buildings of the army barracks."

As they moved on around, Patrick asked, "Is there not anything on this side of the island?"

"No. Just the salt works."

"Salt?"

Emmaline stopped and turned to him. "There are several tidal ponds on that end of the island from which salt is harvested. It has become a big operation, producing jobs and income for the island." She continued walking, coming to the beginning point and turned to him once again. Her foot tangled in her hoop and she put out a hand towards the lantern glass to steady herself. Feeling the beveled glass brought a reminiscent smile.

Patrick saw the curious grin. "What is it?"

"I was just remembering it was a year ago this was installed."

"The lantern? But wasn't the lighthouse built some years ago?"

"Oh yes, it was, but with thirteen parabolic reflectors and lamps. Last year, it was updated with this Fresnel lens. If you look inside you can see it only requires three gas feed flames now instead of the lamps. It was a great improvement in the light and in the work to tend it."

Patrick squinted into the clear center circle of the beehive looking glass cylinder occupying the majority of the space. "You seem to know a lot about it."

She ducked her head in embarrassment. Timidly she looked up, relieved to find he didn't seem to be offended by her knowledge. She was glad he wasn't one of those men who believed women couldn't be smart. "It was a momentous event on the island." She grinned at the recollection. "It was nearly like a parade as the people followed the mule drawn cart carrying the lantern through town. Because Henry volunteered to help install it, Emily and I watched the progress as the lamps were removed and this new lens was hoisted up and put into place. It was quite a production, I assure you. Do you want to walk out on the gallery before we leave? I'm afraid the space is too narrow for my skirts, but you should go out there while you are here."

"Are you sure?"

"Absolutely. I'll wait right here for you to return."

"I would like to." He couldn't pass her, so he walked back the way they had come until he reached the opening passage to the wrought iron balcony surrounding the lighthouse. Stepping out, he slowly made the circuit, enjoying the view again while the island breeze, which blew stronger at this height, tousled his hair. He put his hat back on to keep the hair out of his eyes and held it with his hand to keep it from being blown away. He returned to Emmaline with an exhilarated smile. "I'm glad you insisted. I enjoyed that very much. I only wish you could have joined me."

The side of her mouth twitched. "I wish I could have too."

He waited for her to proceed him down the stairs.

Soon they were back on the ground and retracing their steps. Not far beyond Duval Street they came to be passing fenced in fields. Patrick noted the healthy rows of well-tended grape vines. "He does seem to be doing well."

"Only Uncle Sandy and my mother seem to have the knack for growing more than the native plants on this island."

Patrick held open the entrance gate for Emmaline. A whiff of verbena assailed him as she passed and drew him to follow her as surely as everything else about her. They walked down the wide limestone path to a modest house. Before reaching the porch, a man stepped outside to greet them. He was burly of stature beneath ebony skin, pleasant of face, and full of vigor in defiance of his graying hair. His manner was courtly as he held out his hand inviting them onto the porch. "Welcome, Miss Emmaline."

Emmaline turned to Patrick. "Mr. Johnson, may I present Mr. Sandy Cornish."

Patrick had trouble holding back his shock. He assumed this man to be a slave or servant at least. He certainly hadn't expected the well-respected owner of a vineyard to be a black man. Emmaline had given him no clue. Quickly recovering, he held out his hand. "A pleasure to meet you, Mr. Cornish." A calloused and beefy hand engulfed his.

The heavy dark head gave him a polite nod. "Most folks call me Sandy or Uncle Sandy."

Emmaline turned to Sandy. "This is Mr. Patrick Johnson. He is Smithy's nephew and apprentice."

"Please, call me Patrick since we're not standing on ceremony here."

Sandy gave a nod. "Patrick, then." He turned to Emmaline. "Are you here to pick up your order?"

She smiled. "I am."

"Rest here on the veranda while I get that for you."

Patrick saw the placard advertising a plate of fresh cut fruit for forty cents. He was feeling parched after their walk. "Miss Whitmore, we've come all this way. Would you mind if we shared a plate of fruit?"

Emmaline caught the hopeful look in his eye. "That would be lovely."

Sandy stepped to the side and held the door for them to proceed him into the house. It brought to Patrick's attention the heavy white scaring and mangled end fingers of Sandy's left hand.

As they stepped into the coolness of the house, they were greeted by Sandy's wife, Lillah. Emmaline performed the introductions again and then they were led to the parlor where several small, cloth covered, square tables were situated for customers. Lillah led them to the table by the window. Patrick held the chair for Emmaline before taking his seat. Lillah gave him an approving nod. She handed them a list of available fruits. Patrick cast a questioning glance to Emmaline.

"I have no preference. Order what you like."

He would have liked to try some of everything but limited to one plate and three fruit choices he picked guava, having never tried it before, and two of his favorites, oranges and grapes, from the variety Sandy left at the forge when picking up the ashes.

Not much was said between them while they waited for the fruit, being content to watch the progress of a small blue-tailed lizard outside the window. Lillah soon returned with a plate piled high with the requested fruit and two large bright printed napkins which Emmaline supposed helped to conceal any fruit stains. The oranges were cut into sections and the guava cut in half, making them easier to eat. Lillah retreated to a chair in the corner and picked up embroidery. Emmaline appreciated the gesture of propriety even as it made her feel discomfited. She removed her gloves and laid them on the edge of the table before choosing a grape, delicately placing it in her mouth. Patrick held up the cut guava eyeing it speculatively.

Emmaline smiled. "You can eat the whole thing or just the inside if you prefer." Patrick took a tentative bite of flesh and rind. She watched him chew waiting for a reaction. He gave her a half smile when he was done and then took a more substantial bite proving he liked it.

Patrick swallowed the fruit and politely dabbed his mouth. "It's like a cross between a strawberry and a pear. Not as sweet nor as tart." He frowned as she picked up another grape. "Do you not like them?"

"Oh, I do. I'm afraid of spoiling my dress with the juice."

"Nonsense." He turned to their hostess. "Lillah, would you mind bringing a knife and fork for Emmaline?"

Emmaline ducked her head in embarrassment. She hated for Lillah to go to such trouble on her behalf, but then it seemed to be no trouble as the matron brought them to her from a tray on the sideboard along with a smaller plate.

"My apologies, miss. I should have realized as a proper miss you would need these."

Emmaline gave her hostess a grateful smile as the items were placed before her. She used the knife to keep the half round of guava from moving while she speared it with the fork and moved it to her plate. Carefully, she cut it in half and half again, lifting the quarter piece of pinkish-yellow flesh to her mouth. She savored the burst of flavor all the while conscious of Patrick studying her every move. She wondered what he was thinking.

The fruit in his mouth had grown tasteless as he watched the delicate way Emmaline moved. Her tongue caught a drop of juice on her lip, and he nearly groaned. The desire to kiss the juice from her lips was a physical ache. Eating the plate of fruit became a means of torture for him. He was astounded to realize he was jealous of a napkin for being able to touch her lips. The only way he could finish eating was to studiously avoid looking at her. Conversation became stilted and then dropped altogether.

He breathed a sigh of relief when the plate was finally empty of all except the orange rinds. Lillah led them outside where Sandy met them with a crate of what appeared to be a peck of sweet potatoes.

Emmaline turned to Patrick. "I hope it is not too presumptuous of me to ask if you would mind carrying the potatoes?"

"Not at all." Something to occupy his hands would be welcome.

"Although…" Emmaline frowned. "I suppose I need a pumpkin too."

Patrick gave her and then Sandy a doubtful look. He could carry both, but for how far?

Sandy took pity on the young man. "I can drop both of them off at your house Monday morning if you like. I won't even charge you since I'm headed in that direction anyway."

"That would be wonderful, Sandy. Thank you."

Patrick breathed a sigh of relief as he handed the crate back to Sandy. They thanked the couple for the delicious fruit and bid them good-day. It wasn't until they passed through the gate that they spoke again. He held it for her and was surprised when she turned right instead of back the way they came, but he didn't question her. Instead, he looked down at her, noting how the afternoon sun made her hair blaze like fire. "I liked them."

"They're good people. His story is a sad one, really, though I suppose it does have a happy ending considering he is one of the richest men on the island, but I've heard rumors that before coming here he had to do things, too horrible to repeat, to keep from being taken back into slavery."

"A man of his stature would be highly valued as a slave." Patrick recalled the maimed hand and wondered if it figured into his freedom.

Emmaline turned to the left and Patrick followed. The street was wider than the roughly cleared path they just left and was well maintained. The brush was cut back and the edges neatly trimmed. A house appeared on the left and Emmaline put another foot of space between them.

He chided her. "Afraid someone might see?"

"We are unchaperoned. It wouldn't do to give any suspicion of touching. I have my reputation to protect."

Patrick instantly felt ashamed for his churlish thoughts. "Of course. I wasn't thinking."

They walked a hundred yards or so in silence. Patrick could see a fork in the road ahead and wondered which way they would turn when Emmaline's pace slowed. She was looking off to the right and he followed her gaze to a clearing filled with headstones.

"Do you mind if we stopped here for a moment?"

"Of course not."

She paused to pick three orange flower clusters from a nearby tree. Patrick picked a single flower. He followed her into the cemetery. He certainly wouldn't begrudge her a moment to visit her mother's graveside. She laid the first cluster in front of a stone that read Agatha Whitmore Pary and the second was for Madalyn Grace Whitmore. She knelt to the ground and kissed the flowers before laying them before the third stone for her mother, Betsafina Drake Wheeler Whitmore. It was the newest of the three and the dates made it logical to assume it was her mother's.

Patrick amused himself by reading the dates and inscriptions. Agatha Pary was of an age to be her grandmother. The middle stone caught him off guard. It was a child, less than a year old. He murmured, "There is something tragic about children dying. She was born the same year as you. A cousin?"

Emmaline sadly shook her head. She held out her hand for Patrick to help her up. Softly she said, "Madalyn was my sister. My twin sister."

Patrick turned to her slack jawed. He had of course heard of twins, but he had never met one.

"I don't remember her at all, but I still feel the loss of her. As if a part of me is missing." She turned her gaze to him. "I've never told anyone that before. I've wondered so many times what it would have been like had she lived."

He didn't know what to say to that, so he kept silent. When she was ready to leave he held the flower out to her. "I picked this one for you."

She accepted it with a tremulous smile. "Thank you. Shall we continue?"

He stepped aside. "Please lead the way."

Across from the cemetery, there was another house on the left at the road's divergence. Emmaline veered to the left and in another hundred yards the street straitened again. He recognized the upcoming intersection and realized they had returned to her house. Their time alone had come to end sooner than he was ready. He enjoyed the idyllic afternoon getting to know her and exploring the island. He paused before opening the gate in the picket fence surrounding her house. "Maybe next time we could walk out to see the fort."

Next time. The words sent a thrill through her. "I would like that." She put a hand on his arm to keep him from opening the gate just yet. She waited until his eyes met hers. She spoke with all the emotion churning in her heart. "Thank you, Patrick. I enjoyed today more than any I've had in a very long time."

If not for standing in front of her father's house, he surely would have kissed her and consequences be damned. "I did too." He quickly opened the gate before he did something stupid.

They walked up the path as close as they could without touching. Her father met them at the door.

Chapter 8

Her father's thunderous expression did not bode well. Emmaline felt Patrick stiffen beside her. Together they walked up the steps to the wide veranda. They stopped at the top of the steps, leaving the full distance to the door between them and her father.

Patrick removed his hat and gave a nod. "Good evening, sir." He was met with cold silence. He wished he could take Emmaline's hand for moral support; for her sake or his, he couldn't say. Perhaps both. He didn't think he had ever felt more intimidated in his life than in this moment facing her father's wrath. Anger emanated from him in lashing waves on Patrick's conscious.

Theodore deliberately spoke directly to Emmaline. "Where have you been? The maid returned hours ago. She said she lost sight of you in town."

Emmaline was flabbergasted. Her father had never spoke to her in such an angry tone. Agatha maybe, but never her.

Patrick opened his mouth to speak in her defense.

Theodore gave the young man a scathing look. "I don't want your excuses." He turned to his daughter. "Emmaline, go inside."

"But Poppa...."

"Now."

She didn't dare disobey the steely tone. She cast an apologetic look to Patrick and went inside. As soon as the door closed behind her, she lifted her skirts high and raced up the stairs, startling the maid on the landing, anxious to reach the balcony. She had no qualms with the wrongness of eavesdropping over this conversation.

Theodore stared at the young man before him, expecting him to turn tail and run, but he was made of sterner grit than expected. Patrick steadily held his gaze in return.

Neither man spoke for several seconds.

Patrick's heart was beating so hard he was sure Mr. Whitmore had to hear it. He wasn't sure he was doing the right thing by standing his ground in the face of the elder man's anger, but he refused to back down. Emmaline was too important to walk away. His jaw went slack. When had that happened? When had *like* grown to *love*? Was it today, as she shared the stories of her life? Was it in the moonlight, waiting for the mail ship? Or was it from the first moment they collided in the street and she first lifted her beautiful face to his? He suspected the latter. He loved her. And with that astounding realization, he squared his shoulders, firmed his jaw, and waited for her father to speak.

Theodore's eyes narrowed as he watched emotions play across Patrick's face and then saw him firm his stance, ready to do battle. He registered a nudge of grudging respect for the lad, but it wasn't enough. He couldn't let Emmaline settle for an apprentice who didn't even like his trade. She deserved more than a life of hardship. Hers had been too filled with loss as it was. She would not be a pauper's wife if he could help it. "Go home, Patrick. There's nothing for you here."

"With all due respect sir, there is." Patrick heard a creak in the boards over his head but dared not break eye contact with Mr. Whitmore.

"Brianna may believe you are good for Emmaline, and though I have great respect for your uncle, I know nothing of you."

"What do you want to know?"

Theodore ignored the question. "You can't support her as an apprentice, and you don't seem to have any notion of taking over your uncle's business."

Patrick lifted his chin. "You are quite right, sir. Although forging is a respectable occupation, I don't see myself as a blacksmith."

His candor unexpectedly softened Theodore. "How do you see yourself?"

Patrick realized total honesty was the only answer he could give. "That's just it, sir. I don't know. I suppose I don't have enough experience of the world."

Theodore's respect for the lad went up another degree, but he was not going to give in to sentimentality. He gathered his righteous anger tightly around him like a cloak on a blustery winter's day. "Your experience will not come with hardship for Emmaline. Until you prove yourself a worthy suitor, stay away from my daughter."

Patrick saw no other recourse. He had no argument to present. He would concede – for now. "Good evening, sir."

Emmaline hovered in the shadows of the upper balcony behind a curtain of jasmine, watching Patrick walk away. The slump of his shoulders tore at her heart. A tear escaped to trail down her cheek, followed by another and another. She didn't wipe them away for that would require releasing her tightly clenched hands, and she feared they were all that were keeping her from falling to pieces. Why was her father being so unreasonable? The thought kept running in circles in her mind like a mantra. She flinched at the slam of the study door from the floor below, but still she didn't move from her concealment. She felt as if she would shatter like fragile porcelain if she did.

Below her, Brianna and Garrett returned from taking Eli for a walk. Their laughter cut into her frayed nerves. She envied her sister's happiness. Would she ever find that for herself? She felt it for a brief moment today. But Patrick was surely lost to her now. Her father had made it clear he was not welcome. Why would Patrick dare to defy him? They hardly knew each other. A sob escaped her. And now they never would.

She put a hand over her mouth to smoother any sound as Brianna entered the bedroom behind her and cheerfully called her name. Emmaline didn't answer. She wasn't ready to face anyone, not even her sister. The door to the balcony was open, but it usually was unless the weather turned cold. She hoped her sister wouldn't come looking for her outside. Emmaline's eyes closed on a sigh of relief as Brianna left the room.

A few moments later, she heard Brianna and Garrett talking from their room next door.

Brianna said, "I wonder what has happened. It's not like father to close the study door unless he is conducting business, but I didn't hear any voices. I thought Emmaline might know, but I don't think she has returned from her walk with Patrick."

Garrett said, "Those two have grown quite chummy."

"I do hope something comes of it. His sunny disposition is perfect for her."

Emmaline couldn't hold back the harsh sob her sister's words generated. She fled into her room, through the house, down the stairs, and out into the garden to sink down on her mother's favorite bench in the far corner under the draping canopy of a silver buttonwood. She turned sideways, leaning against the back and arm and cried like she had never done before, not even when her mother died. The unfairness of her father's decision and the possibility that Patrick may be lost to her forever were more than she could bear.

Brianna heard the sob and her sister's flight. She followed her out to the garden, but then kept her distance, giving Emmaline a chance to release the worst of her tears. She knew as soon as she approached her sister would valiantly reign in her emotion. A few minutes later, when she took a seat next to Emmaline, to her utter surprise, her little sister didn't try to hide her tears but turned into the comfort of her embrace. When Emmaline's crying ceased, still she rested her head on Brianna's shoulder.

From over her sister's shoulder, Emmaline watched a rufous hummingbird feed on the last flowering bush of the season. Feeling a little calmer, she gave her sister a rare confidence. "I wish momma were here. She would know what to do."

Brianna's breath hitched at the mention of their mother. She didn't know what was wrong, but it was something tragic for Emmaline to act so emotional. She hadn't seen Emmaline cry like this, at least not since she was a baby, mourning the loss of her twin. "What has happened?"

Emmaline sat up straight. "Poppa turned Patrick away."

Brianna's jaw dropped. "For what reason?"

"He was furious with me for losing our chaperone, but then he sent me in the house and sent Patrick away because he doesn't want to be a blacksmith and doesn't have any other aspirations, but it shouldn't matter. Not yet at least. It's not as if he has asked to marry me. We are just enjoying each other's company."

"I see."

"You do? What can we do about it?"

"That I'm not sure of. You know how set Poppa can be. We will have to change his mind before he will relent."

Emmaline felt so hopeless. "How can we possibly change his mind?"

"I don't know, but one thing is certain. For you to have any future with him, Patrick must figure out what he is going to do with his life."

* * *

December 18th, the 4th Sunday of Advent

Emmaline was not one to cry over things she couldn't control, making last night's onset of tears that much more distressing. She tied the ribbon sash around her waist and walked to the dressing mirror to make sure it was straight and smooth. Why could she not deal with the loss of Patrick in her usual, practical manner? It wasn't as if she was in love with him. Her head came up to stare at her reflection. Was she? No, she couldn't be. They hardly knew each other. It only hurt so much because she had so enjoyed their walk. It was the first day she had felt truly happy since her mother's passing, and so to have it end with a confrontation with her father struck deeper.

She moved to the dresser and opened her jewelry box. The red onyx broach with the ivory carving of Madonna and child drew her attention as if it was the only piece in the box. It belonged to her mother. Normally she wore it Christmas week, starting with the Eatonton Ball just as her mother had always done, but today she felt the need to have this bit of her mother close to her. It was only a few days earlier than usual. Likely no one would even notice except for maybe Brianna.

She joined the family downstairs for breakfast. It was eaten in silence more in reverence to the Lord's Day than due to any tension between them. Emmaline bore no ill will towards her father. She knew he had only her best interests at heart. She was only disappointed he had taken such strong action. They soon left the house to walk to church. Patrick was already seated with his uncle when they entered.

Patrick felt her presence the moment she entered the church. He felt her gaze touch him and turned his head to meet it. She gave him a tremulous smile before turning her attention to the pew. Mr. Whitmore's stern look met his. He bravely held it for a moment before facing forward again. He felt the need to show her father he was more than a cowering lad, but he also understood what her father wanted, and he was right to want it. Emmaline deserved a man who could support her and right now that was not him. He had to figure out how to change his situation. He spent all last night struggling to come up with ideas. The only jobs he knew were of a laborer, and he wanted to be more than that. He didn't have, nor could he afford, the education needed to be a doctor or lawyer but surely there was something else. Reverend Herrick approached the pulpit bringing a temporary end to his musings.

After the service, Patrick hurried from the church to see Emmaline, but he didn't dare approach her. She met his gaze from across the yard and in it he saw the longing he too felt. She was surrounded by her family. There would be no chance for him to even speak to her today. He was about to turn away when he noticed Garrett headed his way after a whispered conversation with Brianna. He moved to intercept him in the yard while surreptitiously watching Emmaline.

"Good Sabbath, Patrick."

"Same to you, Garrett."

Aware of the other parishioners surrounding them, Garrett chose his words with care. He had no desire to stir gossip and even less desire for word to reach his father-in-law that he was conspiring against him.

"My wife thought you should know there will be a concert at the pavilion this evening. She said you would be interested in attending."

Hope took wing in his breast. If the message meant what he thought, there was yet an opportunity to see Emmaline this evening. "Thank you, Garrett. I believe I'm of a mind to attend." There was a spring in his step as he left the church yard.

Patrick returned home with his uncle for lunch but left soon after. He spent the afternoon wandering about the town until it was time for the concert. At first, he had no purpose, but as he pondered his job quandary, he found himself pausing at some of the shops to consider its potential for him. There were several lawyers and a doctor, but he had already discarded those as impossible. There was the coffee shop, a cobbler, a milliner, a grocer, a tinker, a baker, a ship chandler, and of course the military, but none of them appealed.

The sun was setting, and he was feeling defeated as he walked past the burned district on his way to the pavilion where the concert was to be held. He paused at the spot where Emmaline said her father's paper office stood. He did so at first simply to recall their conversation, but as he stood there it occurred to him, journalism was the only thing that sparked any interest before, and it did so even more now. He resumed walking, but now his mind was full of questions. They flowed heavily as he found a post to lounge against and watch for Emmaline's arrival.

* * *

Emmaline tried to hide it, but she had been melancholy all day, and Brianna knew it. Her sister tried several times to cheer her. Emmaline tried to make her believe she had succeeded and in doing so found herself agreeing to an outing after supper. Now she was walking beside Brianna and Garrett, who was pushing Eli in the pram, on their way to a concert being held at the pavilion. If not for her love of music, she likely would have begged off. She really did feel the beginnings of a headache coming on.

A cool evening breeze blew pleasantly against them as they walked into town. The sun had set a while ago and most of the color was gone now too except for streaks of vermillion clouds standing against the royal blue horizon which darkened to ebony above, broken only by the glint of stars and a waning crescent moon. The feathery silhouette of trees rose to soften the harsh lines of the buildings.

They soon came to the outskirts of the crowd gathered around the gazebo-like structure where Whitehead and Front Street joined. It seemed most of the town had turned out to enjoy the Army band's selection of Christmas carols. Torches lit up the perimeter of the gazebo and lanterns within. A few street gaslights and more torches helped to light the perimeter of the gathering. The only other light came from those who carried lanterns.

Brianna put a hand on Garrett's arm to stop him at the outskirts of the crowd. "Let us stay here so the music isn't too loud for Eli."

They arrived none too soon as the uplifting notes of "Joy to the World" filled the very air around them. Many voices joined in to sing the beloved carol. Emmaline noted Eli's rapt expression. He adored music too, leaving Emmaline to suspect her sister chose their position with an ulterior motive. Sure enough as the thought crossed her mind, she felt a presence come up to her side. Emmaline turned her head to encounter Patrick's smiling face and gave him a joyful grin in return. He leaned forward and gave a nod of greeting to Brianna and Garrett. He cast a glance about them. She did as well. There was no one else close to them, and they had the cloak of darkness for protection. Patrick moved another step closer to her side. He then surprised her by reaching for her hand. Wanting the unexpected closeness as much as he did, she curled her fingers around his palm. The shawl she wore was plenty warm for the evening but the heat that suffused her with the hidden intimacy of their entwined hands made her too warm. She lifted her cheek to the cooling breeze and took several deep breaths to calm her racing pulse. Patrick's voice joined the others in singing the final verse of the song, so she did too.

When the hymn ended, Patrick leaned down to speak softly for Emmaline only, "You have a beautiful voice." She whispered in return, "You have a lovely baritone yourself." Then she gave him another one of her smiles. Her upturned face was so close to his, he had but to lean in a little father to kiss her. He was wickedly tempted. Garrett gave him a knowing look that banished the wayward thought from his mind. Patrick guiltily straightened and joined in with the others to sing "Hark! The Herald Angels Sing."

When the band switched to the slow strains of "Silent Night" Patrick began swaying to the music. Emmaline matched his movements, feeling as if they were having their own private dance. They continued to sway when the song changed to "The First Noel." She was almost disappointed when the change in tempo of "God Rest Ye Merry, Gentlemen" ended the movement between them. Almost. She really did love the lively music best. Several more lilting songs followed before the program was closed out with "O Holy Night" once again allowing her and Patrick to sway together.

As the gathering broke up, and they reluctantly let go of each other's hand, Patrick asked, "May I walk you home?"

She held his gaze, relieved to delay their parting. "I would like that." She placed her hand on the arm he held out for her.

Two familiar boys ran past them with a shout and they turned to find Henry and Emily behind them, surrounded by their other three children and Henry carrying Laurie.

Emily said, "It's too bad we didn't find each other sooner. We could have enjoyed the concert together." She peeped into the pram to admire her sleeping nephew, Eli.

Henry nudged her arm. "Don't get any ideas."

She gave him an angelic smile. "Only if it is God's will."

Brianna said, "It would have been nice to be together, but I'm afraid we arrived late and for Elijah's sake we didn't venture close."

Emily said, "Of course, I understand." She turned her attention to the tall gentlemen. "Patrick, did you enjoy the concert?"

"Yes ma'am, I did. It's the first time I've heard such a large band play. Any music put on back home outside of church is with a fiddle and guitar and maybe a mouth organ."

When the others dropped a few paces behind carrying on their own conversation, Patrick asked Emmaline, "How did your father get started as a newspaper man?"

"He had a family friend and mentor who owned a paper and hired him when he graduated from college. He tried his hand at all of the jobs at the paper before discovering an affinity for writing. My sister works for the same paper, although the son is running it now."

Her answer wasn't encouraging. Patrick didn't have any college education. He actually never graduated from primary school, having left early to work in the fields before completing his studies. He didn't have any family connections to aid him either. He wondered if that would prevent him from being a journalist. Other than Emmaline's father, he didn't know any other journalists to ask. He would give it more thought later. Right now he wanted to enjoy Emmaline's company. "Your sister arrives tomorrow, does she not?"

Emmaline's smile grew huge. "She does, and I am so praying she was able to bring James with her."

"Your younger brother, right?"

"Yes, and the apple of our father's eye. He denies having one, but we all know James is his favorite."

"And you're hoping James can pull your father from his

melancholy."

Emmaline didn't think she had mentioned that specific part of her plan to Patrick. "How did you know?"

Patrick shrugged. "It makes sense. I pray it works. I know how worried you are for your father."

She looked up at him with earnest concern. "Thank you."

They were at the corner of Fleming Street where Henry's family would leave them. Emmaline stopped and turned to bid them goodnight. Not long after, they approached the yard of Emmaline's house. Anything more than a hasty goodbye fled Patrick's thoughts as he discerned Mr. Whitmore smoking a cigar on the porch, presumably waiting for his family's return. It crossed his mind to part from her now and save them all from any confrontation, but instinctively he refused to cower from her father. Somehow, he knew it was better to bravely face him than to take the easy way out.

A few blocks away, Henry and Emily walked in companionable silence, content to listen to the excited chatter of their children skipping ahead. It was going to be a while before she would get them settled down to sleep. It was a good thing they didn't have school in the morning. In the momentary glow of a gas lamp, Emily noticed Henry's reminiscent smile. "What are you thinking?"

"I was just remembering how good it felt when Emmaline was a baby and we got her to smile again after losing Madalyn. Do you remember?"

"I do."

"It is the same feeling now to see her smiling after mourning for so long, and it is all because of Patrick."

"You like him." It was a statement, not a question.

"I do. He is good for her."

"I agree. Henry. We must find a way to bring your father around to approving of him."

"We can try, but ultimately, it is up to Patrick to bring him around."

Emmaline bit her lip as she watched her father rise from the wicker chair on the porch. She hadn't anticipated that he would be waiting for them outside. If she had, she would have discouraged Patrick from walking her home. She didn't want to upset her father tonight. Too much was at stake tomorrow with her sister's arrival for him to be in an ill mood. Guiltily, she dropped her hand from Patrick's arm.

Brianna nudged Garrett and gave him a pleading look when he turned to her.

Garrett understood what she asked of him. They needed a diversion. "Patrick, I appreciate you coming to help with the pram. Could you take the front?"

Emmaline and Brianna waited together in the yard as Patrick and Garrett gently lifted the pram with a sleeping Eli up to the porch. The girls followed behind. Patrick held the door for Garrett to wheel the buggy inside. He took his hat off as the ladies approached. Brianna entwined her hand in her father's arm. "Come inside, Poppa. I want to tell you all about the concert."

Theodore patted her hand before dropping his arm to place it at the small of her back urging her to enter the house. "You can tell me all about it in the morning."

Brianna pursed her lips in frustration. She paused before entering the house to give Patrick an apologetic look. "Thank you for your assistance."

"You're most welcome. Good night, Mrs. Cade."

Emmaline eyed the two men most important to her bracketing either side of the door. Tension emanated between them. Her father would not enter the house before her, for that would leave her alone on the porch with Patrick, something he would not allow, not even for a second. She would have to pass the threshold first, and if she did, she would leave Patrick alone with her father, something she was loath to do with the tension flowing between them. She didn't step any closer to the door but turned slightly sideways, putting her shoulder towards her father. She gave Patrick a speaking look, hoping he would understand her intention. "Thank you for your escort, Mr. Johnson, and your assistance. It saved me from any risk of tripping over my skirt if I tried to help with the pram or from having to wake Elijah."

Patrick gleaned Emmaline's intention. He was prepared to face Mr. Whitmore, but he understood Emmaline's reluctance to have him do so. He gently let the door close and took the necessary steps past her to the edge of the porch. He turned to face father and daughter and gave a nod to them both. "Good evening, sir, Miss Whitmore." He turned to descend the steps, donning his hat, and proceeded home in an intentional unconcerned manner, hoping it would give Mr. Whitmore the impression he was not as disappointed as he felt.

Emmaline watched Patrick leave before turning towards the door. As her eyes met her father's, she realized the delay in entering the house had betrayed her true feelings. Her father moved to the other side of the door, taking Patrick's place in holding it open for her, his expression inscrutable. "Come, Emmaline."

* * *

Patrick lay awake, staring at a crack in the ceiling plaster and listening to his uncle snore from the other side of the wall. One question kept circling in his mind: could he write for a paper? Doubts assailed him, but he held on to the fact that one of his teachers praised his essays saying he had a way with words. But could he risk everything on her praise alone? Maybe he didn't have to. He could try his hand at writing an article as if there were a paper to write for. The idea held a lot of merit. The more he thought about it, the more committed he became to the idea.

He needed something to write about. Politics? He shook his head. That wouldn't work. He didn't know enough about the feelings in Key West or those who held office on the island. Even the presidential race was out of his depths. Besides, it had to be of local interest if it was to be for a local paper. It should be something the islanders cared about. Maybe he could interview Sandy. The former slave certainly seemed to be a man with an interesting past, but that was just it, it was past. He wanted something of interest now.

He couldn't come up with any grand ideas, so he decided to think about it some more in the morning. He tossed and turned, trying to sleep to no avail. His mind refused to let it go so he let it wander the same path he took through town before the concert and again, when he reached the burned district, inspiration overwhelmed him. He could write about the rebuilding. Who owned the lots? What were their plans for rebuilding? Would it be the same as before or something better? Or were they selling their lots? What was the future of Key West's prime real estate?

He was relieved to finally have purpose and direction, but still it was a long time before he slept.

Chapter 9

"I think you know my heart isn't in this." Patrick held his uncle's gaze from across the breakfast table.

Smithy gave his nephew a scrutinizing look. "What has heart got to do with it? It's a job. You master the skill. You do the job. Simple as that."

Patrick couldn't hold back his snicker. "I think one must have heart or threat to master a skill, and as I have neither... You must admit my skill is poor at best, Uncle. Surely you've noticed."

"You need more practice."

Patrick rolled his eyes, exasperated. "I don't want to practice. I've found something else I want to try. At least, I think I have."

"Humph."

"Uncle, all I ask is that you give me today to find out. If it doesn't work, no more will be said. I will dedicate myself to improving at the anvil."

"And if it does work, where does that leave me? Short an apprentice."

"I'll still be here to help. Even if my idea works, I may be able to do both." He eyed his uncle who sullenly continued to eat his porridge. "Will you allow me to have the day off?"

Smithy growled, "Do what you will. I've no hold over you."

Patrick grinned. "Thank you."

He walked away from the forge with only the tiniest regret for leaving his uncle to work alone. Last week had been slow in orders so his uncle should manage fine on his own for one day. If not, he would help him catch up when he returned. Patrick figured the best place to start his research was with the city records. Armed with pencil and paper, he expected to spend his morning digging through dusty files. To his surprise, the clerk was knowledgeable and friendly, providing him with most of the information from memory. It gave Patrick a moment's concern that perhaps everyone on the island was as well informed. Though the population was larger than his hometown, it was possible it was the same here as there – everyone knew everyone else's business –

but when he questioned the clerk, he was assured his knowledge was more extensive due to handling the necessary paperwork for lot purchases and business taxes. Relieved he would not have to find another topic, Patrick delved into gleaning all he could from the helpful clerk.

An hour later, he was on his way to start meeting with the owners on his list. He chose Mr. Mulrennon first, having been intrigued by Emmaline's story of his saving the town. It wasn't hard to find him. The maid at his temporary home directed Patrick to find him overseeing construction. Mr. Mulrennon was tall and boisterous of Scotch-Irish descent, making him easy to distinguish. Patrick guessed him to be in his early thirties as he introduced himself and a half hour later knew much of the man's history in addition to his plans for the new hotel and shops he and Mr. Ware and Mr. Carey were invested in. His past history as a compositor for the *New York Herald* was especially intriguing. But what Patrick appreciated most was Mr. Mulrennon's encouragement in Patrick's endeavor. He then offered to introduce Patrick to the next landowner on his list.

And so the day flew by as Patrick met the men of Key West and learned of their visions for the future. He returned home in time for supper, famished and impatient to begin organizing his thoughts into something interesting for others to read. If not encouraging, his uncle was at least helpful in offering to do the dishes even though he had cooked. Patrick knew his uncle hoped this was a passing fancy and his mind would soon return to forging.

* * *

They were finishing tea when it came, the knock on the front door Emmaline had been impatiently waiting to hear. The long-awaited day, nay, the long-awaited moment had arrived. Her eyes met Brianna's, reflecting the same excitement she felt. Simultaneously, they rose from the table and hurried to answer the door. The expected lad of ten or twelve removed his cap and said, "The Nantucket has arrived, miss."

Emmaline removed a coin from her skirt pocket to hand to him. "Thank you, Timmy." The lad scurried off with his new wealth. She and Brianna turned to find their father standing behind them, picking up his hat and cane from the hall table. Emmaline handed Brianna her bonnet with a grin and took hers hanging from the peg on the wall. Garrett had offered to stay home with Eli so the three of them left the house to walk side-by-side down to the wharf.

It didn't take long to find the ship. It was a shiny new steamer anchored at the end of the deepest dock in the harbor. They waited near the dock, out of the way of the workers. Emmaline's heart fluttered in happy anticipation of being reunited with her sister, Agatha, and with anxiety to learn if James was with her. Brianna's arm tightened around hers. A glance at her sister's face proved she was feeling the same emotions. On her other side, Poppa stood stoically beside her showing no emotion. Her messenger had been quick in his task for the gangplank was only now being put into place allowing the passengers to disembark. He must have come running as soon as the ship entered the harbor.

A woman in a cherry red dress waved to shore from the ship's rail. Emmaline couldn't be sure at this distance, but she thought it was Agatha. She waved in return, her heart squeezing in concerned dismay. Brianna waved too as she said in a low voice, "I don't see James." Emmaline realized then how much she had been counting on Agatha to bring him. Her letters seemed so sure of her success that Emmaline hadn't considered she might fail. Tears threatened, but she took a deep breath to banish them. She wouldn't let Agatha see her disappointment for she was happy to at least have both of her sisters for Christmas.

It seemed to take an inordinately long amount of time for the many passengers to make their way from the ship to the dock and then to shore. Agatha was one of the first to disembark but was not among the first to reach them as a sea of faces in somber shades of gray, brown and black travelling clothing approached. As the group neared the end of the wooden planks a pair separated from the rest, one in a red dress, to race towards them with exuberant smiles.

Joy winged in Emmaline's heart robbing her of speech. He was here. Emmaline found herself engulfed in their joint embrace along with Brianna. Together, Agatha and James said, "Merry Christmas!" Emmaline echoed them, her voice choked with emotion. The new arrivals pulled away to cautiously approach their father. Agatha hugged him. James held back until Agatha moved aside and then he held out his hand. Father and son shook hands to outward appearances as if it were any other day, but Emmaline saw the emotion that hovered in her father's eyes. It gave her hope.

James had already made arrangements for their luggage to be taken to the house so the five of them walked back through town, all anxious to get home. The three sisters walked together, arms entwined, with Emmaline in the middle. Father and son led the small group. James filled the air with happy chatter about his experiences at West Point. It seemed the military school was very much to his liking. He was doing well in all his classes. The only downside was his poor marksmanship. He announced his intention to practice every day somewhere out towards the salt pond. Agatha surprised everyone by stating her intention to join him. At their skeptical look, she pulled a small lady's revolver from her handbag. "One can't be too careful walking alone at night in the city."

Theodore gave her a cross look. "Why are you walking alone at night?"

"Meeting deadlines sometimes keeps me late."

"Then someone should walk you home. Kendrick should know better than to let you leave unescorted."

Many arguments leapt to Agatha's tongue, but she willed herself not to speak. She didn't want to have this argument right now. For heaven's sakes, they had just arrived. She turned from her father to link her arm with Emmaline. "So, little sister, what are your plans for our holiday? I'm sure you have it all thought out."

Theodore said, "Agatha, this conversation is only over for now."

She gave him a wink to indicate she expected as much, wickedly knowing he would not like the unladylike gesture.

Emmaline whispered, "Please don't irritate him so." To the group she said, "We start tonight with a welcome home supper."

"Have you decorated?"

"Some."

Agatha squeezed her sister's arm. "Have I a surprise for you."

Emmaline couldn't help smiling at the excited exuberance in her sister's voice. "What is it?"

"Patience little one. All in good time."

Emmaline half grinned, half grimaced, at Agatha's familiar teasing. She hated it, but on the other hand, she was glad to have her home, annoyances and all.

James turned to walk backwards. "Where is Henry?"

Emmaline said, "Working, I'm afraid. He has promised to join us for supper even if his whole fleet of sponge boats sinks today."

Agatha grimaced. "Well let us hope that doesn't happen with all the mouths he has to feed."

The rich aroma of coffee assailed them from the coffee shop just ahead, but it was the men standing outside the hotel on Duval and their heated debate over the Presidential candidates that drew their attention. Agatha grimaced. "I see the war talk is as bad here as it is up north. We must enjoy this Christmas. I see our country headed into a very dark place."

Her pronouncement left a pall over them all. But as was typical with her mercurial nature, her next pronouncement made them all laugh. She waved her hand in front of her face. "My goodness I forget how hot it is here. It was threatening to snow when we left New York."

Upon reaching the house, Agatha went upstairs to freshen up, followed by Brianna to check on a napping Eli. James and Theodore joined Garrett in the parlor and Emmaline went to the kitchen to put together some refreshments. They soon all came together in the parlor to share each other's lives since last they had written.

A knock on the door announced the arrival of their luggage. Agatha rose with giddy excitement, more than warranted the mere arrival of her trunks. She was first to reach the door. As the others trailed into the hallway, they heard her say, "It will be easier to take those around to the kitchen." She then stepped aside to allow the man carrying a tightly wrapped, oddly shaped bundle to enter. "James, will you show this good man to the parlor?"

Emmaline, Brianna, Garrett, and Theodore stepped aside with puzzled faces to allow the delivery man passage. Agatha directed those carrying the trunks upstairs. She called over her shoulder, "James, you wait for me!" Leaving the men with instructions on which rooms to take the trunks, she lifted her skirts and hurried back down the hall to the gathering in the parlor. She moved to the wrapped bundle and turned to face them. By now they all had guessed the surprise. "I brought a Christmas tree!" Agatha turned to help James undo the tightly wrapped sheeting. As it untwisted, the branches sprang free releasing their fragrance into the air.

Theodore breathed in deeply. The smell took him back to childhood hunting trips with his father in the Adirondacks. "Balsam fir."

Agatha smiled. "Yes, it is."

Emmaline and Brianna exchanged a happy look as they noticed their father's pleased expression.

Agatha looked to her sisters. "There are also several buckets of branches out by the kitchen we can use to decorate the house and church."

Emmaline smiled. "I love it. Thank you, Agatha."

Agatha smiled. "My pleasure. I adore Christmas trees. Now, hurry James. We must get this secured in a bucket of water with some rocks for stability."

James shook his head but obligingly did as she bid him. He forgot how bossy Agatha could be.

Agatha turned to her little sister. "Emmaline, what do we have for decorations?"

"Not much, I'm afraid. We do have some cranberries and dried corn from the barrel Grandpa Drake sent. We can string those together and make some gingerbread cookies to hang. The wide ribbon will be needed to make bows for the church garland."

"I suppose those will have to do. Shall we get busy?"

A pan of gingerbread cookies was cooling on the counter in the outdoor kitchen where Mrs. Faraday was preparing their supper, while another was baking in the oven. In the dining room, the girls were working together in harmony, just as they had done in childhood, to finish two more trays. One ebony, one red, and one chestnut head all bent over their work as they put their inherited creativity to use, working the gingerbread dough into as many different shapes as they could imagine with embossed details and a hole for the ribbon to hang them on the tree.

Emmaline sat back and rolled her shoulders to ease the tension while admiring Brianna's scroll work on a heart. Hopefully, the impressions wouldn't be lost when the cookie spread during baking. So far simple markings, deeply cut, had worked best. There was much debate between them whether or not to try adding piped icing for decoration. Agatha was insisting. Emmaline and Brianna were resisting not only because they didn't have the powdered sugar and thought it a wasteful expense to buy it, but they also knew Agatha would lose interest by then, and they would be left doing all the work.

Agatha capitulated. "Well I suppose none of us could do them as well as Momma anyway."

Brianna gave her a sad smile. "You're right. I know I couldn't."

Emmaline leaned forward in the chair, crossing her arms in front of her on the table. In her mind, she saw the delicate white lines accenting the crisp brown cookies of her childhood. "I can't either."

Brianna said, "Do you remember the scrollwork she would put on the bells?"

Emmaline said, "Once she did flower vines on a heart."

Agatha said, "I remember. There was one for each of us that year and each heart was shaped a little differently."

Emmaline sighed. "She had a way of making Christmas special."

Brianna said, "She did. I only hope I can do half as well with my children. So far, I have not."

Emmaline said, "Oh posh! You shaped a train engine for Eli. I'd say that is making it special."

Brianna grimaced. "Only if the smoke stack doesn't fall off."

"I'm sure it will be fine." Emmaline checked her watch fob. "Speaking of which, it is time to pull them out of the oven. Are these ready to go in?"

Brianna carefully added her heart to the tray. "I think so."

The three soon returned to clean up the dining table. The last two trays were safely in the oven, the engine baked up well with smokestack still intact, and their mouths were watering from the wonderful smell of herb-crusted chicken almost done baking in the brick oven.

They finished just as Henry and Emily arrived with their six children. Agatha and James were the center of attention, as expected. Emmaline stood back watching the happy reunion. Henry's youngest two didn't remember their Aunt Agatha. Margaret barely did, but Alex and Ben rushed to embrace their favorite aunt, nearly knocking her off her feet. Ella waited for them to run off again before she approached Agatha and James.

They were called to supper before they reached the parlor. As a special treat, and because they wouldn't all fit at the dining table, Emmaline had dinner served in the backyard at the oversized table under the dappled sunlight filtering through the leaves of the lime tree. She was thankful it was a pleasant evening. The temperature warm enough to not require shawls. The eight adults, four children, two toddlers, and one baby were seated at the benches with Theodore presiding at the head of the table and Emmaline at the foot in heavy wooden chairs brought out for the occasion. The smooth planks of lignum vitae were covered by a cream tablecloth with embroidered edges her mother made special to fit its fourteen foot length. The covered dishes of boiled potatoes, herb roasted chicken, creamed peas, and biscuits waited for grace to be said but first the wine was poured. Theodore raised his glass in a toast once they were all settled. "To family."

The adults echoed him. "To family."

The meal was enjoyed with fanfare and all were in good spirits. Emmaline even noticed the occasional upward lift of the corner of her father's lips. This was what she hoped Christmas would be, a time for her family to enjoy being together, and a step towards healing her father's broken heart. Her eyes met his across the table. Her smile faded under his scrutiny. She wished she knew what he was thinking. Agatha and Brianna's conversation drew her attention, and she soon forgot the odd moment.

Agatha was passionately complaining again of Kendrick's

management of her articles and dismissal of her ideas. "I hate the way he questions everything I do or say. It's as if he enjoys arguing with me."

Brianna simpered. "Perhaps that is the only way he can get your attention."

Agatha's mouth dropped open and as she considered Brianna's words a frown appeared. "No. He doesn't harbor any feelings for me." She straightened her shoulders. "Certainly not. He enjoys arguing for argument's sake."

Garrett said, "If he doesn't respect you, then why don't you quit? There are other papers to write for."

"He doesn't disrespect me, he just makes everything a battle."

Emily couldn't resist teasing Agatha. She kept her eyes on her plate as she softly said, "Love and hate often run a thin line."

From across the table and next to Agatha, Henry smirked.

Agatha eyed her sister-in-law. "There is no love between us."

From Agatha's other side, James quoted, "The lady doth protest too much, methinks."

Agatha scowled at her little brother but then her eye caught Emmaline's amusement and decided a change of subject was needed. "Brianna tells me you have a suitor."

Emmaline felt every eye at the table turn to her. "I wouldn't say that."

Agatha said, "Then what would you call him?"

Flippantly, she replied, "Patrick," and was immediately appalled by her own rudeness. Agatha hadn't even been here a day and already she was a bad influence.

"And when will I meet this Patrick?"

Never, if Emmaline had her way, but she pulled her manners around her like a protective cloak and evenly said, "Most likely at Christmas services."

"Surely you will see him before then."

Calmly she answered, "I don't believe so."

Agatha turned to her sister-in-law. "Emily, tell me you have invited Patrick to the ball?"

Emily lowered her fork of potatoes to her plate. "Of course he is, as his uncle is always invited, although Smithy has never attended before."

Agatha looked to Emmaline. "Do you think he will come?"

"I'm sure I couldn't say."

Brianna smiled. "To see you, I'm sure he will."

Henry said, "Unless his feelings have changed, he'll be there."

Emmaline looked to Henry. "Could his feelings have changed?"

Henry gave her a reassuring smile. "Have you forgotten last night?"

She remembered the feel of Patrick holding her hand. Unbeknownst to her a soft, tender smile gently bloomed on her face.

Agatha was left speechless. Her little sister was in love. Knowing how tender her feelings could be, she couldn't tease her about it. Instead, she sincerely asked, "What is he like?"

Emmaline looked to Agatha in surprise. She was so used to be teased by her that sincerity rang false. She noticed everyone else waiting expectantly. Good manners dictated an answer, so she tried to think of something neutral to say. "He's from Virginia."

Agatha wasn't going to let her off that easy. "Is he a good man?"

"Of course, he is."

"And?"

Emmaline noted the sincere interest in Agatha's demeanor, so she answered in kind. "Patrick is caring and thoughtful, kind-hearted and hard working."

Theodore was arrested by the beautiful smile that lit Emmaline's face simply in saying Patrick's name. He had been watching the conversation with interest. Emmaline's earlier smile as the meal began caught his attention. It seemed as though it had been years since he had seen it. Now, he realized this young man had somehow made her blossom. Maybe financial well-being was not all to be considered. Betsy would tell him happiness mattered more. Right now, in this moment, seeing Emmaline's joyful demeanor, he would have to agree.

Agatha grinned. "You're in love with him."

She didn't want to dignify her statement with a response, but Emmaline knew her sister would not leave well enough alone. "No, I'm not." Agatha's eyebrows rose so she added in defense, "We've only met a few times. We've hardly spent any time together. Certainly not enough to know how we feel about each other."

Emily said, "Haven't you heard of love at first sight?"

Brianna said, "You spent a good portion of Saturday with him."

Emmaline, used to them coming to her defense, gave the pair a discomfited look. Henry received a grateful smile for changing the subject.

* * *

After supper, the family adjourned to the parlor where the lovely balsam fir held prominence by the window. The dried corn had been popped earlier in the day and now a large bowl of popcorn and another of cranberries waited on a nearby table to be strung. There was also the plate of cookies waiting for ribbon to be hung. The candles would be added on Christmas Eve.

Henry's four youngest children stood in front of the evergreen in bewilderment.

Alex turned to his father. "Why is there a tree inside the house?"

Ella had never seen one either, but she had overheard Agatha earlier and in her elder sister wisdom explained it to her brothers. "It is a Christmas tree. You decorate it and on Christmas Eve Santa Clause leaves presents under it."

"Nah huh." Ben always discounted his sister out of hand.

James rubbed Ben's head as he passed by. "Ella's right."

Ella gave Ben a smirk. He stuck his tongue out at her. His mother's entrance made him quickly turn away. She somehow always had a way of knowing when he was misbehaving.

Garrett joined James as the ladies grouped together to carry on their own conversation. Theodore lingered a moment in the doorway.

Henry paused beside his father as they both overlooked the chaotic jumble of family gathered in the parlor. "She did all this for you."

Theodore turned to him questioningly.

"Emmaline is worried about you. She arranged all of this to please you in the hopes it would give you back some of your joy." Henry continued into the room leaving his father to contemplate his words as he would.

Theodore's gaze drifted over the happy occupants. *Give him back his joy.* He lost any joy when Betsy died and in the beginning it was unbearable, but looking at himself now through Emmaline's eyes, he could see he had been holding tightly to his grief like a mantel of protection, only it wasn't protection. It was a wall keeping him from living, keeping him from his family. Betsy would not approve. He had to break free from his melancholy for them, if not for himself.

As if Betsy were speaking to him, he heard her words spoken to his heart. "Look what we have created." Indeed, the room was filled with his offspring; five children, two in-laws, and seven grandchildren. He still has Betsy in them, and they were all here to share their love with him. Certainly, that was reason enough to have joy in his heart. He couldn't live in the past anymore. He needed to live in this moment and embrace the future. How could he have been so selfish to hold his love from them? Feeling ashamed for having hurt those he loved, he vowed then and there to begin appreciating what he had instead of only mourning all he had lost.

Three-year-old Laurie came running to him on his wobbly legs, grinning just like Henry did at that age. Theodore straightened from the doorframe and took a few steps forward to catch him, lifting him into the air before nuzzling his neck, bringing forth giggles that melted his heart. He whispered to himself, "I understand now, Betsafina. I promise to open my heart."

He caught Brianna's gaze from across the room and for a moment he faltered, seeing not her, but her mother. His heart caught. Laurie pointed to the Christmas tree, drawing his attention away from Brianna. He swung the wiggling child into the air again before setting him on the floor. This time when he looked at Brianna, he saw only his lovely daughter and beside her Emmaline gazed at him with a watery smile. He strode towards her and enfolded her into a deep embrace, her head tucked under his chin. "I'm sorry, little one."

Emmaline choked on her tears.

Her father had come back to her.

Her Christmas wish had come true.

Chapter 10

Tuesday morning was bright and clear. Patrick approached the Whitmore house with jittery excitement and nervous trepidation. A lot depended on this meeting going well. In fact, his whole future was dependent on the outcome. The breast pocket of his coat held the crisp, neatly written pages of the fourth draft of his sample article. Actually, it was the sixth if you counted the two times he rewrote it because of copying errors.

The front door opened and Emmaline and her siblings exited the house. The two he didn't recognize must be Agatha and James, expected to arrive yesterday. He stood still, waiting to see if her father was joining them. Disappointment stabbed at him to think he may have to wait longer. As the group descended the porch, relief washed over him not to see Mr. Whitmore. It was just as well they were leaving. He would rather Emmaline not witness his disappointment if Mr. Whitmore didn't like his writing. He was standing in the shadow of a large oleander shrub in front of their neighbor's house. He stepped behind it to watch them pass.

The maid answered his knock and upon recognizing him said, "I'm afraid Miss Emmaline is not at home."

"Actually, I am here to see Mr. Whitmore, if I may?"

"I believe he is in his study. Would you like me to announce you?"

"I think it may be best if you do."

She opened the door for him to enter the foyer. "Wait here."

As the maid left, he moved a few steps closer to the opening into the morning room. On the far side was a portrait above a desk of Emmaline's mother. The resemblance was so strong it could have been a portrait of Brianna, but Emmaline shared her smile, at least the few times he had seen it.

The maid's return made him turn. "Mr. Whitmore is waiting for you in the study."

If he were important, Mr. Whitmore would have come out to greet him. Patrick wondered if he should take that as an intended slight, or if it was another of Mr. Whitmore's taciturn ways. For his intentions, it was best if he held no ill will towards the man, so he put any meaning of the break in protocol from his mind. Mr. Whitmore rose from his desk as he entered the study, which also helped him to forget the slight. Patrick stood just behind one of the chairs facing the desk, hat in hand.

"Good afternoon, Mr. Whitmore."

Theodore was curt and direct, more from habit than disrespect. "Patrick. What brings you here? Has your situation changed?"

Patrick swallowed his pride. "Not exactly."

"Then I don't know why you're here. I haven't changed my mind about Emmaline." Theodore inwardly flinched. That was not entirely true, but the lad needn't know that just yet.

"This visit isn't about Emmaline."

Theodore waited for him to expound.

Patrick nervously turned his hat in his hand. So much depended on the outcome of this conversation. "I came today seeking your advice."

"Then I suppose you should have a seat."

He breathed a sigh of relief as he sat in the chair and put his hat on his knee, but anxiety rose again as Mr. Whitmore remained standing. He garnered all the courage he had as he laid the papers on the desk. He had rehearsed what he wanted to say over and over again, but now, he couldn't remember how to start. "Well, Mr. Whitmore, as you said, I don't want to be a blacksmith, so I've been considering other alternatives. I won't bore you with all my considerations." He faltered in his phrasing. Not a good sign for someone who wanted to use words to earn a living. He kept his eyes on the desk fearing a glance at Mr. Whitmore would make things worse. "That is, after much consideration, I have determined to try following in your footsteps."

Theodore frowned. "Are you hoping flattery will suffice? For I assure you, it will not."

Patrick met his gaze. "No sir, I am in earnest. Being a journalist is the only thing that has sparked any interest for me." He rose, picked up the papers, and held them out for Mr. Whitmore. "I came here for you to read this and to give me your honest opinion. I believe I have what it will take to write stories, I mean articles, but I wanted, well, thought, it best for someone like you with experience to... approve is not the right word."

"You want me to tell you if you can write?"

Patrick's jaw firmed and his words were stiff in defense. "I can write. The question is whether or not I can write well enough."

Theodore eyed the young man. He was no simpering fool to have the courage not only to look him in the eye on Sunday but to face him now. He would give him the respect of reading his paper and offering his opinion. This was probably just a lark and not a serious aspiration but either way, what could it hurt? He sat behind his desk, donned his spectacles needed now for reading, and leaned back in his chair. The title read "Key Westerners Overcome Once More." Not a great title, but not terrible, either. The article started with a brief history of rebuilding after the hurricane of 1846 and then described the events of the fire in May. Patrick told of the plans each landowner had for rebuilding better than before and what it would mean for the islanders. Theodore hadn't intended to read the whole article. He was surprised it kept his interest and had to admit with a grudging respect that the boy had talent.

Reading it had also unexpectedly rekindled his own passion for journalism. He missed the whole process of looking for a good story, researching the details, writing it, and printing it. He missed holding the first copy of a print run, the smell of drying ink, and the pride he felt at seeing the paper he put together ready to share with others. He suppressed his feelings as he considered what to say to Patrick.

"You have good word structure. You picked a topic of interest to your readers, which is vitally important for a journalist. You did research. However, your article is missing a piece."

"It is, sir?"

"You neglected to ask what I plan to do with my lot."

Patrick's heart dropped. He assumed Mr. Whitmore had no plans based on what Emmaline told him. He should have asked. A good journalist would not make such an oversight. "My apologies, sir. It was not intentional."

Theodore laid the papers on his desk and steepled his hands. "I suppose if you had asked, my answer would be nothing. Until now, I had no thoughts of rebuilding."

"And now, sir?"

"There are thoughts. You can write. But there is no paper here to write for, so it will not provide an income. I am assuming you don't have the means of buying the needed equipment to start your own paper."

Patrick's elation at his approval quickly faded as Mr. Whitmore gave him a good dose of reality, but he was not defeated. "No, sir. Could I send articles to another paper, maybe in New York or perhaps in Jacksonville or St. Augustine?"

Theodore's lips twitched. There was the enthusiasm and endurance he wanted to see in the young man. He had a passion for his project and that was key to success. He rose from his desk. "Go find something else to write about. I'll make some inquiries on your behalf."

Patrick rose too, holding his excitement in check. "Thank you, sir."

"Mind you, I'm not making any promises."

"Of course, sir."

Patrick nearly leapt for joy as he stepped down from the Whitmore porch. He could not have imagined this meeting going any better. He returned to the forge, eagerly toying with ideas for another story.

* * *

Tuesday afternoon the girls were coming down the stairs, having taken their packages upstairs from their morning shopping.

Agatha stopped at the landing, barring Emmaline's descent. "I want to meet this Patrick. We should invite him for supper this evening."

Emmaline felt a rush of excitement followed by a dash of cold dread. "Poppa won't approve." Hearing feet tread on the wood flooring, her head swiveled to the lower hall.

Theodore was passing by with a cup of coffee and the paper brought by Agatha on his way to his study. "What will I not approve?"

Before Emmaline could speak, Agatha said, "Inviting Emmaline's friend for supper tonight."

"It is fine with me." He nonchalantly continued walking past them.

Emmaline gave Agatha a piercing look. They were only delaying his fury by not mentioning Patrick by name now.

Theodore murmured as he approached the study, "Bachelors always welcome a good meal."

Both Emmaline and Agatha turned to look at their father's retreating back. Emmaline whispered, "Did he say what I think he said?"

Agatha looked to her with eyebrows raised. "I heard something about bachelors."

"Still, I wouldn't dare invite him."

Agatha grabbed her arm. "I will."

Emmaline turned a pleading look to Brianna following behind her on the stairs. Sweetly she said, "You two go on without me. I believe I'll stay home and look after Eli."

* * *

Each step they took towards their destination increased Emmaline's unease. As if worrying about introducing Agatha to Patrick didn't have her nervous enough that her sister might not like him, which would lead to all kinds of difficulties, she was also fretting over her father's reaction. She eyed the ominous thunderheads gathering above them. The increasing energy in the wind was not encouraging either. Walking to the forge and back would take them nearly an hour. They were sure to be caught in a downpour somewhere in between.

Emmaline stopped, dubiously eyeing the sky. "Agatha, perhaps we should return home."

Agatha turned around to look at her but kept walking backwards. "You are not backing out now."

"But, Agatha, we're going to get drenched. This is not a good idea."

"And when has a drenching ever hurt anyone?" With a flounce of her skirt, she turned around again and continued walking, expecting Emmaline to follow.

With a resigned sign, Emmaline picked up her hem and hurried to catch up to Agatha. They were within sight of the forge when the raindrops started falling. Emmaline looked upon them as a blessing. Now they would appear as two ladies seeking shelter from the storm rather than the interlopers they were. There was nothing between her and Patrick to warrant an introduction of her sister, especially not a contrived introduction. It was humiliating! But Agatha wouldn't care. She doubted if her sister had ever experienced her own humiliation, though Emmaline could say from personal experience, she had certainly dished it out. This moment was bound to be another example.

The increasing rain caused them to dash headlong for the shelter of the forge lean-to. They couldn't help but giggle at their folly. Once out of the rain, they removed their soaked bonnets to shake the water from them. Emmaline cast a glance around the space. Smithy was paused over his work at the anvil, clearly surprised by their appearance. Disappointment struck deep in her chest. Patrick was nowhere to be seen. Perhaps his uncle had sent him on an errand.

Agatha stepped forward with a bright smile. "Hello Smithy. Do you remember me?"

Smithy's mouth quirked. "Quite so, young Agatha Whitmore. Visiting from the big city, are you?"

"Yes, I am. How have you been, sir?"

"Well as can be expected, I suppose. I doubt you are here simply to escape the rain or to visit with an old man. I'm afraid my nephew isn't here today."

Emmaline's heart dropped with disappointment. It was on the tip of her tongue to bid the old blacksmith good-day when her sister spoke up.

"Well that is a shame for I was looking forward to meeting him, and you are a clever man. It was not simply the rain that brought us to you. My sister and I have come to offer you and your nephew an invitation to dine with our family this evening."

Smithy frowned as he gathered the words for a protest.

Agatha would not allow it. "Surely you are not about to turn down a sumptuous meal in the company of friends? I have heard bachelor meals are rather tiresome." He gave her a speaking look of resigned acceptance. "Good. We'll expect you by seven. Now where is this nephew of yours?"

"Right here."

Both girls spun around to find Patrick striding into the shop, dripping wet.

Smithy grumbled under his breath but within Emmaline's hearing, "'Bout time you got back."

Patrick's eyes held Emmaline's with a soft, welcoming look, having every appearance of being happy to see her. Agatha strode forward, her jade green dress sweeping across the dirt floor, to hold her hand out to Patrick. "Nice to finally meet you, Mr. Johnson. I am Agatha Whitmore. I'm sure Emmaline has mentioned me."

The corner of Patrick's lip twitched beneath his mustache. "She has. Nice to finally meet you, Miss Whitmore. I hope your journey from New York was pleasant."

"Please, call me Agatha. It was uneventful sail but still a bit thrilling as it was my first time on a large steamship."

Patrick nodded in understanding. "I agree. I sailed on one from Portsmouth."

"New Hampshire?"

"Virginia."

"Oh yes, that's right. Someone did mention to me your family is from Virginia." Later, she would have to ask him about Harper's Ferry. She didn't want to spoil the day bringing up such an ugly subject now. Agatha shrewdly eyed the young man. There was intelligence in his dark eyes, and a gentleness about his features. Good qualities in a suitor for her baby sister and so unlike the firm angled planes of Kendrick Jenkins. Agatha frowned inwardly. What was she doing comparing this man to her boss? She forced herself to put the irritating man from her mind. She was free from him until the New Year and she intended to enjoy it.

Smithy called to his nephew for assistance. Agatha inclined her head. "Don't mind us. We'll just wait over here out of the way for the rain to slacken."

Patrick nodded to Agatha but turned to speak to Emmaline. "Don't leave without saying goodbye."

Emmaline said, "I promise I won't."

She watched him shrug out of his jacket and hang it on a peg on the back wall. He then rolled up his sleeves as he moved towards his uncle. He picked up a hammer and began working to shape the hot metal his uncle held in place on the largest anvil in the shop. Her gaze caught on the working muscles of his forearms and the bulging biceps that soon filled out his rolled-up sleeve. She had never looked at a man that way until Patrick. Her midsection tightened and her mouth went dry wondering what it would feel like to have his strong arms wrapped around her. Heat rose from her neck to her cheeks as she realized where her thoughts had wandered. She ducked her head and turned to watch the wavering gray curtain of falling rain. What was she doing thinking of a man touching her, much less wishing that he would?

Agatha leaned towards her with a conspiratorial smile. "I like him."

Jealousy flared within Emmaline's breast before her mind had a chance to reason with her heart that Agatha meant she liked Patrick for Emmaline not for herself.

Agatha eyed him appreciatively. "He is strong in physique and gentle in nature."

Emmaline couldn't help turning to look at him again. Patrick happened to glance up from his work and flash her a wink and a grin before returning his attention to the hammer strikes.

"He's definitely smitten with you."

Emmaline blushed a furious red this time.

Agatha smirked. "I wager you'll be married this time next year."

Emmaline was suddenly swamped with sadness and felt tears threaten. "You forget how Poppa feels. He would never allow it."

"Then we'll have to find a way to change his mind. What is his objection?"

"His job as apprentice, but I think more specifically it is his ambition, or the appearance of a lack of it to be more precise."

"And does he lack ambition?"

"I'm not sure. When last we spoke, it seemed more of a lack of direction than ambition."

"He doesn't know what he wants from life?"

"No. Although he has shown interest in Poppa's writing and the paper."

"Has he? Hmm. I shall have to feel him out about it this evening."

"Agatha?"

"Don't worry pet. I won't do or say anything unseemly."

Emmaline was sure she didn't intend to but doubted it was possible. Agatha always managed to say or do something outrageous in the name of helping her sisters.

The passing storm was slackening. In a few moments they would be able to leave the shelter of the forge. Emmaline looked to Patrick again, enjoying watching him work. She hated to leave, but at least she could look forward to seeing him again tonight.

Patrick watched the sisters walk away, skirting around the worst of the puddles. Emmaline's unexpected appearance had brightened his day.

Smithy called out, "Stop pining over the girl and give me a hand. You'll see her again soon enough."

Patrick turned back to the anvil and lifted the hammer in readiness for his uncle to once again remove the heated metal from fire. "How so?"

"We've been invited to supper."

Patrick couldn't help the grin that exploded across his face.

* * *

Agatha set a chair in front of the front door. She gave a quick glance around to make sure no one was watching. Brianna was in the parlor with Garrett and Eli, Poppa was in his study writing letters, and Emmaline was in her room, likely redressing a third time in preparation for dinner. The girl was beyond besotted. Agatha hoped she never got that silly about a man. She lifted the front of her skirt with one hand and held the chair back with the other as she climbed onto the seat. She then took the bundle of greenery tied to a length of ribbon the maid handed to her, followed by two hat pins. Agatha's height allowed her to easily reach the ceiling. Task complete, she carefully stepped down from the chair. She picked it up to return it to the dining room and unexpectedly encountered Brianna.

"Is that what I think it is?"

Agatha merely grinned as she moved around her elder sister.

Brianna chortled. "You bring all the fun."

* * *

Emmaline was first to reach the front door, having anxiously been hovering near the doorway of the parlor in order to hear the sound of the knocker. The maid opened it revealing Patrick's solitary figure waiting in the pooled light of the porch lantern. She stepped aside for him to enter.

Patrick removed his hat before crossing the threshold and strode well into the entry in response to the beckoning look in Emmaline's gaze. He loved her eyes. They were as wide and round as Brianna's and as in her mother's portrait, but where their eyes were blue, Emmaline's were the mixture of green and brown found in a pooling stream. They made him feel at home in spirit as well as in place.

He paused before her and lifted his gaze to the rest of her family gathered behind her. "Thank you for the dinner invitation. My uncle sends his regrets. He was feeling too fatigued to walk so far after being on his feet all day."

Emmaline frowned. "Our intent was for the both of you to enjoy an easy meal you didn't have to cook. Now I fear we have made it worse by taking you from him. If we had known, we could have sent the carriage."

"Not at all. He wouldn't want such charity as a carriage. I left my uncle warming some leftover soup that was not enough to share, so all is well in the end."

"If you say so."

Theodore said, "Come into the parlor, Mr. Johnson, and have a drink while we wait for dinner to be served."

Emmaline exchanged a bewildered look with Brianna and then turned a questioning look to Agatha who shrugged her shoulders. They expected their father to be cordial but cold and standoffish. His unexpected warm greeting took them all by surprise.

Garrett stood in the middle of the room holding Eli, who grinned and kicked his legs, apparently excited to see Patrick, or simply amused by a new face in the room. Patrick stepped forward to greet Garrett and shook the tiny hand Eli held out to him. When the baby reached for him with both arms, Garrett transferred his son to their guest. Patrick placed the baby on his hip and then in mock seriousness asked the tike about his day. He was answered with a bout of gibberish drool that made them all laugh.

Theodore handed Patrick a tumbler of brandy, which Eli grasped the rim of before either man could react. Patrick gave the baby a serious look. "Are you really trying to steal my drink, sir? I have to warn you, I don't take well to sharing. I'm afraid you'll have to get your own."

Eli studied Patrick's face for a moment, as if taking his measure, and then let go of the glass. They all laughed causing Eli to look around the room in bewilderment.

Emmaline's heart lurched at her sudden realization Patrick would make a good father.

When they were called in to dinner, Agatha contrived to seat Patrick on her side of the table, giving her the opportunity to quiz him further. After their father blessed the meal and began passing the serving dishes around, Agatha said to Patrick, "Emmaline tells me you have some interest in being a journalist."

Even duly warned, Patrick was taken aback by Agatha's directness, but on the other hand, he was grateful she brought up the very subject he was most interested in discussing with her. "And she has told me that you are a journalist for the *New York Weekly*. Do you find the work satisfying?"

Agatha gave him a point of approval for being open-minded that she was a female writer. "I do, although I wish I didn't have to get past so many prejudiced men to get answers to my questions."

"I fear it will be a while before men are openly accepting of ladies in the work place. For most, it threatens their masculinity to accept that females are as smart, if not smarter, than them."

Agatha contained her smile of approval. "And where did you come upon such enlightenment?"

"My parents, I suppose. Ma is smarter than Pa in many ways, but she hides it from him, deferring to his judgement. When I asked her why she did so, she explained the importance of a man's masculinity to his well-being and a peaceful home."

Brianna said, "Your mother sounds like a smart and wise woman."

Agatha grimaced. "It must have been hard on her at times."

Patrick nodded. "When it really mattered, she would find a roundabout way to help Pa see what was right, as if he had discovered it for himself."

Agatha said, "You sound as though you admire her for it."

"I suppose I do."

"Would you take issue if your wife was smarter than you?"

Patrick gave her question due consideration. He had never considered the possibility before as he had inherited his mother's intelligence more so than his siblings. "I would hope I could cope with being married to someone smarter than me, but I suppose I hope to marry someone of equal intelligence. Not necessarily equal in knowledge, but at least equals in the ability to absorb and use knowledge."

Emmaline carefully watched the exchange with a keen eye on Agatha. She was pleased to see Patrick's answers garnered her respect. If Agatha stood against him, it would have made a relationship with him difficult at best. Her approval was a relief. The topic of conversation shifted to final preparations for Christmas and the Eatonton ball to be held on Thursday.

Agatha again turned to Patrick. "You will be attending the ball, won't you?"

"I'm afraid my uncle declined the invitation, as usual."

Emmaline felt her heart drop to the pit of her stomach.

Patrick continued. "But while I was conversing with Henry yesterday, I assured him I planned to attend."

The relief she felt caused Emmaline's smile to be brighter than warranted. Realizing how much it revealed of her feelings, she looked down at her plate, but then surreptitiously eyed her father for his reaction. Her eyes collided with his and in them she saw speculation. Heat bloomed in her cheeks. She couldn't imagine what he must be thinking. He hadn't spoken yet, giving her no idea of how he felt about Patrick's presence. Was he hiding his irritation or resigned to Agatha's manipulations?

The conversation swirled around them in benign topics as they finished their meal. Emmaline daintily wiped her mouth before rising. In a blink, Patrick had moved behind her to assist with her chair, usurping her father. Emmaline's eyes rose to see Poppa turn to assist. His face was impassive. Agatha winked at her. Emmaline wouldn't be surprised if she hadn't nudged Patrick in her direction.

Normally, Emmaline would have cleared the dishes from the table before joining the family in the parlor, but to her surprise the maid quietly told Emmaline she would take care of it, leaving Emmaline to follow her family into the parlor where she found Patrick admiring the Christmas tree flanked by Agatha and Brianna.

Patrick asked, "Why isn't Emmaline's Kugel ornament on the tree?"

Brianna had Eli on her hip, holding his hand to keep him from touching the tree. "We all thought it was prettier in the window."

Emmaline said, "The truth is it is too heavy to hang on the tree.

Only the sturdiest of branches can support it and since those are at the bottom within reach of my adorable little nephew, it was safer in the window."

Brianna smiled. "And prettier."

Patrick eyed the sisters. "Emmaline told me her grandmother bought it for her at the Christkindlmarkt. What did she get each of you?"

Brianna said, "I got a gingerbread cookie shaped like a heart, decorated with delicate piping. It was almost too pretty to eat."

They all turned to Agatha. She shrugged her shoulders. "I can't recall."

Brianna said, "I remember James got a bag of candy. I think we all had sweets except Emmaline."

Agatha's brows drew together. "Now that you mention it, I think I may have got candy too. I seem to remember hiding a white paper bag so I wouldn't have to share, since you didn't have to share your gingerbread."

Brianna laughed. "That does sound like you."

James approached them. "Did I hear my name mentioned?"

Agatha nodded. "We were reminiscing over the Christmas in Austria."

Brianna said, "Do you remember the treats from the market? You shared your bag of candy with the rest of us."

Emmaline smiled at him. "You always were the generous one. You got that from Momma." It was said so easily, her name slipping from her tongue without thought or sadness, but it lingered in the air between them. The sadness grew to a palpable shared sense of sorrow.

Patrick felt their loss. "How did she..." Maybe he shouldn't ask. The pain was obviously still raw for them. "Never mind."

Brianna looked at the faces of her younger siblings and decided they did need to talk about it. This Christmas was about healing the family and that was part of the process. Softly she said, "The doctor said it was likely an apoplectic seizure."

Tears pricked Emmaline's eyes as the scene replayed in her mind. "It happened suddenly." She swallowed hard against the painful memory. "She was tending her flowers like she did every morning before the sun rose too high."

Patrick touched her shoulder. "You don't have to..."

Emmaline lifted her watery eyes to his. "I want to. No. I need to share it." She took a steading breath and started again. "It was a beautiful morning. Very pleasant with scattered clouds, birds singing to one another, dappled sunlight touching the leaves and flowers of her garden. I sat down for a moment in the wicker chair, taking a moment to enjoy the peace of it all." Her wistful smile faded. "Mother was walking back to the house with a basketful of cut flowers. She wanted to make an arrangement for an elderly neighbor who was sick. She was always generous with her flowers. She was near the house when she suddenly stopped walking. She got this strange expression on her face, and then she collapsed to the ground." Emmaline brushed at the stray tear running down her cheek.

Patrick had to fight the urge to take Emmaline in his arms and give her comfort.

James said, "I remember hearing you screaming from the yard. I ran out to find you cradling Momma and saying 'please Momma' over and over again."

Agatha caught her father's anguished gaze from across the room, he was as immobile as a statue.

Emmaline lifted her chin. "I sent Jamie for the doctor and to get Poppa from the print shop."

James was nearly in tears. His voice broke as he said, "I ran as fast as I could."

Brianna suddenly understood the burden James was carrying. She transferred Eli to Agatha and enfolded James in her arms. "It was not your fault."

So caught up in her own grief, Emmaline realized for the first time how their mother's death had affected her little brother. She stepped around to see his face and laid a comforting hand on his shoulder. His distress somehow calmed hers. "James, she was gone before I reached her. I didn't realize it until after you had left. There was no saving her." Emmaline had to make sure he understood. "You couldn't save her."

Patrick saw Mr. Whitmore flinch as if he were waking from a dream or in this case a nightmare. He strode forward to wrap his arms around Emmaline and James. He choked on the words, "I'm sorry. So sorry. I've been so sunk in my own grief, I failed to help you deal with yours. I failed you as a father." His voice cracked. "And I swore to never do that again after failing Henry."

Patrick retreated from the group, feeling very much like an interloper. He joined Garrett at the sideboard, absently accepting the drink he was handed, and keeping his back to the others to give them some privacy. Agatha followed him. Garrett raised his eyebrows at her, and receiving a nod, poured her a brandy as well. He handed her the drink and took Eli from her.

Patrick was going to suggest he take his leave when Agatha turned to him and spoke.

"We have you to thank for that." She glanced back at the huddled group, finally openly sharing their pain and sorrow.

At first, Patrick assumed Agatha was reprimanding him, but then he realized her intention was gratitude. He gave Agatha a thoughtful look. He knew she didn't wear her heart on her sleeve, but even so, she didn't seem to be as deeply affected by the loss as the others. "Where were you when your mother collapsed?"

Agatha gave him a saddened look. "I was in New York and Brianna was in Pennsylvania with Garrett." She cast a doleful look over Patrick's shoulder to her father and siblings. "Poppa withdrew into himself, leaving Emmaline and James to comfort each other. Henry was here of course, with Emily, but not living in the house. I don't think they knew how badly they have suffered. None of us did. We were aware Poppa was drowning in sorrow, but I don't think we really understood how much Emmaline and James were still grieving. It's good they are all finally acknowledging it openly. Now they can heal." She raised her glass slightly towards him. "Thank you."

Patrick shook his head. "All I did was ask a question."

Agatha gave him a half smile. "Sometimes that's all it takes to open the floodgate."

Patrick set his glass on the sideboard. "Perhaps it's time I leave."

"Don't you dare."

Patrick blinked at the forcefulness of Agatha's protest. "Why not?"

She smiled. "Look. They are all smiling. Now we can enjoy the evening. Do you play cards, Patrick?"

"Some."

Brianna approached followed by the others. "No card games tonight, Agatha. We need something more uplifting after that bout of tears. Shall we sing carols?"

Emmaline's arm was entwined with her father's in the first comfortable closeness Patrick had seen them share. "Oh please, Agatha, let's sing."

"Very well." Agatha moved to the pianoforte in the corner. Once seated, she turned to query what to play and noticed Patrick's surprise. She shrugged. "I don't sing, so I learned to play in order to make my contribution."

Emmaline gave him a fetching grin. "She plays quite well when she puts her mind to it."

Agatha smirked. "What shall it be, sister dear?"

"You know which one."

"So I do." She turned around and set her hands to play her little sister's favorite Christmas hymn. What followed was a rousing rendition of "Joy to the World" led by Emmaline's soprano and joined by Theodore's baritone, James, Patrick, and Garrett as a trio of tenors, and Brianna's alto. Several more songs followed before Agatha declared she had played enough.

Reluctantly Patrick announced, "I should be getting home before it gets much later. My uncle likes to start work early in the morning."

Emmaline said, "I'll walk you to the door."

Behind them, Agatha and Brianna exchanged an amused look.

Before opening the front door, Emmaline turned to Patrick. "Thank you for coming. I enjoyed the evening."

"Even the tears?"

"Yes, even the tears. They were... restorative, I suppose." Inwardly, she groaned as Agatha and Brianna peaked around the corner of the parlor door. Agatha's sly smile gave her pause for concern.

Agatha's eyes lifted to the ceiling. "I believe you are standing under the mistletoe."

Brianna bit her lip to keep from grinning. "Tradition calls for a kiss. It's bad luck to refuse, Emmaline."

Patrick felt a thrill at the idea of kissing Emmaline, but it was quickly subdued by Mr. Whitmore's entry into the hall.

"What's this?"

Brianna laid a hand on her father's arm and softly said, "A bit of harmless fun, Poppa."

James said, "Agatha brought home some mistletoe."

Theodore's eyes lifted to confirm there was indeed mistletoe above his youngest daughter's head. Inwardly, he groaned. *Why couldn't she still be his little girl?*

With no interference forthcoming, Patrick turned to Emmaline, noting the pinkish hue imbuing her cheeks, endearing her even more to him. He leaned down to her, fully aware of their audience at the other end of the hall. She turned her expectant face up to his, her lips slightly parted, her eyes betraying her nervous anticipation. He badly wanted to kiss those soft, pliable lips, but he had yet to win her father's full approval, and he would not jeopardize it by taking too much advantage of the moment. He tilted his head slightly to lightly press his lips to her cheek, the cheek facing the door, so there would be no question in her father's mind.

Emmaline was both relieved and disappointed he chose to kiss her cheek. She didn't want her first kiss to be under the very noses of her family, but Good Lord, how she wanted this man to kiss her. Even so, to the family what must have looked like a simple kiss was anything but. The brush of his whiskers and mustache was followed by the soft press of his warm lips to the hollow beneath her cheek bone. The movement of his lips as he applied the kiss sent tingles racing down to her toes as he pulled away. It was a moment before she gathered enough wits to open the door and wish him good-night.

She was aware of her family vacating the hall while she had yet to move from the door, her eyes vacantly staring at the far wall. Patrick kissed her. It may have been induced by mistletoe, but the soft look in his eye as he leaned down told her he wanted to kiss her as much as she wanted him to do so. Her hand drifted to her cheek as if to hold onto the sensation.

Coming to her senses, she climbed the stairs to her room. Her emotions were too raw to go back to the parlor. Tonight, she had been kissed and as thrilling as that was, it was the earlier emotional moment that mattered more. She felt as though she and her father, and James, had found a measure of healing from the overwhelming grief they had carried for the last two years.

Chapter 11

Wednesday evening was subdued in the Whitmore house compared with the emotional upheaval of the night before. The family was gathered in the parlor after supper. Theodore was smoking his pipe and reading his paper. Brianna and Garrett were playing with Eli. James and Agatha were playing chess and Emmaline was finishing the last of the embroidering on a smock for her youngest niece, Henrietta. On the tea table was the remains of a plate of cookies and peppermint sticks, evidence of how Brianna and Emmaline had spent their afternoon. It was only a sampling of their baking. The rest was carefully stored away for their Christmas celebration.

Brianna suddenly announced to the room, "We need to have a family portrait made." Everyone looked to her, but no one spoke. "Do you remember? Momma asked for it several times that last year, but there was always something keeping one of us from being there. We are all together now. Henry came home from the sponge grounds today to attend the ball and doesn't plan to leave again until after Christmas, so sometime between now and then, we must have one done."

Emmaline murmured, "To honor her."

Brianna nodded. "Yes."

Theodore put down his paper. "I agree."

Agatha sighed. "It seems to me, it would make the most sense to have it done before the ball when we're already dressed up in our finest."

James said, "Moffat and Simpson's may not be open. Don't they usually attend the ball as well?"

Theodore said, "They do, but maybe we could make a private appointment say an hour before they plan to leave."

James said, "I'll go by there in the morning and ask."

Theodore smiled at the grown-up response from his son. "Shall we go together?"

James smiled. "I would like that."

Brianna frowned. "What of Henry and Emily? They may be needed to help with final preparations for the ball."

Theodore rose. "Then I shall visit Henry now. Best to know sooner rather than later if we must postpone."

* * *

The excitement in the house was palpable as everyone was busy getting ready for the ball, and for their family portrait beforehand. The studio and participation of Henry's family was secured. All they had to do now was arrive on time and there was not a moment left to spare. Emmaline nervously fidgeted again. Brianna sighed heavily. "Em, I can't get this right if you keep moving." In her hands, she held the ribbon and flowers she was artfully weaving into the crown of braids atop Emmaline's head.

Emmaline caught her sister's gaze in the mirror. "I'm sorry." She couldn't help it. Tonight was one of the biggest celebrations of the year. The Eatonton Ball was a huge event for the islanders. It was held the week before Christmas every year since the first anniversary of Henry and Emily's marriage, fourteen years ago.

Invitations were coveted and necessary for the limited space inside the house. Outside was a secondary venue for all those who wished to join but didn't have an invitation. There were tables of simple fare and an abundance of beer and wine set up in the yard where those in attendance could dine (albeit standing) and listen to the music.

For those invited, they would dance in the lavishly decorated ballroom to the strains of a seven-piece orchestra from Charleston. Every windowsill, candle sconce, chandelier, table, and alcove would be adorned with island greenery, hot house flowers, scented candles, ribbon, and threaded beads. Her mouth watered just thinking of the late supper to come, imported from New England. It was tradition to have clam chowder, roasted turkey, creamed potatoes, cranberry-orange relish, and to follow, roasted chestnuts and a variety of trifles. Oh, and how could she forget the deliciously fruity and effervescent champagne punch?

It was her mother's favorite event, making tonight bitter-sweet as memories of her excitement in getting ready for the ball entwined with Emmaline's excitement of the moment.

"There. I'm done." Brianna stood back to admire her work. Emmaline leaned closer to the mirror, turning her head this way and that, to see the delicate white flowers and blue ribbon adorning her head. "Now to get you into your gown without musing it."

Emmaline eyed the dress on the hanger, suddenly recalling her last fitting. "You better tighten my corset else you'll never get the buttons done up."

"If I do, you won't be able to breathe much less enjoy your supper."

"Such is the price of fashion, I suppose."

"Thank heavens I am considered a matron. I don't think I could abide such restriction. You best hold on to something while I pull the strings."

* * *

Patrick was glad his uncle let him leave the forge early. He needed a full bath, a good trim, and fresh clothes. Unfortunately, it didn't occur to him until he was climbing the flight of stairs to his room that he didn't have any suitable clothes for a ball. His spirits fell so fast he felt it in the pit of his stomach. What was he going to do? Even his Sunday best could hardly be called a suit. He opened up the box on the stand by his bed and removed all of his savings. He hoped it would be enough.

Five minutes later, Patrick stood outside the tailor shop eyeing the window display. If the man was willing to let him buy it, would it even fit? What choice did he have? The ready-mades at the mercantile were work clothes. He needed a gentleman's suit with a jacket, vest, and properly fitted pants. If this didn't work, he wouldn't be able to attend the ball. He took a deep breath and entered the shop. The bell above the door jingled, announcing his arrival.

* * *

The Whitmore family gathered on the piazza in front of Moffat and Simpson's Photography Studio. Emmaline's insides fluttered in excitement. She had never had her picture taken. The family had their portrait painted not long after James' birth. All she remembered was having to stand still for what seemed like hours upon hours in an uncomfortable dress and shoes. She inwardly laughed. She was again wearing an uncomfortably tight dress and shoes. She pressed a hand to her middle. It was hard to breath in her taut corset. She wasn't sure it was worth it, even though her mirror reflected an enviably narrow waist.

The group studied the various photographs pinned to two boards hanging on either side of the door while they waited for Henry's family to arrive. They easily recognized most of the studious faces of friends and neighbors. Some were of the army soldiers currently or previously stationed at the barracks.

Emily soon arrived with the children, all impeccably dressed. Little

Margaret and Henrietta spun around for their aunts to show them how their new dresses flared out when they did so. Theodore was first to ask, "Where is Henry?"

Emily jostled a fussy Laurie as she answered, "He'll be here soon. He was needed back at home. He said we should go in and get situated."

Theodore said, "Very well." He opened the door and proudly watched his family file past in all their finery. Emily wore an elaborate golden gown. She held Laurie's hand as he followed her, proudly wearing his first skeleton suit of olive green. Margaret and Henrietta followed in pale dresses layered in flounces, Ben and Alex wore matching vested suits and long pants, making it even more difficult to tell them apart. Theodore found it hard to believe they had outgrown knee-length breeches. Ella Rose startled him even more, looking older than her years in a nearly full-length pink dress. She was followed by Brianna in a forest green gown, Agatha in garnet, wearing his aunt's cameo rose at her throat, and Emmaline in royal blue. His chest burst with pride. His girls had become such lovely ladies inside and out, even if Agatha still had her caustic moments.

His eye caught on the broach Emmaline wore at the center of her neckline. The ivory Madonna and child on red onyx in a gold setting was set off well against her gown. It brought to mind the first time he saw Betsy wearing it. It was their first Christmas together.

Emmaline noticed her father staring at her chest. She looked down hoping she wasn't indecent. The décolletage of her gown was entirely improper for walking about in the light of day. She found her bosom adequately covered by the fichu she donned before leaving the house. The wink of gold beneath it enlightened her. She covered the broach with her hand and looked to her father, wanting to say something to lighten his mood. "You don't think it comes across as too patriotic, do you?"

Theodore blinked and raised his eyes to Emmaline's. It took a moment for her words to register and another to realize she was referring to the combination of red, white, and blue. The corner of his lip lifted. "Would it matter if it did?"

She smiled. "No."

Emmaline went inside, followed by Garrett, carrying Eli in a white dress. Eli reached out to Theodore with a chubby hand and then leaned towards him. He took the child from Garrett, endeared by his grandson's preference for him. James, in his freshly pressed suit, held the door for him to enter and then followed him inside.

His family filled the front room with hardly any space to spare. Mr.

131

Moffat soon appeared to usher them into the studio. He and Mr. Simpson then spent a good deal of time arranging them in various seated and standing positions with Theodore in the center still holding Eli, who refused to be taken from him. To avoid a tantrum, he was left in his grandfather's care.

Emily leaned towards Emmaline to whisper, "Henry said it will take less than a minute to take the photograph. I can't imagine it. That everything about us will be captured within that box so quickly."

Having overheard, Agatha said, "Not everything about us. Only a likeness. It can't grasp our personalities. Not yet anyways. Who knows what will come one day."

Mr. Simpson said, "And where is Mr. Henry Whitmore?"

Henry appeared just then. "Here I am."

Mr. Simpson turned to direct him. "Oh good. Please take your place behind your wife. Stand behind her right shoulder if you would please, sir." When Henry settled, he gave the group one last critical look, then turned to finish setting up the camera box, making sure they would all fit within the frame of the picture.

Without moving her head, Emily asked Henry, "Were you able to help him?"

"I believe so. I didn't wait to see the results."

Mr. Moffat looked them over with an eye for details. He straightened the boys' shoulders, adjusted the baby's dress, brushed lint from Theodore's shoulder, and fixed the hem of Ella's gown. Receiving a nod from Mr. Simpson that all was ready he said, "Serious faces now."

Snickers were heard from the twins and instantly silenced by Henry's terse, "Boys!"

Mr. Moffat held up his hand. "Ready? Now remember. You must hold absolutely still until I say." He then ducked beneath the light-blocking black cloth behind the camera box and removed the lens cover from the front.

They ended up taking three photographs because Elijah kept fidgeting. It was with a sigh of relief that they were released from the unnatural poses they were holding. Theodore settled the bill, and then they walked together down Whitehead Street to the Eatonton home. The ball was not due to start for more than two hours, but it had been decided the walk home and then back to the Eatonton's would be even more uncomfortable in their finery.

Upon reaching the grand house, Emily's mother, Abby, led the ladies upstairs to a room she had set aside where they could remove their dresses and loosen their corsets during the interim. They could even take a nap if they so desired, as the ball usually went well past midnight. The younger children were ushered to the nursery and turned over to the care of their nanny to change them into play clothes and keep them occupied for the evening. The older children also changed and entertained themselves. They would all have their supper in the nursery tonight. Servants hired for the event fluttered about the downstairs rooms tending to all the last-minute details under the butler's calm direction.

The men were directed to Max's study for drinks and cigars, and perchance a friendly game of poker. There they found Emily's father, Max, her four brothers, Christoff, Thorn, Nate, and Jacob, and Patrick waiting for them. Henry eyed Patrick's borrowed attire with a critical eye. The jacket was tight across his shoulders and his upper arms, and the pants were a tad too short but otherwise it would do for the evening. He clapped him on the back. "I told you it would be a close fit."

Patrick said in a hushed tone, "Close does not begin to describe it. I'm afraid to move my arms too much for fear I'll split a seam, but I do sincerely appreciate the loan of it."

"It was fortuitous us running into you like we did. I know Emmaline would have been greatly disappointed if you had not attended."

Patrick knew he would have been too. He wasn't sure he wouldn't have attended anyway just to see her. With barely held impatience, he tracked the slow rotation of the hands on the grandfather clock as he made a valiant effort to keep up his part in the gentlemen's conversation.

* * *

At the appointed hour, the Eatonton family gathered in the foyer to greet their guests. Emmaline and her sisters lingered in the bedroom, taking their time to redress. Ella hovered nearby, eagerly offering assistance where she could, entranced by the grandeur of the whole affair and lamenting she was not old enough yet to attend. She couldn't wait for the day when she could wear a full-length gown. Emmaline remembered when she once felt the same as Ella. She didn't bother telling her the added weight of the extra material, the larger skirt, and the tighter corset made a ladies dress uncomfortable at best, and she would do better to enjoy her freedom while it lasted, knowing how little it mattered to her when she was told as much.

Giving one last check of her reflection in the cheval mirror, she followed her sisters out the door and down the front staircase to join the gathering guests. Emmaline paused halfway down, her gaze sweeping the gathering in the foyer in search of one face in particular. She found him standing against the door jamb at the entry to the formal sitting room watching her. The corner of his lips lifted in a smile meant just for her. Her heartbeat quickened. As she continued down the stairs, she noted the ill-fitting and outdated tailored clothes he wore. He must have borrowed them. It hadn't occurred to her that he might have trouble finding clothes for a ball. She was glad he found something that fit well enough to attend. The evening would have been ever so dull without him.

Patrick worked his way around the crowded foyer to meet Emmaline at the bottom of the steps. He held out his white gloved hand for hers, closing his fingers around her gloved ones with a gentle squeeze. He admired the way her simple gown of deep blue enhanced her figure and offered a striking contrast for her auburn hair. The bodice draped low from her shoulders and across her bosom, giving him a tantalizing view of her décolletage from his height. Desire, unlike any he had felt before, swept over him. His jaw clenched as he tried to wield control over his reaction.

Emmaline frowned. "Is something wrong, Patrick?"

He willed himself to smile lightly. "No, nothing is wrong. You look beautiful. Will you honor me with the first dance?"

"I would like that."

They moved past the reception line to make their way into the ballroom where they joined Brianna, Garrett, Agatha, Christoff, and Thorn. The latter looked resplendent in his captain's uniform. James joined Nate and Jacob and a few other young fellows on the far side of the room.

Brianna addressed the elder Eatonton brothers. "Are there any ladies in particular you gentlemen hope to see in attendance tonight?"

Christoff said, "No one in particular for me. I plan to dance every dance with someone different."

Thorn huffed.

Brianna turned to Thorn. "There is not a lady for you?"

Christoff scoffed. "Thorn hasn't been interested in anyone since..."

Emily arrived in time to hear the last part of the conversation. She gave Christoff a scorching look and purposely interrupted him to admonish her brothers. "What are you standing here for?" She waved her hand towards the others in the room. "Go. Circulate. You can stand around like wallflowers later. Right now we have guests to greet." She cast a welcoming smile for the others in the group and then followed her brothers.

The Eatonton Ball was Emmaline's favorite of the season. She could spend the night just admiring the lavish dresses. Few would dare to wear anything but a new frock to this ball. The gentlemen were elegant as well in their black well-fitting pants, matching dress-coat and vest with pleated white shirts and cravats or their freshly pressed uniforms. Well, she could spend the night admiring others, but then she would miss the dancing and she loved to dance, except if she had a bad partner. She looked up at the man beside her. She dearly hoped he was a good dancer.

A thrill raced through Emmaline as the signal was given for the ball to begin. Patrick offered his arm with a lighthearted smile. "Shall we?"

She gave him a teasing grin. "We shall."

They lined up with the other dancers and it was then it occurred to Patrick the dancing here may be different then the jigs and reels they did back home. He nervously glanced at Emmaline standing across from him. He hoped he was not about to embarrass himself.

Theodore scanned the ballroom looking for Emmaline, expecting to be her partner for the first dance. He found her with Patrick, in line with the other couples for the quadrille. He felt disappointed to have been replaced for the opening dance, but watching the way she smiled at Patrick and the way he tended to her gave his father's heart a measure of peace. Agatha stepped up beside him.

"They look well together."

"Hmm."

Agatha's mouth quirked at her father's typical response. "Could I take her place?"

Theodore turned to Agatha with a frown. "What do you mean?"

"I know you usually dance the first dance with Emmaline." He had done so since her youngest sister's debut in the ballroom. "She appears to be otherwise engaged. Will you dance with me instead?"

Theodore raised a hand to caress Agatha's cheek. How typical of her to ask for what she wanted rather than wait and be disappointed. He hated to admit it might not have occurred to him to seek out his middle daughter as a partner. "I would be honored to dance with you." He let his hand fall, knowing she did not tolerate tenderness for long, and offered his arm to escort her to a place in the dance.

It didn't take long for Patrick to learn the subtle variants in the dance. He was soon able to move with confidence and enjoy the looks and touches they were freely able to share with the movements of the dance. Everything about Emmaline enticed him whenever he was with her, but tonight, she seemed especially enchanting. He was going to have a hard time leaving her side when the dance came to an end. Even the swirl of her dress as it brushed his leg begged him to stay by her side.

All good things must end, and all too soon for Patrick, the final notes from the orchestra drifted away. He and Emmaline lingered in each other's gaze a moment before she said, "You best escort me to my father before we draw too much attention."

"Of course." Patrick willed his legs to move. As they walked towards Mr. Whitmore, he asked, "When may I dance with you again?"

"We can only share one more dance, so it must be a waltz, don't you agree?"

"Yes. A waltz, most assuredly."

"I believe there is one planned for right before supper."

When they reached her father, Patrick reluctantly parted from Emmaline. Her father gave her his arm and escorted her back to the center of the room for the next dance.

Agatha drew his gaze from watching Emmaline's departure. "Shall we join them?"

Her directness still surprised him, but he had no qualms accepting her suggestion. They joined Emmaline and her father to make a set of four, ensuring he and Emmaline would interact in the movement of the dance.

The third dance they were on opposite ends of the room. Patrick mis-stepped several times for trying to keep his eye on Emmaline and the young man she was dancing with rather than focused on his partner.

On the other side of the ballroom, near bank of open windows, Thorn intentionally approached his father conversing with a distinguished man wearing the uniform of a high-ranking navy officer. He was the father of a certain young lady, and Thorn was intent on gaining a proper introduction. He was so single-minded in his purpose it had not yet registered with him why it was so important he receive the introduction. Her beauty struck him from the moment he first beheld her entering the ballroom on her father's arm. He was determined to dance with her, but not just any dance. He wanted to waltz with her. Simple hand touches were not enough. He wanted to know the feel of her in his arms.

Max curiously eyed his son, wondering at his appearance by his side. Normally, they rarely saw each other during the ball. The intensity of his gaze upon his companion was stranger still. "Commander Kent, may I introduce my son, Sergeant Hawthorn Eatonton."

"Good evening, Sergeant."

"Good evening, Commander Kent. A pleasure to make your acquaintance. I understand you will be in command of these waters for the foreseeable future."

"That is so."

Thorn wanted to ask directly of his daughter but instinctively knew that would be detrimental. "Will you be taking up residence on our island?"

"I have let a house for myself and my daughter. Ah, here she is." He held his arm out for the diminutive blonde to join them. "Annabelle, you've met our host Captain Max Eatonton, and this is his son Sergeant Hawthorn Eatonton." He looked to the younger man. "I present my daughter, Miss Annabelle Kent."

Thorn bowed to the enchantress with the crystal blue eyes, golden hair, and porcelain complexion looking like one of his mother's prized figurines come to life in a pale blue dress. "I am pleased to make your acquaintance, Miss Kent."

Annabelle said, "As am I, Sergeant Eatonton."

Max said, "And this is my eldest son, Captain Christoff Eatonton. He commands the flagship of our merchant fleet."

Thorn was caught unaware of his brother's arrival. His surprise turned to dismay as he noticed Christoff's intent interest in Miss Kent.

Annabelle politely regarded the elder brother. "It is nice to meet you as well, Captain Eatonton."

Christoff said, "How do you find Key West, Miss Kent?"

"It is quite delightful."

"Where is it you call home?"

She gave him a beguiling smile. "Right now, it is Key West."

"And before?"

"A multitude of places, but if you mean where did I grow up, I suppose that would be Baltimore."

The next dance was being assembled. Christoff bent low before her. "Miss Kent, may I have the pleasure of this dance?"

Annabelle accepted with good grace but was secretly disappointed it was not the other brother.

Emmaline was winded after the third set. She declined the next dance and sought refuge with Emily by the open window. Her tight corset made it difficult to catch her breath. Vigorously, she waved her fan and waited for her heartbeat to slow. Fortunately, she was not lightheaded. The idea of fainting in a crowded ballroom horrified her.

Emily looked at her with concern. "Will you be alright?"

"Yes. I just needed a moment to catch my breath."

Emily signaled to a nearby server who soon brought cups of cool and refreshing punch.

Emmaline saw Patrick pass by dancing with another and watching her with concern. She gave him a reassuring smile. They both hated the rules that kept them apart. If they could do as they wished, they would share every dance together, but it was unseemly for them to dance more than two dances together, especially since the ladies were greatly outnumbered by the men. She sipped her punch as she watched the couples turn about the floor. Across the room, one gentleman had yet to take his eyes from a certain lady dancing with another man.

Emmaline said in an aside to Emily, "Who is Christoff dancing with?"

Emily followed her gaze to her brother dancing with a delicate looking blonde in a light blue gown heavily decorated with ruffles, lace, and bows. "Annabelle Kent. She is the daughter of Commander Kent. His fleet arrived last week." As she spoke she became aware of the same oddity that Emmaline had noticed and a pleased smile spread upon her face. "It appears as though Thorn may finally be over his infatuation for Brianna."

"Brianna? Are you saying Thorn held tender feelings for my sister? I thought it was the other way around."

Emily nodded, but her gaze was still fixed on her brooding brother. "It was in the beginning but as soon as Brianna turned from him, Thorn finally took notice of her. I believed he still did until this very moment. He took it hard when she married Garrett." Her gaze turned soft. "This is the first time I've seen him take an interest in any other lady."

Emmaline shook her head in bewilderment. "I can't believe I was never aware of it."

"I'm not surprised. Thorn rarely shows his feelings."

"He seems to have let his guard down tonight. Anyone can see Miss Kent has caught his attention. Did Brianna know?"

"Of Thorn's change of heart? I'm not sure."

Emmaline studied the smiling face of Christoff's partner as they danced past. She was very pretty. "Have you met Miss Kent? Is she nice?"

"Only upon introduction. We did not say more than a few innocuous words to each other. She spoke well and fortunately does not seem to be as reticent as my brother."

"That is good. Could you imagine if he and his wife were both alike in that regard? There would be nary a word spoken between them."

"Speaking of romance and such. You have a gentleman headed your way."

Patrick was making his way around the dancers to Emmaline, determined to be at her side when the next song started, knowing it was to be a waltz, having consulted earlier with the conductor.

As the music ended, Christoff escorted Miss Kent back to her father. She was disappointed not to see Thorn waiting there for her, but her spirits soon lifted as she saw him approach with a determined stride and two cups of punch.

Her welcoming smile was all the encouragement Thorn needed. "I thought you might like some refreshment."

"That was very kind of you, Sergeant Eatonton."

Thorn offered the other cup to her father.

Commander Kent's lips puckered. "I can't abide such sweetness."

Max said, "If you would care for something stronger, we could go to my study for drinks."

"Yes, thank you. Annabelle?"

She cast a glance in Thorn's direction with a raised eyebrow. He couldn't mistake her meaning. "Miss Kent, may I have the pleasure of this next dance?"

"You may." Thorn offered his arm with a bland expression, but inside he was tumultuous with joy for having achieved his goal.

Max and the commander watched their children leave, one in wonder to see his son so taken with a lady and the other in dismay to realize his daughter had more than a passing interest in the low-ranking army officer.

The orchestra was taking a short break. Thorn and Annabelle sipped their drinks while they waited for the next dance to begin. They were half facing each other and the room, watching the other guests as they mingled.

Annabelle eyed the handsome man standing next to her. "Do you always get what you want?"

Thorn's eyes widened. "What do you mean?"

"You can't deny you manipulated an introduction to my father with the express intention of gaining an introduction to me, followed by a dance, and unless I miss my guess, you wanted a waltz in particular."

Thorn's mouth dropped open at the accuracy of her assessment. It was as if she had read his mind. Gathering his pride, he firmly closed his mouth. To denounce her was futile. She had surely seen the truth in his reaction. "Do you mind so much? I could return you to your father."

Her eyebrows rose. "Honesty. That is quite refreshing. Many a man would deny even what is so plainly true."

"I am not most men." Something in her expression briefly changed. It was like a spark of hope that withered as soon as it was born. Beneath the strength she projected, Thorn sensed a wounded animal.

Annabelle gauged his sincerity. He seemed true, but she knew all too well the deception of appearances. "But you just did what many have done before, manipulated a situation for your own benefit."

"True. But it is my intentions afterwards that differs, for now, all that matters is pleasing you."

"Pretty words, Sergeant Eatonton, but in my experience men use a woman's tender feelings against her to get what they want."

Again, he sensed the wounded soul within. Softly, he said, "A true gentleman would not."

"And are you a true gentleman?"

"I hope to prove myself so, in your eyes if in no other."

Annabelle felt her heart dangerously swell with feeling. To break the spell, she looked away as she took a sip of her punch.

Emily and Henry approached. Thorn could well guess his sister's intent was to assess his feelings for Miss Kent.

Across the room, Patrick's heart took a galloping leap as Emmaline moved to fill his open arms as the first notes of the waltz filled the air. One delicate gloved hand rested on his upper arm, the other nestled into the palm of his hand. His other hand cupped her shoulder blade and as one they moved with the music as he led them around the floor. The tempo spoke to him. One, two, three. One, two, three. She felt so right in his arms. Together, they glided about the room, lost in their own fairy tale.

Emmaline felt as if she were floating on air. The music and Patrick's arms carried her about the room, oblivious to anyone else. It was all she had dreamed it would be. It wasn't perfect. They had the occasional misstep, and he landed on her foot once, but it was still the best dance of her life. She wanted to close her eyes to savor the moment but feared she would misstep. The consolation of staring into warm brown eyes that saw only her was not so bad.

Thorn swept Annabelle into his arms at the orchestra's first notes. It was the first time he had danced the waltz with anyone other than the Whitmore girls. It was different. With all but Brianna the steps had been carefully measured, limbs stiff and uncomfortable, and even with Brianna, he was never fully at ease. There was always the feeling of being too intimate. With Annabelle it felt like they were made for each other. He wished he could pull her closer. Their steps felt natural. She gracefully followed where he led. One, two, three. One, two, three. He wished the song would never end.

Thorn asked, "How long will you be staying in Key West?"

"I am leaving after the holidays."

Thorn's heart plummeted.

As all things must, the dance came to end. It was followed by a call for supper. A subdued and melancholy Thorn led Annabelle to her seat and found his place card disappointingly at another table. His thoughts were filled with how to see her again before she left the island. Not coming up with any answers, he was poor company for his dinner companions. Patrick, on the other hand, was delighted to discover he was seated next to Emmaline. They talked of all sorts of things as they enjoyed the delicacies of the meal. It was with great effort they occasionally turned away from each other to politely speak with the guest on their other side.

At the meal's end, Emmaline hated to be parted from Patrick. It would be unseemly to dance with him again and she found no joy in dancing with any other. She was considering pleading a headache and asking her father to leave early. But the thought flew from her mind with Patrick's request.

"When the ball is over, may I escort you home?"

"I would like that."

Her joyous smile lingered with him as he impatiently waited for the evening to come to a close.

Thorn hovered on the edge of the ballroom. No amount of coercion from Emily could get him to mingle. He had eyes only for Annabelle. He had asked for another dance, but found she was promised for the rest of the evening, so he intended to be on hand the moment of her departure for one last chance to speak with her.

Emily picked up a cup of punch and joined Brianna standing near the refreshment table. "It seems as though Emmaline is as taken with Patrick as he is of her."

"Indeed."

"Do you think anything will come of it?"

"I do believe wedding bells are in her near future."

"And your father, will he approve?"

"Not at first, but I think Poppa is coming around to him."

Emily watched her father-in-law as he conversed with a nearby group of gentlemen. "Your father seems different tonight."

"You noticed it too?"

"It's hard to miss. There is still sadness in him, but he is not as despondent. He has danced with me and mother and you and your sisters, which is more than can be said of last year."

"He danced with our neighbor's wife too."

"Oh my. And look! There he goes now escorting one of the widows to dance."

"By the look on his face, he wasn't given much choice."

Emily laughed lightly. "Knowing her, that is likely very true."

Brianna eyed another couple dancing past and the brooding stare from across the room following their every movement. "It appears a lady has at last caught Thorn's attention."

"So it seems. Unfortunately, I just learned she will be leaving the island in a fortnight."

"That is too bad. Perhaps you should befriend her to keep them connected."

Emily smiled broadly. "Brianna, what a clever idea. I shouldn't interfere, but I believe I will."

Emmaline was disappointed when the last strands of music faded and the ball was officially over, and yet relieved. Her feet were sore, her legs ached, but mostly she couldn't wait to be rid of her dress and corset to properly breathe again. But that would come later. First, she would walk home with her family on the arm of the most handsome man in the room.

Patrick approached the Whitmore family gathered near the grand staircase where Emmaline first appeared this evening. Her father was placing her shawl across Emmaline's shoulders.

Agatha asked, "Mr. Johnson, did you enjoy the evening?"

"I did, thank you. And did you?"

"Yes. The food was splendid and the company fine, as always."

They moved to the door, pausing to bid farewell to their hosts. Except for the grandchildren asleep in their beds upstairs, the entire Eatonton family was gathered in the foyer bidding farewell to their guests. The Whitmore's were the last to leave.

Together, Patrick and Emmaline stepped out into the night. The waning moon was nearly spent, only the barest sliver showed on the eve before the new moon, allowing the stars to shine bright, but still they couldn't compare to the lady by his side. Patrick laid his free hand atop the gloved one resting upon his forearm. He was rewarded with Emmaline's glowing smile as they passed beneath the gaslight of the front piazza. They descended the steps preceding James, Agatha, and Mr. Whitmore. Garrett and Brianna returned home shortly after the late supper so Brianna could tend to Eli and allow the housekeeper who was watching him to go home.

Emmaline breathed deeply of the salty air. There was a contentment about her she hadn't felt in a long time and it had everything to do with the man by her side. She wanted to invite him to join the family for Christmas Eve. He was already expected for Christmas Day. She hesitated in consideration of her father. His spirits were lifted and the holiday was going well. She didn't want to risk upsetting him by including Patrick in what had always been a private family evening.

Patrick and Emmaline were both startled by Theodore, speaking from behind them.

"Mr. Johnson, have you made any progress on your second article? Do you have a subject?"

Patrick shifted them to walk beside the others. "I do have an idea. Henry has agreed to take me out and introduce me to sponge fishing. I was thinking of writing a brief history of how much the industry has grown and how he sees it expanding over the next decade."

Theodore nodded encouragingly. "Do you think you could finish drafting it by tomorrow?"

Patrick's breath hitched with excitement. "I believe so."

"Good. Then bring it by the house on Saturday."

"But that's Christmas Eve, won't I be disturbing you?"

"So it is." Theodore cast a questioning glance to his daughter and saw a hopeful yearning in her eyes. "Would you care to join us for supper and festivities before church services? Your uncle is welcome to join us if he likes."

"I would like that very much, sir. Thank you."

Joy burst in Emmaline's chest knowing she would see Patrick again the day after tomorrow. Christmas this year was turning out to be everything her heart desired and then some.

Chapter 12

Friday, Emmaline rushed through her morning chores, anxious to make one last shopping trip in town. It occurred to her last night, rather the wee hours of the morning as she tried to fall asleep after the excitement of the ball, that she needed to purchase a last minute gift for there was not enough time to make something other than food, which did not appeal. She knew what she wanted to purchase.

Any other time, her sisters would join her on the excursion. Today, she intended to go alone. Brianna would not approve of her idea. As it turned out, Agatha found her as she was donning her gloves and hat.

"Where are you going this morning?"

"I have an errand in town."

"I think I'll join you. I could use a good long walk to clear my head."

Emmaline would have refused, but knowing Agatha it would cause a scene and likely end up with Brianna joining them. "Very well. But I'm leaving now."

Agatha stepped to the foyer table and picked up her gloves. "I'm ready."

Emmaline led them out the door. She turned north on Whitehead Street.

Agatha interrupted Emmaline's thoughts. "How are we going to present our gift to Poppa? It's not as if we can hang it on the tree or even beneath it."

"Henry has made arrangements to store it at Mr. Tift's warehouse. He said he would work out the means of presenting it to Poppa."

"That makes sense. Are you sure Poppa will appreciate it?"

"Appreciate it, yes. He will know what it took for us to get it for him. What you are really asking is if it is what he wants and not just my idea of restoring his sense of purpose."

"That is pretty much what I am asking."

Emmaline shook her head. "I'm not sure. It could be a very bad idea."

"Even if it's not what he wants, I doubt Poppa would look upon it as a bad idea."

"I suppose we'll find out soon enough."

Agatha studied Emmaline's taught shoulders. "By the way, where are we going?"

"The milliners shop."

"Something for you or a gift?"

"A gift."

Agatha got the message in Emmaline's succinct reply. They lapsed into a comfortable silence until they reached the shop. Inside, Agatha turned towards the ladies' section, expecting Emmaline to follow, but she did not.

Emmaline's feet followed her gaze to a particular display. She knew exactly what she wanted. From the moment she climbed from her bed, she had been trying to come up with something special for Patrick. It had to be special. Because of him she was the happiest she had ever been. Because of him, her father was once again talking about newspapers and writing articles. Because of him, Christmas would feel like Christmas. When inspiration finally struck, she tried to dismiss it as too forward. But her heart was set on it. And besides, she may well be falling in love with him, so it didn't matter to her if the gift would be considered inappropriate.

Emmaline stared at the assortment of top hats before her. She hadn't realized they came in such a variety of fabrics and heights. Agatha joined her after circling the store's displays.

"Poppa hates top hats."

"It's not for Poppa."

"Then who? It's too expensive for you to give to Garrett, and I doubt he would like it either."

"It's for Patrick."

Agatha's mouth went agape. "I don't stand much on ceremony, but even I know a gift of clothing, even head covering, is too personal. It's not a proper gift for a man you're not related to, much less barely known for a month."

Emmaline absently said, "I feel as if I've known him all my life."

"Even so, to give him anything it should be something you made."

Emmaline brought her full attention to her sister. "Don't lecture. That's the very reason I avoided Brianna."

"If you are set on..."

"I am."

"Then may I suggest that one? It will work well with his height and long face."

"Thank you."

* * *

Patrick spent Saturday morning anxiously rewriting his article again. He wanted it to be better than it was before presenting it to Mr. Whitmore. So much hung in the balance of his approval. Finally, the position of the hour hand on the clock forced him to be satisfied with what he had. If he spent any more time on it he would be late.

He washed, shaved, and dressed with more care than he ever had in his life. When he was done his uncle eyed him critically. "You know what you're doing boy?"

"Not really, uncle. I'm just praying my efforts are enough. Are you sure you don't want to come?"

"I'm sure."

Patrick clenched his jaw, hating the words but knowing he needed to say them. "Then, I should stay. I shouldn't leave you alone on Christmas Eve."

"Nonsense. What do you think I've done all the years before you arrived? You go on. I'll see you at service this evening."

"Yes, sir, very well. Thank you, sir."

"Stop sir-ing me and get on with you. Don't ever keep a lady waiting." His voice trailed off as he added, "That way leads to heartache."

Patrick paused in buttoning his boot. The tone of his uncle's voice hinted at a story behind his words. He wanted to ask him about it, but he was in a hurry. He hoped he could find another opportunity later.

Patrick inhaled the comforting scent of pine emanating from the wreath before him as he waited for someone to answer the door. Nervously, he shuffled his feet and fiddled with the paper sack he carried. He was every bit as nervous this time as he was in presenting the first article. Maybe more so.

Emmaline's smiling face appeared in the opening as the door swung wide to admit him. Instantly, he felt calmer about the article and yet more excited to be with her again.

"Come in. Poppa's waiting for you in the study."

Patrick's stomach clenched. "I'm not late, am I?"

"Oh no. You're fine. Can I take your coat?"

Patrick looked down, considering his shirt and vest. He supposed it was appropriate enough. He first handed her the paper sack. "This is for you."

Emmaline smiled. "Thank you." Eagerly she unfolded the opening. Inside was a variety of candies from the apothecary. It must have cost him a nickel, maybe even a dime for the bag was quite full. She looked up with bright eyes. "What a treat! That is so very generous of you."

He slipped his arms from the lightweight dress jacket and handed it to her. "I thought you would like to share them with your nieces and nephews."

She smiled. "How thoughtful." She hung the coat on a peg and then led him to her father.

A half hour later, Patrick went in search of her, feeling as if he had won some grand prize. Not only did her father like what he had written, especially the part about the high quality of Key West sponges, he also promised to send it to all his contacts. And the best part was his confidence that Patrick would be paid for his writing. He was well on his way to being a journalist, and he felt like celebrating. He wanted nothing more than to share his good news with Emmaline. Instead, he was intercepted in the hall by her brother and brother-in-law.

Henry eyed his clothing with disdain. "You got a change of clothes with you?"

Puzzled, Patrick said, "No."

Garrett clapped him on the back. "I'll lend you some of mine."

"Why do I need other clothes?"

"You can't go fishing in that getup."

"I didn't know I was going to be fishing."

Henry said, "It's a Christmas Eve tradition. I'm surprised Emmaline didn't mention it."

Garrett said, "Come on up to my room. We'll get you squared away."

Patrick shook his head, "Where's Emmaline?"

Henry said, "Oh, she and the ladies went to decorate the church and visit the orphans. If the fishing's good, we'll be back before they are."

Patrick came downstairs wearing work trousers and a loose shirt. Henry and Garrett led him from the house, west on Southard Street to the beach in front of the fort. The other two turned south but Patrick stopped and stared at the impressive brick structure rising from the water a thousand feet offshore. He had never seen anything like it. Why would they build a fort in the harbor and not onshore?

"Come on, Patrick."

Reluctantly, he turned to follow his companions to a rowboat breached on the beach. He eyed it skeptically, vividly recalling the seasickness that plagued him on his journey from Virginia. "Can't we fish from shore?"

Henry smirked. "You can't catch conch on a beach. Can you swim?"

"When the occasion calls for it."

"Good. Climb aboard. The sooner we get out there, the sooner we can be done."

Henry rowed them to his favorite hunting ground where the waves gently flowed over a bed of turtle grass. He and Garrett stood up on either side of Patrick, rocking the boat. Patrick tightly gripped the sides while he watched in stunned silence as they stripped off all their clothes and jumped into the water. Both came up sputtering.

Henry said, "It's as cold as a witch's tit."

Garrett shivered. "You say that every year."

Patrick dropped a hand into the water and pulled it out with a shake. The water was cold.

"Because it's true every year. Patrick, what are you still doing in the boat?"

"Not turning blue, for one thing."

"Well if you're not going to help hunt, make yourself useful and fill the bucket with water."

Patrick scanned the boat, perplexed, then he looked under his seat. He pulled the bucket out and filled it with water. There was a precarious moment he thought for sure he was going to turn over with the boat. He watched the other two swimming about below the surface. Pretty soon, one and then the other came up holding large mollusks. They handed them to Patrick to put in the bucket. Each was more than twice the size of his hand. It was cone shaped with a spiky spire, sand colored on the outside, but the lip of the shell opening were beautiful polished shades of blush to pink where the grayish sea snail retreated. "What are they?"

"Queen Conch," said Henry before he dove back down.

They brought up seven more before Patrick helped them back into the boat. They shook their heads sending a shower of water droplets over him. "Ahh, that's cold!"

Garrett said, "What? You think you shouldn't share in the torture?"

"No, I don't."

The two dressed quickly and sat back down, picking up the oars, and to Patrick's relief the boat glided rapidly across the water back to shore.

"What are you going to do with these?"

Henry glanced over his shoulder. "That, my friend, is our supper. It's a family tradition to have Momma's conch chowder on Christmas Eve. It was her specialty."

A half hour later, Patrick was not allowed to escape his introduction to harvesting conch meat. He was very appreciative of the borrowed clothing by the time he finished.

* * *

Emmaline tried to hurry her sisters and niece along, anxious to see Patrick again. They were returning from a traditional family visit to the orphans, bringing them most of the cookies and peppermint candy they had made earlier in the week. This year was Ella's first to join them, and she offered her own special gift by reciting the poem "A Visit from St. Nicholas" from memory, faltering only once as she said 'mamma in her 'kerchief'. It was received with resounding applause and so many requests for her to repeat it that she could hardly refuse the poor dears.

Ella said, "I am so glad they liked the poem. I forgot all about it mentioning parents until I came to the line about them. I was so afraid I would hurt their feelings since they don't have any parents, but it didn't seem to bother them."

Emily ran a hand over her daughter's head. "I'm sure you have given them dreams of a happy family of their own along with the dancing sugar plums."

"But isn't that sad for them to dream of something they won't have tomorrow?"

"Are you sad about the things you dream of having but don't?"

Ella gave it serious consideration. "No, I suppose not."

"Momma, can we stop to buy some candy?"

Emmaline quickly looked to Emily and shook her head.

Emily said, "Not now, Ella. I think your aunt is anxious to return home."

Emmaline let the excuse stand. She didn't want to spoil the surprise of Patrick's candy.

They entered the house the same time as the men were headed upstairs to change. Emmaline nearly collided with a very smelly Patrick.

Brianna's nose turned up at the smell of salt and seafood. "Oh. I know what you boys have been doing. It looks like Patrick got the worst of it."

Garrett said, "It was only right since he refused to brave the water."

Agatha said, "Sounds to me like he was the only smart one. One of these year's you'll catch your death of cold."

Henry repeated the same line he often said in return. "Nonsense. We were warm again before we reached the shore. Isn't that right Garrett?"

"Speak for yourself. Brianna, I think you need to come upstairs and tend to your husband. I'm still mighty chilled."

Patrick watched the playful banter with interest and a touch of sadness. It was similar to what he shared with his siblings and suddenly he was missing them, but then he caught Emmaline's warm gaze. He ruefully looked down at his shirt. "I can't stand this another moment. I need to change." He started up the steps but turned back and winked at Emmaline, enjoying the blush that bloomed in her cheeks. He came down again not ten minutes later and joined the family in the parlor.

Emmaline crossed the room to greet Patrick. "You look better, smell better too." She blushed, as she realized mentioning the smell of him was improper for a lady. "Would you come help with the candles?"

"Of course."

They walked over to the tree where Agatha and Emily were attaching candles on one side. They took position on the other. Emmaline picked up the lit candle and chose a branch. They worked together to secure short unlit tapers to the branches with melted wax. Ella helped by handing them the candles. Her brothers and sisters were scattered about the room playing with various toys and games. Brianna entered the room with a subdued Eli, having just awoken from a nap. Ella began softly singing in a clear, sweet voice the "Coventry Carol."

When the song ended Emily said to her daughter, "That was beautiful."

Patrick and Emmaline added their praise.

Emily said, "Let's sing a cheerful song next."

Ella thought for a moment and began "Hark! The Herald Angels Sing." The others in the room soon joined in, as did Henry, Theodore, James, and Garrett, drawn from the study by the lively singing. A few more carols saw the candles done and the group stepped back to admire their work.

Margaret asked, "When will we light the candles?"

Henry brushed his daughter's head. "After supper, when it gets dark. Do you remember why we put candles on the tree?"

"Because the Christ child is the light of the world."

"That's right."

Emmaline turned to Patrick. "I think now would be a good time for your gift." She retrieved the paper bag from where she had tucked it away on the side table.

Emily eyed it with concern. "If that's what I think it is, you'll spoil their appetites."

"Nonsense. One piece each won't do any harm. Besides, better before than giving it to them afterwards and spoiling their sleep."

Emily blanched. "I concede your point."

Emmaline smiled. She then opened the bag and held it out. "Children, look what Mr. Johnson brought for you?"

Happy moments passed in the serious choice of candy flavor.

Emily shook her head at them. "Don't you have something to say to Mr. Johnson?"

Sheepishly, Ella and the boys thanked him, mimicked by the younger siblings. It was soon followed by the sticky faces and fingers of the younger ones, which Emmaline assumed responsibility for cleaning with Patrick's aid in holding a squirming Laurie.

Patrick then turned to face the group. "I think we need some entertainment. Henry, Garrett, will you join me?"

Both men hesitated.

He smiled. "I assure you it is a more pleasant task than the one you took me on earlier."

They reluctantly stepped forward and were brought into a whispered conference before turning to face the others. Patrick then led them in a rousing rendition of "God Rest Ye Merry, Gentlemen." They received applause and cheers at the song's end. Not to be outdone, Alex pulled Ben and his Uncle James forward to take their place and gave a comical version of "We Three Kings" sung in the deepest voices they could muster. When they were done, Ella and the twins argued over what song to sing next.

James held up his hands, silencing the trio. "I know a new song."

Ben and Alex simultaneously said, "You do?"

James grinned. "I do. The brother of a fellow West Pointer learned it for a hometown play. It's such a catchy tune, soon we were all singing it. Do you want me to teach it to you?"

Three loud voices cried, "Yes."

"It's called "Jingle Bells" and it goes like this…"

Theodore couldn't help but smile at his family's antics, inspired by Patrick.

Patrick.

He turned to look at the young man standing beside Emmaline. He enlivened this family. He helped pull him and Emmaline from their sorrow. He was a good man. He should tell him so. Theodore moved to his daughter's side and held his hand out to Patrick.

Patrick eyed him questioningly but took the proffered hand.

Theodore said, "I wanted to say thank you."

"For what, sir?"

"Emmaline and I have been like ghosts in this house. We've been going through the motions of life but not really living. You have brought joy and laughter back into our lives."

"Surely, your family is responsible for that, not I."

Theodore tilted his head to the trio trying to out-sing each other. "James may have taught them the song but you started that, not James or Henry or any of the others. You."

At the increasing volume of the singers, Patrick worried Mr. Whitmore might be getting irritated, especially when he had to raise his voice to be heard. "I'm sorry, sir."

Theodore shook his head. "No need to be sorry. They are having fun. It's been too long since anyone had fun in this house. You brought that back, and I wanted to thank you."

Emmaline was overwhelmed with hope, joy, and profound relief. Patrick had found a way to win her father's approval.

Patrick breathed a sigh of relief. He had gained Mr. Whitmore's acceptance and, unexpectedly, his gratitude as well.

Emily forestalled her children from starting the song a fifth time. "How about something else? You can sing that one again tomorrow."

Ben broke out with "Joy to the World" and the others picked it up as loudly as they had just finished the last.

Emily looked to Brianna, hoping to use Elijah as an excuse to quiet her exuberant youngsters, but she found the baby excitedly clapping his hands. Resigned, she and Brianna shrugged their shoulders and joined in the singing. Afterwards, they played parlor games the rest of the afternoon until they were called to supper with the setting sun.

After Theodore said grace, the meal proved boisterous as well, but was enjoyed with relish and a touch of sad nostalgia for the one who wasn't with them. In memory of Betsy, they enjoyed the conch chowder and crusty, fresh bread.

Patrick's first sampling of the chowder was cautionary, having handled the slippery meat, but he was comforted by all the familiar vegetables. He sipped the first spoonful of broth and was delighted with the savory tomato base with a hint of spiciness. He dug out a bit of the meat. Expecting it to be chewy, he was surprised by its tenderness. From there, he finished his bowl as eagerly as the rest and was rewarded with a second serving.

After the meal, the family returned to the parlor for the tree lighting. Henry and Theodore lit the tapers as the others watched and the room began to glow.

Light from the darkness.

Henrietta let go of her mother's hand to toddle over to her father and raise her arms. Charmed as always when she favored him, he picked her up. Not to be outdone, Laurie did the same. Henry leaned down to take him up in his other arm. The wonder on his children's faces filled his heart with joy.

When the candles were all lit, Emmaline led them in singing a few solemn hymns as they stood around the tree.

Theodore felt blessed to finally be able to appreciate his family without the bitterness of loss. If Brianna looked most like their mother, Emmaline sounded most like her. Especially when she sang. Her sweet voice commanded rapt attention just as her mother's did. He was happy to have these living, breathing parts of Betsy still with him.

After the hymns, Theodore picked up the family Bible, the one containing all their names and births, and seated himself. His grandchildren gathered at his feet to listen to him read of Christ's birth.

When Theodore closed the Good book, Henry and Emily rose. It was time to put the younger children to bed. They and the three eldest would join the family later at the evening service.

While the others were preparing to leave, Emmaline asked Patrick, "How would you be celebrating today if you were home?"

"Very much the same. We would have a tree, and sing carols, and father reads from the Bible before bedtime and again Christmas morning. We go to church on Christmas day. I suppose we would have gone Christmas Eve too if we lived closer to the church. I suppose the biggest difference is I don't have any nieces or nephews so no little children."

"The little ones do change things, don't they?"

"They do, and for the better."

"Do you want children?" The question made her blush. "I mean, one day, eventually, after you marry."

The corner of Patrick's mouth lifted at her embarrassed rambling. "I do." He waited but she pressed her lips without saying anything else. He couldn't imagine her not wanting children so he asked, "How many children would you like?"

"I haven't given it any thought. A few, I suppose. More than two would be nice. And you?"

"However many I am blessed with will be fine with me."

Agatha surprisingly interrupted them. "What are you discussing?"

Emmaline flushed beet red. "Nothing of importance."

"By the look on your face, I'd say you're in danger of needing a confession."

Patrick didn't like Agatha's teasing. "I assure it was nothing so improper as to require confession."

"Then what were you discussing?"

Emmaline said, "Children" at the same time Patrick said, "Nothing of concern to you."

Agatha smiled, "I see." She held Patrick's gaze a moment before walking away.

He was very afraid Agatha had seen more than he intended to reveal, especially to her.

The house grew quiet with the departure of Henry and his family. Agatha coerced James into a game of chess. Brianna handed Eli to her father so she and Garrett could play a game of backgammon, leaving Emmaline and Patrick at loose ends.

Emmaline suggested, "We could play piquet."

"Or we could just talk."

"We could."

And they did. They spoke of childhood, favorite foods, memories, and such. Patrick described his parents and each of his siblings for her. So intent were they on each other that the peal of bells calling the islanders to worship took them by surprise.

They walked the short distance through the moonless night by candlelight, joining the other gathering parishioners, each carrying a candle. The many together lit the church's interior. The service began with lighting all the candles of Advent and ended with an exodus of candlelight and song spreading out from the open doors of the church. In between were the Bible readings of faith and belief, evil and strife, and a joyful birth to deliver all from sin.

Solemnly they walked back to the Whitmore home.

Patrick, having entered last, stopped in the foyer with his hat in hand. "I suppose I should be going home."

Emmaline turned to face him while Brianna and Garrett took Eli upstairs and the others went into the parlor. Emmaline looked over her shoulder, wondering if she could ask Patrick to stay a little longer. She was surprised to discover they were alone in the foyer.

Patrick's eyes fervently held hers for a moment before they moved up to the ceiling. Her gaze followed to find the twigs of greenery above her head. How could she have forgotten the mistletoe? Her lips parted and her breath froze as she brought her eyes back to his. She licked her suddenly dry lips, bringing his attention to them. He stepped closer and sent an anxious glance over her shoulder. She turned her head as well to confirm they were still alone and unobserved. Her eyes came back to his, surprised to find him closer still.

His hand reached for hers and the jolt of tactile pleasure sent her heart racing faster. She had removed her gloves as she entered the house, and he wasn't wearing any either. His warm fingers lightly brushed the back of her hand and curled around to her palm, anchoring her to him as he slowly breached the distance between their lips. In anticipation, she lifted her face to his. Her eyes fluttered closed. He pressed his lips to hers, and time slowed for just that moment. When he pulled away, she opened her eyes to find him intently watching her.

Her first real kiss.

A kiss that devastated all her senses and sensibility.

Emmaline's mind couldn't get past the fact it had finally happened, and so unexpectedly. She stood there, looking at Patrick, with no other thought except, *he kissed me.*

Patrick was overwhelmed. Rather than satisfying him, the kiss awoke needs he didn't know he had. He wanted her with an ardor and desire not felt before. He knew it as sure as the sun would rise in the morning. Emmaline was his one and only love. Tomorrow he would ask for her father's permission to formally court her.

He felt behind him for the door. If he didn't leave now, he was going to kiss her again. "Good night, Emmaline."

"Good night, Patrick."

He held her hand for as long as he could, only letting go as he crossed the threshold. She closed the door behind him and turned to lean against it. She touched her lips in wonder.

He kissed her.

What did that mean? Would he ask for her hand? Would her father give his blessing if he did? The questions circled in her mind as she floated up the stairs and prepared for bed.

She relived the kiss over and over as she drifted off to sleep and dreamed of Patrick.

Chapter 13

The light of morning brought insecurity to Patrick as he dressed for church. Last night's surety of his love for Emmaline hadn't faded, but it did not take into account her feelings. What if she didn't feel the same? The need to see her, to speak with her, to know how she felt about him grew to desperate proportions in his chest. Somehow, he had to see her alone or at least separated enough to discover her true feelings. But it was Christmas. It was a day for worship and family. It wasn't likely they would have a moment alone after church or dinner. He was already dreading the hours between when he would be without her. He would likely have to resign himself to waiting until next weekend to ascertain her true feelings.

Emmaline ran her hands one last time over the front of her billowing forest green skirt before turning from her reflection in the cheval glass. Her movements were no different from any other Sunday, but the day was far from ordinary. It was Christmas day, and Patrick had kissed her. The memory of that kiss was never far from her mind. She couldn't wait to see him again. She was very thankful that it was Sunday, and they would soon walk to church where she hoped Patrick would be waiting for her. Surely, he was as anxious to see her as she was to see him.

On her father's arm, Emmaline impatiently matched his gait as they sauntered to church followed by James, Agatha, Brianna, and Garrett, who was carrying Elijah.

Theodore felt his daughter's angst. "What is it dear?"

Surprised her feelings had communicated to her father, Emmaline was at a loss as to what to say.

"Is it Patrick?"

Her gaze flew to his. Were her feelings so transparent? "Yes."

"Perhaps we should invite him to visit after services."

"I would like that very much." It made her extra thankful she and Brianna decided to save the cinnamon bread for a treat after church.

They turned the corner of the church yard and her heart leapt, for there was Patrick, waiting for her by the gate. She wanted to run to him but restrained her steps.

Theodore's deep voice said, "Merry Christmas, Mr. Johnson."

"Merry Christmas to you, Mr. Whitmore, and you, Miss Whitmore."

Emmaline smiled. "Thank you, Mr. Johnson."

The pleasantries continued as the others were greeted in similar fashion. Finally, Emmaline could ask, "Mr. Johnson, do you have plans after the service?"

"No."

"Would you like to come visit with us? We will be serving fresh cinnamon bread and Jamaican coffee."

"How could I possibly turn down cinnamon bread?" Or her. "Thank you for the invitation."

"Your uncle, of course, is welcome too."

"I will ask him."

Reverend Herrick gathered the congregation from the yard to begin the service. Patrick paused at the Whitmore pew to give Emmaline a smile which was warmly returned and then proceeded to sit with his uncle.

The service was joyful in celebration of Christ's birth. Afterwards, the congregation filed out in high spirits. Patrick once again joined the Whitmores in the church yard with his uncle. Smithy tried to decline their invitation but was soon persuaded by Theodore to join them. It was worked out that Smithy and Patrick would make a short detour home before proceeding to the Whitmore house.

The Eatonton family approached. They would be joining the Whitmore family later for Christmas dinner, as it was their turn to host this year. Emily's parents, Max and Abby, led the group of thirteen. In unison, the elder Eatontons greeted the Whitmore family with a cheerful, "Merry Christmas." Henry and Emily naturally moved to stand between the two families as the bridge they were between them. Henry heartily shook his father's hand and kissed the cheeks of each of his sisters. The older teenagers, James and Jacob, left the families in pursuit of two young ladies of interest while Agatha proceeded to question the other Eatonton brothers on their work and love interests. She enjoyed her inquisition until Christoff turned the questions back on her. Emily's young children milled about the legs of the adults, impatiently waiting to return home to play with their new toys waiting for them under the Christmas tree.

Emily said, "I'm looking forward to dinner. Mother made a new recipe for dessert using the pecans Uncle James sent us. It required the rest of the molasses to make the pie, so I sure hope it's worthy."

Abby said, "My uncle sent the recipe as well. It was created by his cook, Jemima. He assures me it is a heavenly treat."

Max said, "The aroma from the kitchen would attest to his claim. It made my mouth water."

Theodore said, "How is James Bennington these days? He must be nearing eighty now."

Abby said, "He turned eighty-one this year. Cousin Robert writes that he is as spry as ever."

Max gave Abby a comforting look knowing the mention of her uncle brought to mind her dearly departed father. Over her shoulder, he saw Commander Kent and his daughter speaking to the reverend. An idea occurred to him. He turned to Theodore. "Could I have a moment of your time?"

"Of course."

Max explained his intentions and gained Theodore's approval as the two men walked over to greet Commander Kent and his daughter.

After an appropriate amount of small talk, Theodore asked, "Commander, if you have no other plans, you are most welcome to join our families for Christmas dinner at my house."

The man looked to his daughter and receiving her slight nod, he accepted the invitation. Max and Theodore returned to their group moments later.

The children's impatience was not lost on the adults, and so the families soon parted. Henry and Emily sent their children home with her parents so they could stay behind with Henry's family.

Henry spoke to his siblings, "I was thinking now might be a good time."

Theodore watched in confusion as looks passed between his children. "A good time for what?"

Agatha said, "To take a walk into town."

That confused Theodore even more. "Whatever for?" They knew as well as he, all the shops were closed on Sunday, especially being Christmas.

Henry said, "You'll see."

Theodore took his cue from Henry's mischievous tone. He suspected there was a gift for him involved, so he fell in step without further question. It was Christmas after all. Brianna sent Garrett and Eli back to the house so the baby could take a nap, then she and Agatha each took one of their father's arms as they followed Henry and Emily. James and Emmaline trailed behind.

Henry brought the group to a halt in front of the locked doors of Asa Tift's salvage warehouse. Much to Theodore's surprise, Henry produced a ring of keys and opened one of the double doors for them to enter. The amount of trust Mr. Tift placed in his son made his father's heart proud. Henry led the family deep into the shadowed interior to a large, shrouded object. He turned to face them, motioning to his siblings. Brianna, Agatha, James, and Emmaline stepped forward to flank him. Theodore waited in curious suspense to learn what all the fuss was about.

Henry said, "Poppa, this gift is from all of us. We hope it pleases you. As you can see it would hardly fit under the tree."

Whatever the object was, it was as tall and as wide as a man. Theodore looked from one face to the next of his children and saw their faces filled with expectation, hope, concern, and a touch of anxiety. The gift must be something extraordinary. They moved aside, creating a path for him to step forward and remove the covering. He gave a good pull on the oilcloth with both hands, allowing it to pool at his feet. Beneath it he uncovered the last thing he would have guessed – a new printing press. No wonder it was here at Tift's warehouse. He stared at it a moment trying to decide how he felt. Overwhelmed for sure, but also touched that they would give him back the chance at doing something he loved when that very thing had taken so much of his time from them, especially Henry. This gift was no small expense, either.

Brianna said, "Poppa?"

He blinked away the moisture in his eyes and turned to face them. "Thank you." It was all he could say. Anything more and he feared he would end up blubbering like a baby.

Agatha stepped forward. "We hoped if we took care of the press, you could afford to rebuild the shop. Plus, Kendrick has promised to send a supply of ink and paper when you are ready for your first run."

Theodore nodded. "There will still be many other expenses like furniture and typeset, but, yes, with this gift you have made it possible to reopen the print shop. Thank you. It is a very thoughtful and generous gift."

Emmaline said, "Do you really like it? Do you really want to reopen the shop?"

Theodore looked to his youngest. "Honestly, I have been considering it, but I wasn't sure until this moment." He turned his head towards the mass of wood and metal looming behind him. "Looking at this press brings to mind all the anticipation and pride of printing a good newspaper. I look forward to the day it gets put to good use. It is a wonderful gift. I am very blessed in my children."

Henry said, "We are blessed by our father."

Agatha said, "Enough sentimentality. We have guests coming. We should get back home."

Theodore grinned inwardly at his daughter's reminder of her namesake. Even after all these years, he still missed his Aunt Agatha and her meddlesome, contrary ways.

Emmaline trailed behind the rest of the family as they started out of the warehouse. She was thankful her father liked his gift. The strong sense of relief she felt made her realize how worried she had been that he might not appreciate their gesture.

Theodore felt his youngest's presence behind him. He paused to allow her to pass him and noticed her thoughtful expression. "What is it, sweetheart?"

"Just pausing a moment to be thankful."

"What are you thankful for?"

"Having the family together, for the joy of today and all that it means, but to be honest, I'm mostly thankful you liked your gift."

"Why wouldn't I?"

She bit her bottom lip, anxious about revealing her heart. "The way you have been the last two years, the anger you felt at losing the shop... I was worried you wouldn't want to rebuild it, that you wouldn't want to go back to being a newspaper man because you..." She ducked her head unable to finish.

He lifted her chin to meet his eyes and waited for her to continue.

"Because you missed Momma and blamed me."

"Blamed you for your mother? Of course not."

"No. Blamed me for losing the paper."

"The fire took the paper."

"Yes, but because of me you weren't there to fight the fire because I begged you to stay home."

Theodore's heart clenched in shame for all the ways he had failed his little girl when he had vowed to do better after being gone so much during the Florida War. He pulled her into his embrace, gently cupping the back of her head and holding it to his cheek. "Sweetheart, I never blamed you. You had every reason to ask for my attention. If anyone is to blame for anything, it is I for abandoning you."

Emmaline struggled to hold back her tears. Tears for the pain of lost closeness with her father these past two years, tears for relief of the guilt she had carried since May, and tears of joy to once again feel the tenderness and devotion of her father's love. She kept the tears in check with a willful determination of avoiding explanations to her siblings.

Theodore waited until Emmaline broke their embrace. He peered into her hazel eyes, just a little deeper green than his, and was relieved to see the haunted pain had been banished. "Shall we join the others?"

Not yet trusting her voice, Emmaline nodded.

Outside the warehouse, Henry and Emily parted from the family to join the rest of the Eatonton's. The rest of the family walked back to the house, arriving at the same time as Patrick and Smithy. Emmaline felt a thrill to see him. It didn't matter that they had parted less than an hour ago. To be with him again brought her joy.

Patrick pressed his hands against his coat pockets as he walked towards his love, reassuring himself the gifts were there. He really hoped by day's end he could bestow both of them upon her. It would depend upon her father's acceptance.

At the edge of the yard, Mr. Whitmore and his family greeted them as if they had not just left each other at the church. They were welcomed into the house with fanfare and led to the parlor where Theodore and James engaged them in conversation. Emmaline and Brianna went to the kitchen to gather refreshments.

Patrick broke away from the men when Emmaline entered the room carrying a cloth covered platter. She set it down on the side table and turned to him. Her movements stirred a hint of cinnamon in the air and his mouth watered.

Emmaline smiled timidly. "Hello." She didn't know what else to say.

He couldn't help but smile to receive a third greeting from her today. "Hello." He lowered his voice for her ears only. "You look beautiful."

Shyly Emmaline ducked her head. "Thank you." She looked up through her lashes. "I'm so glad you came."

"Not half as glad as I am that you invited me, uh, us." His hand moved to his pocket. "I have something for you."

"I have something for you as well, but we need to wait. We haven't exchanged family gifts yet, well, except for Poppa's." Her smile widened as her voice lifted in joy. "We took him to Tift's warehouse after church to show him his gift. He was pleased with it."

"Why was his gift at a warehouse?"

"It was too large and heavy to move here only to take it back to town for storage."

"You gave him a gift he has to store?"

"I never told you about it?"

"No."

She was surprised she hadn't mentioned it to him. "My brothers and sisters put in together to give him a new printing press."

Patrick felt a kick of excitement. The printing press may mean Mr. Whitmore would reopen his paper and just might give him a position as a staff writer. "I definitely would have remembered if you told me that. I am sure your gift pleased him. Your father did mention to me that he saw no point in rebuilding without a printing press."

Emmaline grinned with happiness, relieved to know her father truly did appreciate their gift. "When did he tell you that?"

"The day I brought the first article for him to read."

Garrett left the room to help Brianna bring in the coffee. They returned a moment later. The family gathered around the sideboard eager for the special treat that was to tide them over until the large meal to be in two hours' time. Patrick and his uncle hovered in the background, but Agatha and Emmaline insisted they come forward.

Mr. Whitmore offered a short prayer of thanksgiving for the food, fellowship, the gift of his wife Betsy and her legacy of children and memories, and most of all for the gift of a savior, Jesus Christ.

"Amen," echoed around the room.

Agatha took a bite of bread and a sip of coffee before she set them down on an end table and said, "It's time for gifts."

Her pronouncement garnered smiles and laughter from her family. Emmaline came to sit on the sofa next to Patrick, just as he hoped when he chose his seat. She leaned a little closer as she said, "Agatha is always impatient when it comes to gifts."

Agatha approached with a gift in hand in time to overhear her. "You, sister dear, are just as impatient. The difference is you have the manners to restrain yourself and I don't." She placed the gift on Emmaline's lap.

Brianna said to Agatha, "You have the manners, you just choose not to use them."

Emmaline gave Patrick a shrug as if to say this conversation was a common one.

Agatha had yet to move away. With excitement in her voice she said, "Go on, Emmaline. Open it."

The gift felt like a rectangle box. It completely covered her lap. She pulled the ends of the ribbon and, with Patrick's help, unwrapped the brown paper to reveal a wooden box. She turned it so the catch faced her and opened it. Inside she recognized the Brewster stereoscope from a magazine advertisement. Beside it was a number of stereo cards. She looked up at her sister with awestruck wonder. "This is amazing. How did you know I wanted to see one? I didn't mention it in my letters. Or did I?"

"No. It just seemed like something that would catch your fancy."

Patrick helped hold the viewing box while she inserted the first card with a double photograph of Battery Park in New York. She lifted the box, placing the lenses to her eyes. She wasn't sure what she expected to see but the dimensional image took her by surprise. It was if she was standing in front of the building, except of course for the lack of color, but still, it was amazingly real looking. She passed the box to Patrick as the others in the room gathered around to take a turn.

While the family was distracted by the stereoscope, Patrick rose to retrieve one of his gifts from his coat hanging in the foyer. When he returned, Emmaline was waiting for him in the parlor doorway holding a large, awkwardly wrapped package in both hands. He took it from her expecting it to have some weight, but it was surprisingly light. In exchange, he handed her a smartly wrapped flat square package. He waited for her to open hers first.

Emmaline admired the bleached paper packaging tied with a pretty green silk ribbon. It was the fanciest wrapped gift she had every received. Patrick must have paid extra for the store clerk to wrap the gift. It touched her that he would spend the extra amount to please her. Slowly, she undid the wrappings, prolonging the anticipation. Inside was a card paper box. She removed the lid to find a handkerchief of the finest cotton with bobbin lace and pink embroidered roses. She lifted it from the box, which she placed aside, to feel its delicate textures.

Her shining eyes lifted to Patrick's. "It is exquisitely beautiful. Thank you."

"It was the best one I could find in the mercantile."

"You didn't have to spend so much. It's so fine, I'll save it for Sundays and special occasions."

"Nonsense. You shouldn't save it. You should carry it every day." Her doubtful look made him add, "I insist."

"We shall see." She gave a nod towards his gift. "Now you. Open yours."

Patrick shifted the box to one arm so he could remove the wrapping.

"Here, let me help you." Emmaline tucked her new handkerchief in her dress pocket and helped him remove the leftover yarn she used for string and the sack paper. They were careful not to tear such a large piece so it could be reused.

Patrick held the hat box before him in awestruck wonder. Unless she had used the box for something else, and why would she when it was clearly brand new, it contained a hat. Not just any hat, but a top hat. A coveted top hat. How had she known? His eyes met hers and his smile burst from the excitement he was holding back. With shaky fingers he undid the strap closure and opened the box to reveal a sleek beaver skin top hat with a black silk band. He lifted it from the box, which he set on the floor. He turned the hat round and round in his hands admiring the sheen and the crisp, perfectly formed rim. He wanted to try it, but it was impolite to wear a hat inside.

Emmaline didn't have to ask, she could see the look of adoration in his eyes. She hadn't been wrong. A top hat was his heart's desire, at least one of them.

It occurred to Patrick that Emmaline bent a rule of propriety by giving him the hat. Why would she risk censure unless she really cared for him as much as he cared for her? "Emmaline?"

"Yes?"

James appeared from behind her. "What do you have there, Patrick? Egads! What a nice hat. Emmie Grace, did you give that to him?" He put his hands on his hips. "Where's mine?"

Emmaline playfully nudged his arm. "You would never wear something so fine."

"I might, if you gave me one."

"Well I didn't, so we'll never know, will we?"

"I suppose not. Try it on, Patrick. Let's see how you look."

Patrick needed no further encouragement. He flipped the hat onto his head. He straightened it, and then tipped it to the slightest angle. He returned to the foyer to see how it looked in the looking glass. As he studied his image, Emmaline's appeared behind him. "What do you think?"

"It suits you. You look like a man of the world."

How did she know that is what he wanted; to be a man of importance, of commerce, instead of a laborer? He turned to her and removed the hat. She was close enough to the mistletoe he would have claimed a kiss if not for their growing audience. Her brother and two sisters were watching from the parlor doorway.

"Thank you, Emmaline. I will treasure it always."

"As I will my handkerchief."

She said it in earnest and meant it with her heart. The generosity of her gift made him consider giving her the necklace before speaking with her father. If he refused him, he would not be able to give it to her afterwards. Respect for her father restrained him. Instead, he gestured with his hand for her to proceed him back to the parlor.

They returned to the sofa and watched the other family members open their gifts. Smithy was startled when Emmaline placed a gift in his hands. "It is from all of us to you. We are thankful to have spent more time getting to know you in recent weeks."

"You shouldn't have done anything. There was no cause to give me a gift."

"You are a guest in this house and we had a feeling you might be here while the family exchanged gifts. We didn't want you to feel left out, so my sisters and I all had a hand in making you a gift."

His gaze passed from one lady to the next. "You made something for me." He was touched by the thoughtful gesture. It had been decades since he had received a gift from anyone. Smithy undid the wrapping to find a tobacco bag as fine as any he had ever laid eyes on. He had to clear the emotion from his throat before he could speak. "Thank you." It was the most sincere gratitude he had felt in a very, very long time.

Emmaline could see the deep well of emotion he was trying to hide. "You're welcome." She gave him a smile and returned to the sofa.

Patrick leaned closer to whisper, "I've never seen him like that." He turned his head to catch her gaze. "You are a very special lady, Emmaline."

He was enjoying spending the holiday with her and her family. His only disappointment was he had not found time to speak with her father and so the necklace was still in his pocket. The rest of the family carried on light conversation punctuated with laughter. His uncle seemed to be enjoying himself too. He and Mr. Whitmore got along well, being of similar temperaments.

Shortly after the clock struck half past twelve, the Eatonton family arrived. A plethora of coats, hats, and gloves were dispensed with in the foyer before the Eatonton family joined the others in the parlor to await the call for dinner. As the gathering swelled, Patrick sighed with resignation. There would be no chance to speak privately anytime soon. He could only hope that later he could seek a moment of Mr. Whitmore's time. Meanwhile, he lingered beside Emmaline, content to share in her enjoyment of the festivities.

Another knock sounded at the door, surprising everyone in the room except Max and Theodore who went to answer it. None were surprised more so than Thorn to discover the latest arrivals were Commander Kent and his daughter Annabelle.

Thorn started to approach them but checked himself. He didn't want to appear too forward in his attentions towards Annabelle. Christoff had no such compunctions. He was first to greet her father upon entering the parlor.

Greetings turned into conversations that ebbed and flowed about the room with so many gathered; eighteen adults in all plus the six children. The parlor normally felt spacious but between all the guests and the Christmas tree it was uncomfortably crowded. Emmaline was glad she had devised a scheme that was sure to please everyone. Her maid, Jane, gave her a nod from the doorway that all was ready in the yard. Emmaline gave a nod to Ella who promptly gathered her siblings and led them from the room.

Emily asked, "Where are the children going?"

Emmaline smiled. "Outside. Ella and I arranged for the children to have a picnic with the help of my maid who had no family to share Christmas."

"How thoughtful. I know they will enjoy themselves."

"And not be underfoot."

Once the food was taken to the dining room, Mrs. Faraday and her daughter who came to help left to spend the rest of the day with their family, taking with them enough extra servings of the meal to feed them as a bonus for the sacrifice of their time during the holiday. Emmaline checked the final details and then alerted her father it was time.

Theodore rose from his seat. "James, will you bring the two bottles of wine on the sideboard, please?" As his son turned to do his bidding, he addressed the room. "Our dinner is ready. Shall we adjourn to the dining room?"

Emmaline led them into the room. "We will not stand on ceremony today. Please, sit where you like."

The table was fully extended to seat twenty. It was set with linen, her mother's fine china, gleaming silverware, two multi-tiered candelabras, and adorned in the center with mingled branches of holly and pine. It was also laden with dish after dish of their favorite holiday fare starting with a platter of carved turkey at either end of the table so as to be easy to pass. There was a steaming bowl of mashed potatoes and beside it a savory gravy made from the meat drippings. A bowl of green beans tossed in fresh butter, a basket of yeast rolls, a platter of roasted fish, and another of baked sweet potatoes rounded out the main meal. The sideboard held a dish of sweetmeats along with the pecan pie and cookies for later. The enticing aromas made Emmaline's mouth water in anticipation.

Theodore seated Emmaline at her usual place at the foot of the table and went to stand behind his chair at the other end. He gestured for Commander Kent to take the chair to his right. He seated his daughter next to him. Christoff eagerly took the seat on her right. Max sat across from the Commander to give aid in holding the conversation. Since his brother took the seat he wanted, Thorn followed his father so he could sit across from Annabelle. Brianna was quick to notice their honored guest was surrounded by men, so she led the way for Garrett to sit her next to Thorn, giving Annabelle feminine company. Nate sat next to Christoff, then it was Agatha, Emily, Henry, and finally Patrick on Emmaline's left. She asked Smithy to sit on her right hoping to make him feel more comfortable in the crowd. Abby, Jacob, and James took the remaining seats between Smithy and Garrett.

Theodore said, "Please join hands and let us pray." When the circle was complete, he said, "Our heavenly father, we thank you for the gift of your Son and the everlasting life he assured for us. May we never take it for granted. We thank you for these family and friends with whom we share this celebration and for the abundance of good food to nourish us. May our hearts always be mindful of your blessings and the needs of others. Amen."

"Amen," echoed from the others.

The passing of dishes and filling of plates set the informal tone, allowing for conversation to flow across the table as well as to one's neighbors. The food and company were enjoyable, but Patrick was anxious for it to end, and so time seemed to move slowly. Emmaline warned him there would be a competitive game of charades after the meal, which would further delay his mission.

Emmaline leaned a little sideways to whisper, "Is something wrong, Patrick?"

He gave her a reassuring smile. "No, not at all." He made a point to participate more in the conversation.

Henry said to Patrick in an aside, "You seem tense. Does that mean you are contemplating asking a very serious question?"

Patrick looked at Emmaline's brother in dismay. "Is it so obvious?"

"Yes."

"Do you object?"

Henry gave him an assessing look before answering. He liked Patrick and he was good for Emmaline. He had never seen his sister as happy as she had been these last few weeks. "No."

"Will your father approve?"

"That's hard to say." Henry's gaze went to his father at the other end of the table. His spirits were lighter, but did that mean he was ready to let Emmaline go?

"He rightfully has concerns about my ability to provide for her."

"It was the same for me in courting Emily. I had to prove myself to her father."

Emmaline frowned to see the serious concern on Patrick's face. "What are you two discussing?"

Henry captured Emmaline's gaze. "I'm just getting to know your Patrick better."

She opened her mouth to deny he was 'her Patrick' but then thought better of it. It was Henry's way of avoiding answering her. She decided it might be best to let the question go unanswered. At least Henry and Patrick seemed to be getting along. Her brother's approval was important to her.

Henry said to Patrick, "Poppa showed me your article. It was great. You made what I do sound like something special. Heck, you made me seem larger than life."

Patrick grinned. "Maybe you are."

Emmaline laughed. "Don't go giving him airs. He'll start lording it over us."

Patrick was taken with her laughter. It was the first time he heard it. He dearly wanted to bring it forth again but couldn't think of anything clever to say.

When Emmaline saw that all at the table were finished eating, she rose from her seat, signaling the end of the meal. The men all promptly rose as well and helped the ladies with their chairs.

Theodore said, "Gentlemen, will you join me in the study for a cigar and brandy?"

The Commander said, "Certainly, but I do hope you have some scotch as well." His jovial tone took any possible insult out of his words.

Theodore replied in similar fashion. "I believe we can find a dusty bottle around somewhere." Max, Smithy, Garrett, Nate, Jacob, and James followed them. Patrick was the last man to leave the room. His eyes searched Emmaline's as he whispered, "Must we be parted?"

She gave him a gentle smile. "It is only for a little while so that we ladies may clear the meal since the servants have the day off. It's..."

"Part of the tradition." He finished saying it with her. "Alright then."

Emmaline caught Abby's eye and gave a nod towards Annabelle, prompting Abby to say, "Miss Kent shall we adjourn to the parlor?"

Emmaline said, "Emily, you should join them. We sisters can take care of this."

"Nonsense, four is better than three."

They made quick work of scraping and stacking the dishes and then carrying them out to the kitchen. In no time at all they joined the other two in the parlor. Emmaline carried a tray with two steaming tea kettles to add to the rest of the tea service waiting on the sideboard.

In the study, the men were being entertained with Commander Kent's exploits during his long career in the navy. He held the rapt attention of Max and his sons, as well as some common ground with Theodore's experiences during the Seminole War.

Smithy and Patrick stood together in a corner. He leaned close to whisper to his nephew while keeping his eyes focused on the main conversation. "You haven't spoken with him yet, have you?"

Patrick's brows knitted.

Smithy said, "Mr. Whitmore. You haven't told him how you feel about his daughter."

"I haven't had a chance."

"You find one, boy, and don't lose your nerve when you do. Girls like her only come around once in a lifetime. Well I know it."

It was the second time his uncle had hinted at a lost love. He wanted to ask what happened to her, but now was hardly the time and place for confessions of the heart.

Smithy said in a faraway voice, "I waited too long to speak for her, and I lost my chance. She married another."

Patrick's anxiety increased. He wanted things settled between him and Emmaline. The sooner, the better. He could only hope to find a moment of Mr. Whitmore's time after the Eatontons departed.

The ladies were soon heard returning to the parlor. When the cigars were finished, Theodore gestured for the Commander to proceed him from the room.

Smithy told his nephew, "Stay here." He then moved sprightly from Patrick's side to intercept Theodore. A look and a nod in Patrick's direction and Emmaline's father held back from leaving the room. In seconds, Patrick had the private moment he had been waiting for, but the unexpectedness of it rendered him speechless.

Theodore faced the young man and waited. It was something he was good at, had in fact perfected it during his career as a journalist, and he wielded it now. He was pretty sure what Patrick's intentions were. He was not going to ease him by starting the conversation. If the lad wanted his daughter's hand, he was darn well going to have to summon the nerve on his own to ask for it. But Theodore's patience was only going to last for so long.

Patrick took a step forward. His eyes met Mr. Whitmore's and in them, while expecting censure, he somehow found strength. "Mr. Whitmore, you told me before I had to find purpose, and I believe I have. I realize that purpose has yet to produce a living, but you have been encouraging in the belief that it could. Now that you have a printing press and can rebuild, that means seems even more likely, if I am not presuming too much."

Theodore's chest eased. He was asking for a job, not for his daughter. Or not yet, at least. "I see a lot of potential in you and passion for the story. If you are willing to help me rebuild, and I mean do the hard labor of building, not just gathering subscriptions and putting out a paper, then perhaps it could lead to a partnership, provided your writing continues to improve."

Patrick eagerly took another step forward. "Sir, yes, sir. That is a very generous offer and more than I expected, sir."

"We shall see how it works out. We can settle the details later."

"Thank you, sir."

"Hmm." Theodore turned towards the door.

Panic bloomed in Patrick's chest. "Sir? If I may have another moment of your time?"

Instantly, Theodore's chest tightened. He turned back to the young man.

Patrick's words were rushed. "Sir, I..." He swallowed around the knot in his throat and tried again. "Sir, may I have your permission to court Emmaline?"

Chapter 14

The words echoed in Theodore's head. *Sir, may I have your permission to court Emmaline?*

Theodore was relieved Patrick wasn't asking to marry his youngest daughter, at least not yet, but it was coming one day soon. He gave the young man a shrewd look. "Haven't you been courting her?"

"No. I wouldn't say so. I have been getting to know her, and in these last few weeks, I have grown quite fond of her. If truth be told, I am in love with her and wish to marry her, but I felt it was too soon to ask for her hand considering my circumstances. Besides, I don't know if she feels the same, so I am asking permission to formally court her, to openly woo her."

Theodore could find no fault with Patrick's request. His selfish fatherly desire was to turn him down out of hand. He put himself in Patrick's shoes and allowed himself to remember how he felt before he proposed to Henry's mother, his first wife, Margaret and to Betsafina; those anxious, tumultuous, feverish feelings that were so hard to contain. He saw them now in Patrick's eyes. This man cared deeply for his daughter and wasn't that what every father wanted in a son-in-law? As much as he wanted to keep Emmaline to himself, he knew the time was coming he would have to let her go. At least it wasn't today. He gave Patrick a nod.

After long, arduous moments of silence, the nod caught Patrick by surprise. "Yes?"

"Yes."

The rush of excitement had Patrick running for the door before his manners made him pause and turn.

Theodore said, "Go on." He smiled to himself as he watched Patrick disappear.

Emmaline's gaze was drawn to the door at Patrick's appearance. She had been anxiously awaiting the return of the men and when they appeared without Patrick and her father, her anxiety increased. She excused herself from the conversation with Annabelle and Emily to intercept him before he got too far into the room. His joyful smile took her by surprise and erased her trepidation.

Patrick said, "Is there somewhere we can talk?"

Emmaline's eyes left his at her father's appearance behind him.

Theodore said, "Emmaline, have you shown Patrick the view from the cupola?"

She shook her head, puzzled that her father was suggesting something that would give her and Patrick a private moment. Surely not. Was she expected to invite others to join them? "No, I haven't."

"You should do so. I'll send Agatha along as chaperone."

Emmaline's jaw dropped. She watched her father cross the room to speak privately with her sister who then headed their way. She turned back to Patrick. What in the world had he and her father spoken of in the privacy of the study? The answer set loose a wave of butterflies in her midsection. She placed a hand against it to steady herself. Was she about to be betrothed?

Patrick held his hand towards the parlor doorway. "Will you lead the way?"

Emmaline silently led the three of them up the two flights of stairs. Patrick took the lead at the attic stairs and undid the hatch opening. He stepped out into the sunny December afternoon and felt the salty wind ruffle his hair. He breathed deeply of the pleasurable smell of the nearby ocean. It smelled cleaner on this western side of the island than it did at his uncle's shop, which stood closer to the north-east shore. He turned to offer his hand to Emmaline and then to Agatha as they moved from the stairs, over the hatch threshold, and onto the decking beneath the cupola. It amazed him how they could do so gracefully with their billowy skirts. Together the three of them admired the view as they explored the walkway following the ridgeline on either side of the cupola. The children's laughter rose from the yard below.

Patrick was trying to decide how to break away from Agatha when she suddenly gave him a wink and moved off to the other side, leaving a good ten yards between them.

Emmaline smiled, "Finally, a moment alone."

"You wanted that too?"

"Of course. I mean, I love my family and I enjoy being with them, and even the Eatonton's, but I have to admit I have been longing for a moment alone with you."

Softly he said, "Me too."

She wanted to ask what he and her father discussed, but she was also nervous of the answer. She couldn't think of anything else to say. Her mind refused to think beyond what he may be about to ask her.

Patrick reached into his pocket for the small gift-wrapped box he retrieved from his coat before meeting her in the parlor. "Emmaline."

She saw he had something in his hand, and her heart stopped. She didn't know how she would answer him. She cared for him deeply, but did she love him enough to pledge her life to him? Did she know him well enough for that? If her father gave his permission for him to ask, could she put her trust in his opinion?

"I have another gift for you but I felt I had to ask your father for permission before I gave it to you." Patrick held out his hand to her with the box upon his palm.

Emmaline's eyes met his. The deep sincerity within them should have calmed her but still her hand shook as she lifted the small package from his hand.

At her continued hesitation, he said, "I meant to only give you the handkerchiefs but when I saw this, I felt as though it belonged to you and no other." He really shouldn't have spent the money. Saving it to buy a ring later would have been more prudent, but the stone spoke to him.

Emmaline undid the bow and removed the red silk ribbon, handing it to Patrick. The red felt covered box was not wrapped, it simply waited for her to gather the courage to open it. Slowly she lifted the top off. Inside, nestled in a layer of cotton, lay a pendant. It was a beautiful green cabochon shaped gem nestled in a gold setting with two gold beads in line beneath it, the final one slightly smaller than the one above. It was not an engagement ring as she feared. Quixotically, while relieved, she also felt strangely let down. Or did he mean for the necklace to be an engagement gift? Some men did not give rings.

Patrick felt the need to fill her silence. He hoped it was not an indication of her displeasure. "The green of the stone with its hint of brown is the very shade of your eyes. That is why I felt it belonged to you. The jeweler told me the stone is a tourmaline mined in Paris, Maine."

Emmaline lifted her eyes to his. "Patrick, what did you ask my father?"

"For permission to court you."

"Oh." Court, not marry. "So if I accept this, than we will be officially courting?"

"Yes. I mean, no. The necklace is a gift with no expectations attached. I asked your father for permission to court you, so it would be appropriate for me to give it to you." He paused for courage because the next part was so very important to his happiness. "Whether or not we are officially courting is entirely up to you. I know how I feel about you. I haven't so much as looked at another since the moment we bumped into each other." He wanted to take her hands, but they still held the necklace and box. "Emmaline, I am in love with you. I want to marry you one day when I can support you as you deserve. Until then, my greatest desire is that you care for me enough to allow me to court you."

He loves me!

He wants to marry me!

Her fears of a moment ago vanished. Somehow in the moments since she took the box from him, her feelings for him had solidified from a vague notion of maybe falling in love to the solid surety there would never be another man for her. Brianna's words came to mind. She said when you're in love, his world becomes your world, you would do anything to make him happy, and you would never want to part from him. With an undeniable strength, she felt all that now and more. Patrick was her one true love, her husband to be, her soulmate. There would be no other.

His dear brown eyes held hers both hopeful and worried. She had the power to ease him and now she wanted nothing more than to do just that. "I love you." She felt the truth in the words and had to say them again, infusing them with the depth of her emotions, so he would believe them too. "I love you, with all my heart."

Patrick's head doubted her first declaration, but his heart felt its equal in her second affirmation. Joy winged in his breast.

She loves me!

It felt as natural as a sunrise to lean down and kiss her, sealing their declarations of devotion.

Agatha gave them a moment before clearing her throat. "Ahem."

Reluctantly, Patrick pulled away from Emmaline's sweet lips to give Agatha a sheepish grin. He turned his attention back to Emmaline and lifted the pendant from its box. He stepped behind her and lifted the necklace over her head.

Emmaline touched the cabochon as it settled against her dress in the vee of her bosom. She felt the warmth of his hand brush against her nape as he secured the clasp. The small intimacy was every bit as potent as his kiss and she wanted more of both. She was beginning to suspect that a lifetime of them would not be enough.

Patrick moved around to stand before her. It was just as he suspected. The gem was a perfect match for her eyes.

Emmaline turned towards Agatha. "What do you think?"

"It suits you."

Patrick said, "Shall we show your father?"

Emmaline looked to him. "Must we return to the others? It's so peaceful up here."

Patrick lightly laughed in agreement. "Yes, I think we must."

Emmaline knew he was right.

The rest of the Eatonton visit was a blur of conversation, charades, and too much wine. It was a relief to all the guests to step into the cool evening breeze for the return home. The Commander and Annabelle left in their borrowed carriage. Smithy said his goodbyes and headed straight home, claiming too much excitement in one day for his old bones. Patrick stayed awhile longer, refusing to be parted from Emmaline any earlier than necessary. He stayed for a quiet evening of conversation and a light supper, after which Emmaline walked him to the door as she did the night before, well aware of the mistletoe.

Patrick smoothed a stray lock of hair from her temple. "Merry Christmas, darling."

Emmaline raised a hand to cover her pendant and her racing heart. "Merry Christmas, Patrick."

Patrick too was well aware of the greenery hanging above Emmaline's head. He kept a wary eye on the parlor doorway, hoping they would be granted a few moment's alone to say good night. He bent his head to hers and kissed his future wife with cherished tenderness. He looked forward to a lifetime of Christmases spent with her.

Theodore stepped into the hall fully expecting to see Emmaline in Patrick's arms and yet totally unprepared for it. He cleared his throat as he approached. They guiltily stepped apart.

Emmaline was quick to come to Patrick's defense with a pointed look above her head. "Mistletoe."

"Indeed. I can see I'm going to have to keep my eye on you two."

"It was Agatha's doing."

"And that doesn't surprise me either." He looked gravely at Patrick. "Shall we meet tomorrow morning to discuss our project in detail or would you prefer to wait until the New Year?"

"Tomorrow is more than fine with me, sir."

Theodore held out his hand to Patrick. "Good night."

"Good night, sir. Good night, Emmaline." Patrick stuffed his old cap in the pocket of his linen coat and picked up his new top hat, stepped out onto the porch, and proudly placed it on his head. He tipped it to Emmaline. "Merry Christmas."

Emmaline couldn't help her proud smile for her well-chosen gift. "Merry Christmas." She stepped to the open door and watched his retreating back for a moment before shutting it. She turned to face her father. He didn't move to allow her to pass. Instead, he picked up the pendent from her chest.

"He has good taste in jewelry, if not the good sense to hold onto his money."

"But you approve of him, Poppa?"

"I do, simply because he makes you happy, but that doesn't mean I'm ready to see you married."

"I'm not ready to be married."

"I have a feeling you will be when the time comes that he asks."

"You think he will?"

"I know he will."

His assurance brought an uncontrolled satisfied smile to her face. Even though Patrick said he wanted to marry her, it was comforting to have her father believe in his intentions. Emmaline studied her father's face. The deep etching in his brow was gone and there was a light in his eyes she hadn't seen since her mother was alive. "Did you have a good Christmas?"

Theodore solemnly nodded. "I did thanks to you." Because she brought the family together, his heart was healing, his spirits were lifted, and he was looking forward to the future with purpose. He still ached for Betsy, but his grief no longer had the power to keep him from living.

"It wasn't just me."

"No, but without your instigation, it wouldn't have been the same." A thought occurred to him. "I have to admit, it is Patrick's desire to write as much as the printing press that has rekindled my desire to print the newspaper."

"That is a good thing."

"Yes, it is. To have purpose and a loving family is a very good thing."

Patrick walked home under the starry night sky with the barest sliver of a waxing moon. Joy filled his heart. A month ago he left home uncertain of his future. Tonight, he felt blessed to know what he wanted from life, who he wanted to spend it with, and to know she loved him too. What more could a man ask for?

The End

Become a Key Friend

You can sign up to receive email updates on upcoming books, contests, sneak peaks, promotions, and more.

Visit www.susanblackmonauthor.com for more details

Check out the 'Behind the Scenes' page for more details, photos, history, resource lists, character lists of who is real and who's not, and many other behind the scenes extras.

See my Pinterest boards for images of people, places, and things that have inspired the writing of each book.
www.pinterest.com/susanblackmonauthor

I hope you enjoyed reading

Once Upon an Island Christmas

Please consider posting an honest review on

Amazon and/or Goodreads

Your recommendation is the highest compliment.

Read on to catch a sneak peek of

Divided Love

The next installment of the Key West series

Divided Love

Sunday, November 18th, 1860

A clear and starry night encompassed the island of Key West as twenty-three year old Nathanial Eatonton rested his forearms on the black iron railing of the lighthouse gallery. He watched the waxing quarter moon set behind the partially built brick fort rising from the water nearly a thousand feet from the shore. Some wondered if the fort would ever be finished. The Corp of Engineers had been working on it for fifteen years. Fourteen, if one discounted the first year's progress swept clean by the hurricane of 1846. With all the talk of war and secession, Nate wouldn't be surprised to see the pace of work increase soon. Beyond the fort, he could barely discern the moving sails of passing ships keeping distant from the light he tended. It made him feel good to be doing something to keep them safe. It also made the ache in his arm from cleaning the glass a worthy sacrifice.

A cool ocean breeze wafted across the tops of the trees and ruffled his blond curls. He impatiently brushed his hair from his eyes. He needed a haircut. Nate breathed deeply of the refreshing salty air as he walked around the gallery, overlooking the trees and roof tops of the island settlement. He was enjoying being the temporary assistant light keeper. He wouldn't mind having the job permanently. He relished the quiet solitude while the rest of the islanders peacefully slept.

The sudden rise of squawking birds taking flight in what was otherwise a peaceful night drew Nate's attention to the vicinity of the army barracks on the north shore. What could have startled so many of them? He listened intently for any clues. The island had no large predators. Years ago it could have been Indians or pirates, but the pirates were long gone, and the Indians subdued. It was nearing midnight. What sort of nefarious man could it be now?

As the birds settled back down, Nate could discern the faint cadence of men marching and the hushed call of orders.

Why would the army be on a midnight march?

As far as Nate was aware, they had never drilled at night, and they hadn't patrolled the city streets since before he was born, during the Second Seminole War some thirty years ago. Normally, around the barracks and fort construction camp, nighttime guard duty was almost nil. The most the town ever saw of the uniformed men was an occasional dress parade on the grounds of the barracks. What was different tonight?

Curiosity pulled at him to investigate. The lighthouse wouldn't need tending again for a few hours. Nate rapidly descended the spiral stairs of the brick tower. If he could find his brother, Thorn, an army sergeant, perhaps he could satisfy his curiosity.

Nate was relatively sure the patrol would follow Southard Street at least as far as Duval Street, so he planned to cut across lots to intercept them. With the moon having already set for the night, it was difficult to see where he was going. He made his way by following the dark outlines of well-known landmarks, occasionally tripping over roots and stumbling in holes. He didn't let it deter him. He was enjoying the challenge. It had been a long time since the days when he and his brothers would sneak out after dark on some imagined adventure.

He pushed aside the large fans of a Thatch Palm and stepped out onto the smooth limestone of Simonton Street. He followed it to Southard but instinct made him check the route from the barracks before rounding the corner of a fenced yard. No more than a block away, the patrol moved towards him carrying bedimmed lanterns. Suddenly realizing it may not be prudent to be caught by the patrol, Nate moved into the concealing darkness of a locustberry bush. He didn't want to be questioned. His purpose was to question his brother. He watched as the men approached. He knew from Thorn, about forty men were assigned to the barracks. He judged the patrol to be made up of only about half that many.

The men marched past wholly unaware of his presence. In the meager light reflected upon his face from the lantern he carried, Nate recognized Thorn's superior, Captain Brannan, leading the troop. There was another junior officer walking beside the small regiment but it wasn't his brother. After they passed, Nate continued watching their progress. They didn't turn towards town but continued straight. Their obvious destination was the fort camp. It brought to mind his earlier thought about the pace of work increasing. Maybe Captain Brannan was bringing these men to start early in the morning. It seemed odd, but what other reason was there for their transition? A new supply of bricks did arrive yesterday. It would only stand to reason to put as many men to work as were available. But why move the men late at night?

When the patrol was out of sight, Nate walked in the opposite direction leading to the barracks. He had no qualms about standing outside of the junior officers' sleeping quarters and whistling for his brother's attention.

* * *

Sergeant Hawthorne Eatonton stood rigidly straight in his uniform observing the night patrol from the veranda of the officers' quarters. The guards were nothing more than moving silhouettes under the dark sky. Normally, he would enjoy star gazing on such a night, but tonight was no ordinary night. A half-hour ago Captain Brannan put him in charge of the barracks before leaving with half the men headed to the fort. His last order was to double the night watch as a precaution. It was likely unnecessary. They didn't expect any resistance, at least not right away, but Thorn had a feeling from this night forward nothing would be normal again.

One of the guards called out, "Halt! Who goes there?"

Thorn peered intently into the darkness in the direction of the call. His hand reflexively went to the hilt of his sidearm. Had he been lax in thinking there would not be trouble tonight? Was there even now a resistance gathering in the darkness? There was no time to signal an alert to the men in the enlisted barracks. He hurried down the wide steps and across the open field of the parade ground to reach the guard now speaking in normal tones. He was still too distant to hear what was being said. He arrived at the edge of the grounds to find it was a single intruder. He slowed his pace to a more dignified walk and approached the guard who looked relieved to see him. He understood why when he saw the other man's face.

"What are you doing here?" Nate was the last person Thorn expected to see.

"I came to see you."

"At this time of night?" He was doubtful but then a troubling thought occurred. "Is something wrong?"

"Not with me, but I came to ask you the same thing."

Thorn turned to the soldier intently listening to them. "Carry on, Private Bass." He gestured for his brother to follow him.

Nate said, "Sorry about that. I was trying to slip past the guards. I didn't expect the second patrol. What is going on to cause such high alert?"

Thorn stopped and turned to frown at his brother. "How can you not be aware?"

"Aware of what?"

"Of the election and its consequences."

Nate dismissed his brother's concern. "Of course I heard about the election. What has that to do with midnight marches and extra patrols?"

Thorn loved his younger brother but his blithe attitude could be exasperating. "It means all the talk of succession is very likely to soon become action. The south will never accept Abraham Lincoln. Trouble is coming and Captain Brannan means to be ready."

"You think there is going to be fighting here? On this island?"

"It's possible."

"Why? We're not important."

"We have something of value. The fort will control the harbor. Control of the harbor controls shipping and controls access to the Gulf of Mexico which controls supplies to the south. Captain Brannan means to keep that control in the hands of the government. It will not fall to any Rebels under his watch."

"You sound as though you admire the man."

Thorn resumed walking. "I do."

"But surely you don't expect anyone on this island to challenge you?"

"We don't know what to expect. It is only prudent to be prepared."

Nate looked over at his brother's profile. Thorn's nature had always been serious but the rigid line of his jaw and stiff posture now made him appear neigh unapproachable.

Thorn said, "Go home, Nate. You have no place being here."

Nate mockingly teased him with a salute. "Well, sir, yes sir." They had reached the street entrance to the barracks grounds. Nate nodded to the guards as he passed. He turned to bid good-night to Thorn, but his brother had already turned away. Nate turned again and made his way back to the lighthouse.

When the news of the presidential election arrived with the mail steamer from Charleston, Nate didn't give it much thought. Politics tended to bore him and what real difference was one candidate over another anyway. It seemed to him Congress had the power. But, in general, much of what happened on the mainland had little to do with him. He was content to earn his living, tease the ladies, and go about his life with little concern for the world at large. He couldn't do anything about it, so why worry about it. Thorn, on the other hand, seemed to thrive upon taking up the weight of the world upon his shoulders.

Barbara Mabrity, the seventy-eight year old light keeper, met him at the top of the lighthouse steps. "Where did you go?"

"To see my brother."

"Did you find out what all the commotion was about? Seems to be quite a fuss going on over at the fort."

"Captain Brannan took half his men from the barracks to the fort. Seems he means to secure it for the Union."

Mrs. Mabrity's mouth puckered. "Is that a fact?"

"Yes, ma'am. What are you doing up here? Did something happen while I was gone?"

"I couldn't sleep so I came up here. I was surprised to find you gone, but no, nothing was wrong. I have to say, I knew the news of the disappointing election was going to spark some tempers, but I didn't expect to see a line drawn in the sand so soon."

Nate grimaced. "I didn't expect it all."

"Well, nothing to be done about I suppose but to grin and abide it."

"Do you think the southern states will cede from the Union?"

She said, "Time will tell the tale." But her eyes revealed a look of resigned acceptance of the inevitable.

Mrs. Mabrity soon returned to the house leaving Nate alone with his thoughts. He didn't dwell on the nation's worries. Watching the wind dancing in the trees and studying the constellations were enough to occupy him. He wished he could keep the job of tending the light, but it belonged to Mrs. Mabrity's grandson, Robert Fletcher. He was on leave to visit his family in Miami. Barbara Mabrity was to travel with him, leaving Nate fully in charge of the light. Unfortunately, she was feeling poorly when their departure day arrived. She chose to stay behind declaring the travel to be too much for her tired old bones. Nate considered it nothing short of amazing that nearing her eightieth year, she still held the position of light keeper. He only hoped he was as spry when he reached her age and that he should live so long.

For the first time in his young life, he truly enjoyed the work he was doing. Not that he minded sponge fishing with his brother-in-law, Henry, but spending weeks at a time on a boat far from shore was not what he wanted to do for the rest of his life. Unlike his eldest brother, Christoff, he did not inherit his family's love of the sea. His father was a fisherman, wrecker, and merchant captain over the course of his life and even now at fifty-nine he was a harbor pilot so he could still sail daily while appeasing his wife by keeping close to home. Christoff captained one of the fleet of ships encompassing the merchant business began by Nate's maternal grandfather and which his father inherited through marriage. The fleet transported a large variety of goods among many ports around the world but most important was the Southern cotton and specifically the cotton from their great uncle's plantation in

Montgomery.

How would the coming conflict affect their trade? Darn, he didn't want to think about it, but there seemed to be no avoiding how much the possibility of war could affect their lives.

* * *

The sun rose on Monday morning bringing with it a cloudy sky and a blustery wind. Nate finished the last of his chores and bid good-day to Mrs. Mabrity. He was headed home for a healthy plate of flapjacks before going to bed. Passing by the side yard of the St. Paul rectory he came across Constance Jamison on her way to the market with fresh baked bread to sell. He was introduced to her a few weeks ago at a church social, having just moved to Key West to care for her aging, eccentric aunt. He was happy to find Miss Jamison alone and headed in the same direction. He hoped it would give him a chance to get to know her better. It had been awhile since anyone new came to live on the island, especially not so close to his age. He was intrigued by her.

Nate tipped his hat to the petite blond. "Hello, Miss Jamison."

She gave a nod of acknowledgement as she continued walking but not a word passed her lips.

Nate would swear she was intentionally treating him as if they had never met, just to annoy him. If it had been anyone else, he would have thought her shy, but he knew from their first meeting, Miss Jamison didn't suffer from shyness. He caught up to her and fell in step beside her. "May I walk with you?"

He waited in vain for her to speak.

Constance cut her eyes to the unwanted man beside her. She had gleaned from their first meeting, Nathanial Eatonton was a man used to getting attention from women. And was it any wonder with his good looks? She could well imagine the chubby-cheeked, smiling cherub he must have been as a baby that would have had every momma cooing and pinching his cheeks. The golden locks and laughing blue-eyed boy would not have been starved for affection. And his cocky attitude was confirmation enough, he had always drawn the admiration of girls, likely even before coming of age. Good looks were not going to sway her. She would keep walking as if he wasn't there. Surely he would grow bored and move on.

Nate surreptitiously studied the lady by his side. For all appearances, Constance was a serenely proper young lady. He had a suspicion demure would be a better description. He smiled as he thought of something clever to say. "I hope you don't mind escorting me home. It's been a rather tiring night keeping the light. I might lose my way." He saw the corner of her lip twitch and was pleased. Except that she still remained silent.

"Penny for your thoughts?"

No answer.

"No thoughts? Or perhaps, too many thoughts to choose. Should I try guessing them?"

Constance tried to remain aloof, but she was finding his attempts to draw her out amusing.

Nate said, "You must be thinking how did I get so lucky as to gain the attention of the most handsome bachelor on the island."

She couldn't restrain her short burst of laughter, but she refused to give him the pleasure of a reply. She rolled her eyes and said nothing.

"Hmm. Do you not consider yourself lucky, or is it that you don't consider me handsome?"

Silence.

"Well, I have been told often enough that I am handsome, so it must be the former, though I can't imagine why." His house was just ahead.

Constance mentally shook her head. He certainly would never be accused of being modest.

"I am afraid our time has come to end for I have reached my destination. Thank you most kindly for your escort." He stopped at the walk to his front door, but she continued on without hesitation. He called after her. "Can I expect the same tomorrow?" He waited in vain. "I will accept your silence for agreement." He doffed his hat. "Until tomorrow."

Constance fully intended to walk another route tomorrow.

Susan Blackmon

Love in Key West series

Salvaged Love

Love in Key West – a novella

Love Again

Enduring Love

Once Upon an Island Christmas – a novella

Divided Love
2021

ABOUT THE AUTHOR

Susan Blackmon has enjoyed reading historical novels all her life. With a talent for writing it was only natural for her to try her hand at creating one of her own. All that was missing was inspiration. An unexpected cruise ship detour to Key West and a few history tours later, Max and Abby's story began.

When Susan isn't writing, she enjoys being with her family, hiking waterfalls, reading, scrapbooking, and escaping to the coast every chance she gets.

Visit www.susanblackmonauthor.com to learn more about her books or to find your favorite way to connect via social media.

www.ingramcontent.com/pod-product-compliance
Lightning Source LLC
Chambersburg PA
CBHW021040130626
46552CB00005B/1938